Magical Lover

by

Karilyn Bentley

Magical Lover

Cover Art by *Tamra Westberry*

The Wild Rose Press
PO Box 706
Adams Basin, NY 14410-0706
Visit us at www.thewildrosepress.com

Publishing History
First Faery Rose Edition, 2011
Print ISBN 1-60154-962-8

Published in the United States of America

"I know enough to realize she denied you," the stranger growled at Lord Simon, his voice gentling as he turned to Keara. "She will take me though, won't you?"

Keara locked her gaze on the stranger, drawn by his green eyes that looked so much like her own. She had never seen green eyes on anyone else, but knew what they meant. Remembered what her grandmother had told her about them.

"Green eyes are the mark of evil, girl," the old woman liked to say. "Be wary of them."

The wind whipped the stranger's hair about his face. A chiseled jaw topped by firm lips that whitened around the edges and a long straight nose comprised a face tightened in anger. His compelling eyes bored into hers.

She couldn't stop staring at those eyes, all the while his fingers continued their steady pattern against her mark, sending sensuous feelings coursing through her veins.

A stranger or Lord Simon? The man whose touch sent zingers of pleasure throughout her body, or the possibly crazy but socially acceptable man who might have her best interest in mind. *Did she actually think that?*

There was no choice. It took two tries to get the words out of her dry mouth.

"I'll take you." She lifted her chin toward the stranger and said a silent prayer he would spare her life.

Praise For *MAGICAL LOVER*

"*MAGICAL LOVER* sweeps you away to a rich, fantasy world filled with magic, mystery and unforgettable characters."
~*Trinity Blake*

"I didn't want the story to end. It's a magical blend of romance and fantasy!"
~*Angela Hicks*

"Sexy and spellbinding!
~*Christie Gibson*

Dedication

To my wonderful husband for all his support.
And to the world's best critique group:
you guys are the greatest.

Chapter 1

"Thoren and Enar," Alviss's voice resonated with a power and strength that belied his withered appearance. "The task chosen for you is to travel to Cautasia. We've had reports of a Halfling boy who needs to be brought to us."

Thoren schooled his face into a mask of indifference. Thank the Goddess he would be leaving the Draconi lands for a while. Spending an entire season placating his father's desire for him to find a lifemate had worn on his nerves. Not that finding a mate was bad, but he'd prefer to find her in his own time.

Didn't his father understand he enjoyed reconnaissance missions? That if he found a mate he would have to abandon what he loved doing? Maybe the old male understood and just didn't care.

Sometimes he wondered.

The Goddess smiled upon him when none of the females in any of the villages had tested as his mate.

Just when he'd become resigned to meeting more fawning females, Alviss, the leader of the Council and the oldest living Draconi, saw fit to telepathically call him and his best friend, Enar, to the Council's Chambers and give this latest assignment.

Judging by Enar's expression, his best friend would rather fight an army alone than have anything to do with the males that sat on the Council.

Unlike Thoren, Enar had enjoyed the Draconi

females' charms a bit too much.

"Cautasia?" Thoren crossed his arms, bunching his biceps. "Why would a Draconi plant their seed there?"

"I do not know why any Draconi male would choose to lie with a non-Draconi female and have offspring, but so many of them do. Which is why we need you," Alviss looked between Enar and Thoren, "to bring these Halflings back to us. Draconi cannot live without other Draconi."

"My son needs to find a mate. He is nearing his Change. This mission will distract him from that search," Balthor clenched the arm of his carved chair, thin lines forming around his mouth.

Thoren held his breath. *Father only wants the best for me.*

Maybe repeated use of that phrase would stop steam from building in the back of his throat every time his father insisted he find a mate.

Honoring his father by consenting to his request was one thing. Having to like it was another.

If only that old Seer hadn't told his parents on his hatching day that his mate would be special, Balthor might not be so insistent about the search. And with his thirtieth hatch-day come and gone, Balthor stepped up the mate-finding crusade, fearful Thoren's Change would come before he found one.

He should worry about that logic. Draconi males generally found their females prior to Changing. Prior to the doubling of their magical abilities. If he didn't find his own mate, he'd have to use a priestess for the ritual. The problem came if no female could be found. That unpleasantness he refused to think about.

But most males didn't go through the Change until their mid to late thirties, which meant he still had a couple of years left. Plenty of time to make his father happy by settling down.

Maybe by then he'd be more in-touch with the find-a-mate program.

"It shouldn't take two of our best spies long to discover the location of a Halfling child, who his father was, and bring him back. Your son may continue his search when he returns. Any other concerns?" Alviss's stare could have melted ice.

Thoren released his breath as the chamber remained silent. His father didn't look too happy, but he'd get his way in the end. According to the now-dead Seer, Thoren's mate was out there and he had no choice but to find her.

A Draconi male was nothing without his mate.

Even Thoren knew that truth.

"Good. It is settled. You two will leave immediately and may the Goddess bless you on your journey." Alviss dismissed both Thoren and Enar with a nod.

Thoren returned the nod to the thirteen males, both Draconi and Watchers, who composed the Council. Alviss and six males from each of the two races were sworn to oversee the safety of the Draconi people.

Thoren enjoyed serving his people. Traveling to different lands, meeting new people, and discovering plots to attack the Draconi all ranked as some of his favorite things.

So far, no plots.

Lately, though, his missions centered on the recovery of Draconi Halflings—those children left behind by a liaison with a Draconi male and a woman of a different race. Seemed like the males in recent generations had become bored with Draconi females and rested their scales in someone else's cave.

That he'd never understand. But without irresponsible males, he'd have no job.

Smiling, he strode out the door, squinting at the

sudden change in light. Even a dragon's eyes took several seconds to adjust to changes in lighting.

"Finding Halflings can go bugger itself." Enar strode across the stones paving the walkway. "I was beginning to enjoy myself trying to find you a mate."

"I feel bad for you, I really do." Thoren placed a hand over his heart. "Bedding forbidden females in secret is such hard work."

"Stop being such a wit."

"Why? It's my specialty."

Enar snorted. "We'll go back on the hunt one day. Then you'll see females prefer me."

"You know what they say about forbidden fruit. That's the only reason you're able to turn their heads. Really though, how do you convince them to bed you? They know non-Draconi males are forbidden."

Enar shrugged as he continued to move forward. "It's nothing."

Thoren shook his head at his friend. Tall, with blond hair that fell to his shoulders and a physique that would scare a seasoned warrior, Enar nonetheless possessed something that caused Draconi females to chase after him.

And the females knew better than to hope for any lover other than a Draconi one. Enar knew better too. Not like that knowledge stopped the Watcher.

Thoren let a lot of societal rules slip when it came to Enar. They both knew that Draconi females were revered. That their magic was often stronger than the males', and for this reason they needed to be protected, and kept from all males except Draconi.

Societal law insisted Draconi females only choose lovers from among the Draconi males and not other races, including the Watchers. Talk about a double standard. No one cared if the males bedded and impregnated non-Draconi females. Provided the offspring came back to live with the Draconi.

"What if someone finds out about all the Draconi women you've bedded?"

Enar waved a hand. "Don't trouble your puny little mind over it."

"Puny?"

"It means small."

"Uh-huh. We're not discussing my mind. We're discussing you."

"You're discussing me. It's lonely having a conversation by yourself."

"I'm not having a conversation by myself. I'm trying to tell you to watch your step when it comes to Draconi females. They should be cherished."

"I never said they shouldn't be cherished. I cherish them quite well while they're under me. It's just when you get them upright that I have a problem." Enar laughed, slapping Thoren on the back.

Thoren shook his head. "Fool, you keep talking like that and it'll come back to bite you."

"Ooow, a throw down between me and the Fates. Who do you think will win?"

Thoren shook his head. "Sorry, but I'd have to go with the Fates. They've been around longer."

Enar threw a hand out toward Thoren. "I see how you are. Are you ready to go conquer Cautasia? Who knows? They might even have women I'll like."

****

Ah, morning. Shallow streams of sunlight whispered across grasses. Leaves tinted red-orange, glistened with dew. The stench of raw sewage permeated her senses as she strode through the alleys, heading for the town gate.

Keara coughed. Someone really needed to do something about the sewers. For the past week, the town of River's Run had smelled like a dump, but no

5

one made a move to do anything about it. Didn't they know all that backed up sewage caused disease?

A glance behind her showed Jamie, her apprentice, walking the same way, hand over mouth and nose, but everyone else seemed unaffected by the stench. Why did smells bother her so much? If the people lingering about were any indication, no one but the two of them noticed the sewers had sprung a leak.

Once through the gates the air improved enough for Keara to stop holding her nose.

"What are we looking for, Keara?" Jamie walked along beside her, hands stuffed in his pockets, staring at the ground.

She ruffled his hair. He shrugged his shoulders and grinned, turning his steel gray eyes to meet her gaze. Point accomplished.

"We're just replenishing our stock."

Why she bothered remained a mystery. Few came to her apothecary shop since her grandmother died, and as a result, most of her supplies remained unused. But her grandmother had always taken her out during autumn to gather herbs, and old habits died hard.

Jamie nodded, kicking stones as he came upon them.

"Are you bored?" Keara smiled, touching his shoulder.

His eyes met hers, full of hope. "Well then, why don't you run on ahead? Just don't run out of my sight."

"Thank you!" He took off, running as fast as his little legs would carry him.

She had found him not far from this very place the day her grandmother died. Half starved and frightened, he lifted scared gray eyes to her face, raking his gaze over her clothes as if taking in her worth before throwing himself into her arms.

Keara had always wanted a child, a wish she knew she'd never have. Few in the town could stand being around her. Truthfully, most thought her a witch and only abided her presence out of respect for her grandmother.

Respect that fizzled with the old woman's death.

Walking through these woods and discovering that filthy child had been the best moment in a day filled with grief.

First thing she did was march him to the town square and claim him for her apprentice.

Then she insisted he take a bath.

"Hey, Keara! Watch!"

She looked up at Jamie's call and caught her breath. *Oh my Goddess, he's going to fall!*

Jamie hung from a tree limb by one hand, swinging toward the trunk, then away, toward it, then away.

Keara held her breath as he let go of the branch he held and hurdled through the air until he caught another tree limb. Her breath vacated her lungs on a wheeze.

"Jam—"

"Did you see me? I flew—" his words ended in a scream as the branch he held snapped, sending him falling to the ground.

Praise the Goddess he didn't fall far. She raced to him, dropping to her knees, running her hands over his body. He blinked, mouth working like a baby bird as he tried to draw breath into stunned lungs.

The only injury she saw was on his hand from where the branch skinned it. Holding his palm, she ran her other hand over it, drawing his injury into herself, changing it, until his skin smoothed out, not even a scar remaining.

Jamie's lungs kicked in and breath wheezed through his lips. He stared at his hand then smiled at her.

"Think you can teach me that one?"

Keara sat back on her butt, rocking onto her back so she lay beside the boy. Healing, even easy healing like Jamie's hand, exhausted her. At least he hadn't died.

She gathered just enough strength to reach over and whap his arm with the back of her hand. "That's for scaring the breath out of me. What if you had died?"

"You would've healed me."

"What makes you say that?"

"I know. You're good. I watch you."

"Don't say things like that. People wouldn't like it."

"I know that, too. I'm smart. I know what you are also. Boys see things, you know."

Keara turned her head to him. For once he met her gaze without being prodded. How did he know? She had healed him and this wasn't the first time, but the rest of it?

"And just who do you think I am?"

"You'll see. I'm figuring you'll find out soon. You'd know too if you'd bother to look. Adults don't always see things like they should. That's why I'm glad I'm a kid. I see all things."

"So you're the Goddess, eh?" Keara put a hand on his stomach and tickled, producing giggles.

"Stop that!" He shoved at her hand. "Don't be silly. Know what else I know? Lord Simon wants you for some reason."

She knew this too. And a strange thing that was. Why would a noble like Simon bother with a shop owner like her? It just wasn't done. Which was probably why so many tongues wagged over the matter. Simon was a nice enough looking man, but something lurked under the surface that gave her chills.

A very bad kind of chill.

She swore the man was slightly mad, just like his father before him. The old man went completely crazy before he died, screaming about men turning into large scaly beasts. Bizarre.

On the other hand, if she married Simon the townspeople would have no choice but to respect her. She could keep her shop, have the priests stop preaching against her sinful coloring, and be part of the town.

She considered it for all of two seconds. Was societal acceptance worth being chained to a crazy man she didn't love?

She wasn't that desperate...yet.

"Jamie, how on earth would you know what Lord Simon wants?"

He shrugged, his small shoulders flattening grass as they moved. "I told you. I see things. Don't fall for him, all right? He's not normal in the head."

"Isn't that the truth? Thanks for the advice. I think I'll lie here for a bit. I'm tired. Don't go wandering off and no more trees."

"Uh-huh. Whatever makes you happy."

Keara closed her eyes, ignoring Jamie's words and their implied meaning. Hopefully whatever mess he got into while she rested wouldn't be too bad. Boys.

****

"Eww. This town smells like raw sewage. Why would anyone want to live here?" It had been a night and half-a-day and the smell remained strong. Thoren looked around at the stone buildings, teetering in disrepair. The breeze on his sweaty brow felt cool, but the air reeked of sewage and who knew what else.

Enar shrugged. "How would I know the ways of superstitious townsfolk? You'd think they'd never seen a traveler with the way they look at us. The only thing semi-decent in this town is the women and even that's a stretch. And to make matters worse, although how they can get worse with no decent women, there is no evidence of a Halfling child like you claim you sense."

Thoren looked at his best friend. Enar's blue eyes twinkled. In this backward town of short people, both men stood out like a ray of sunlight through dark clouds. Muscles rippled under black leather, generating stares in the sea of brown cloth. Assessing glances of women. Hostile snarls from men. A seasoned spy didn't feel fear, but he'd be glad when they left this place.

"Just because you can't sense another's magic, doesn't mean the child isn't here." Thoren wrinkled his nose as a rank town specimen brushed against him in the crowded lane. "Some of us have better noses than others."

"Well, it doesn't take a good nose to know this town has sewer problems. The stench is giving me a headache."

"Didn't the apothecary give you something for that last night?"

"Oh, yes. I take back what I said about the women here. At least one of them is attractive. Not interested in me, though. Maybe you'd be more her type."

"I'm not interested in non-Draconi females. What would possess a male to come to Stenchville for a woman? What's wrong with our own females? I just don't get it. Although I'm glad someone did. If not for the mystery male, I'd still be hiking around Draconia making Father happy."

"Balthor wouldn't be the only one happy."

"Who says I'd invite you along?"

Enar's eyes popped wide. "What? Deny me my only pleasure in life?"

"Females are not the only pleasure in your life."

Thoren gestured to the broadsword hanging down Enar's back. They both enjoyed fighting, although Enar's sword skills outweighed Thoren's. Not that he minded. After all, lobbing magical energy balls at his opponent beat learning swordplay. "A sword is a sword no matter how it's used."

"You got me there."

People ran past them, jostling each other as they raced down the small lane.

"Wonder what's going on?" Maybe the townsfolk finally decided to do something about the clogged sewers.

Enar shrugged as murmurings from a restless crowd drifted down the lane. No sense in joining a riot that didn't apply to them. It sounded like the whole town came out for a shouting match. As Thoren started to turn down a side street, he heard a panicked female voice shout above the ruckus.

"I will not take you!"

The riot just became his problem. Something in that voice ignited a desire to protect her. He had no choice but to shove his way through the throng of people.

"Hey, it's not our...bugger it. Don't wander in there without me." A rush of air announced Enar stepping behind him.

Not that he needed the Watcher. He was a male on a mission to defend that female.

What in the Goddess's name was he thinking? Enar ran into him as Thoren stopped mid-stride. This was not his fight. These were not his people.

"I said I will not take you. Let me go!"

And the choice was taken from him. Her voice struck a chord inside him, banging around, charging his anger. Fight and protect. Kill and save.

"What are you thinking?" Enar grabbed his arm and Thoren whirled, his lips pulled back, teeth exposed.

Enar dropped his arm and took a step back. "All right. Knock yourself out, dragon."

Two shoves later Thoren stood at the edge of the crowd, looking at the female and a man standing in the middle of the town square. The man faced them. Tall for one of these townsfolk, he wore a clean, brown tunic embroidered in gold. Black pants tucked into leather boots that reached mid-calf. His brown, limp hair hung to his shoulders. Brown eyes narrowed on his prey as a menacing smile played across his features. One hand grasped the female's arm.

The female faced away from Thoren. She also wore a brown tunic and black pants, her tunic belted about her waist, a variety of small pouches hanging from the belt. Braided red hair streamed down her back, stopping short of her waist. Her body strung taut as a bow, as if waiting for a strike, verbal or physical.

She needed him. She needed him to save her. She needed him to obliterate the man. Why he felt this way was the mystery of the day. The man needed to be introduced to vengeance dragon-style.

Right when he started to make his move, the voice of a boy shouted over the roar of the crowd.

"She said, leave her alone!"

"Step back, Jamie. Now!"

The female turned toward the boy, gesturing with her hand for him to move back. The boy—who Thoren guessed to be only ten—didn't budge. Stood stock still, fists balled at his sides, jaw thrust forward, a lot of stop-messing-with-her on his face.

The boy was two steps away from getting knocked down by the man in the square, when a woman of pale beauty jerked him back. An ice goddess. White blond hair surrounded a pale face, the only colors bright blue eyes and ruby red lips.

Thoren heard Enar gasp and mutter,

"Exquisite."

Was his friend actually showing an interest in the blond woman during a time like this?

Thoren growled at Enar. Growled? Since when did he growl at his best friend? What was it about the redheaded female that made everything inside him turn into a dragon on the warpath?

The man laughed. "Yes, Jamie, step back. This has nothing to do with you. Not now, anyway." He smirked at the red-haired female as she yanked out of his grasp. She tried to back up, only to run against the teeming mass of townsfolk. She turned, as if to judge the distance she had left and her gaze slipped by Thoren, not noticing him.

But he noticed her and fury ran through his muscles, charging him, demanding a fight between him and her captor.

Steam rose in the back of his throat, his fists cranked into hard knots as he spat out a small plume of smoke.

"What in the name of the Goddess do you think you're doing?" Enar hissed. "It's just some townswoman. Some *non-Draconi* townswoman."

"Can't you see what she is?"

Enar raised an eyebrow. "The apothecary?"

"Start thinking with the head on your shoulders and look at her."

"She's a witch the priests warned you about," the soon-to-be-dead man yelled, his cry egging on the crowd. They responded with a deafening yell. "But as my wife she will put the mantle of a witch aside. Ignore her denials to have me and you will no longer have to deal with the witch for she will have her magic purged when she joins with me."

The crowd hooted and hollered, clapping loudly. The man grabbed her left arm, in the process shoving up her sleeve, displaying the Draconi mark for all to see. Delicate, spindly lines curved around her forearm, stemming from the dragon's tail centered halfway between wrist and elbow.

"By the Goddess, why didn't the Council know about her?" Enar gasped, now clearly in line with the rescue plan.

The man holding the female ran his finger over the mark, smirking as she gasped and tried to pull away. A red cloud dotted Thoren's vision and he swallowed the steam threatening to come out his ears.

"Does anyone have any objection to me taking this woman?"

Thoren saw her bent over, gasping for air, and he knew pain shot through her body from the bastard's touch on her mark. Red haze glittered at the periphery of his vision and he stepped forward. This time Enar didn't bother to restrain him.

"I object. The female belongs to me. I will take her."

Chapter 2

The female belongs to me. I will take her. Keara managed to raise her head, despite the pain flooding her body from Lord Simon's touch. She wasn't sure what was more horrible, Lord Simon trying to claim her for a wife or a stranger doing the same thing.

She should have stayed in the woods with Jamie, but how was she to know that Simon waited for her when she came through the gates? He had the crowd riled into a frenzy and although she ran down the nearest alley, she had been captured and dragged to the town square. Thank goodness Lily had been in the crowd and had taken Jamie.

Soon the crowd would turn on Lily too, if their ranting about the women's differences were any indication. Keara knew no one would help them, that they faced the end of their lives. For a moment, panic seized her. What would happen to Jamie if she died?

And then the stranger spoke.

Keara twisted her head, wondering if the melodious rumble of his voice matched the rest of him. Yes, it did. Her mouth opened and for a moment she forgot to breathe.

She looked up his body as he stepped beside her. Tall, with long, flowing black hair and muscles that rippled under black leather, he looked like a god come to life. A muscle in his jaw twitched as he placed a hand on Lord Simon's wrist, twisting the lord's hand away from her arm.

The pain stopped flowing through her and Keara

sighed in relief, her knees buckling under her. Still holding his hand around Lord Simon's wrist, the black-haired stranger placed his other hand upon her arm, keeping her on her feet, his thumb tracing her mark gently.

Another sensation slammed through her and replaced the mind-numbing pain, sending shivers down her spine and tightening her lower belly. She never realized touching the cursed mark could bring such pain, or such pleasure.

She pulled her gaze from the stranger with an effort to see Lord Simon sputtering in outrage, his wrist twisted at an odd angle.

"You...you challenge me for her? You know nothing of our ways!"

"I know enough to realize she denied you," the stranger growled at Lord Simon, his voice gentling as he turned to Keara. "She will take me though, won't you?"

Keara locked her gaze on the stranger, drawn by his green eyes that looked so much like her own. She had never seen green eyes on anyone else, but knew what they meant. Remembered what her grandmother had told her about them.

"Green eyes are the mark of evil, girl," the old woman liked to say. "Be wary of them."

The wind whipped the stranger's hair about his face. A chiseled jaw topped by firm lips that whitened around the edges and a long straight nose comprised a face tightened in anger. His compelling eyes bored into hers.

She couldn't stop staring at those eyes, all the while his fingers continued their steady pattern against her mark, sending sensuous feelings coursing through her veins.

A stranger or Lord Simon? The man whose touch sent zingers of pleasure throughout her body, or the possibly crazy but socially acceptable man who might have her best interest in mind. *Did she actually think that?*

There was no choice. It took two tries to get the words out of her dry mouth.

"I'll take you." She lifted her chin toward the stranger and said a silent prayer he would spare her life.

He smiled, a predatory gleam of teeth, before turning his glare back to Lord Simon, pushing the man back by his wrist before releasing him.

Grabbing his injured wrist with his good hand, the shorter man snarled at her rescuer. "Fool! You don't know what you are getting. She—"

"Quiet!"

Keara, along with the mob, stood frozen. A hush fell over the crowd as they stared in shock at the black-haired man who dared address Lord Simon in such a way. But then, Keara reasoned, if he truly was evil, what did he have to fear from this crowd? What did he have to fear from anyone? What would evil do when he discovered what she really was? Would he see her as a kindred spirit since she shared his eye color, or would he punish her?

She shuddered. Maybe going with him wasn't such a good idea after all. *Too late now.*

Tall, dark and possibly evil glared at the crowd. "Move!"

Immediately the mass parted, allowing them to pass through. His hand wrapped around hers, leaving her mark throbbing without his touch.

Once they left the town square and horde, she heard footsteps behind her and turned her head, only to come to a complete stop when she saw the giant walking behind them.

Keara remembered having the same reaction to the man the night before when she treated him for a headache. She had never seen anyone so tall or muscular in her life, not to mention his eyes. They were the color of the rivers after the snows melted. The same color as her friend Lily's. His hair was darker than Lily's pale blond, though. And his skin tanned a deep bronze, set off his blue eyes. Until a few minutes ago, she classified him as the most attractive man she ever laid eyes on, but the raven-haired stranger took that designation now.

Ferociousness seeped from Blond Giant's pores, even when his eyes twinkled as they did now. Gulping, she lowered her gaze, afraid of offending him further.

"What's wrong? Why are you stopping?" Raven-haired, Jaw-dropping Gorgeous stopped moving and looked over his shoulder at her.

"She is taking in my manly appearance," Blond Giant's eyebrows waggled. "Which, as you know, is much better than yours."

"You'll have to excuse my friend. His thoughts about himself are larger than his size."

Keara grinned at their banter. Maybe her life would be better with this stranger.

It couldn't get much worse.

"I'm sorry. I've never seen men as large as you."

Blond Giant coughed.

RJG's eyes twinkled as he glanced at his friend. "Large, eh? I can see we're going to get along just fine."

Three blinks later and warmth flooded her face. What a way to embarrass herself. At least her captor-husband-rescuer continued as if he hadn't seen her blush.

"I'm Thoren and this is Enar. I'm afraid I didn't get your name."

"It's Keara the Apothecary."

"Well, Keara, we'll be taking you with us when we leave—"

"And my bride price." He should know, even if she had to interrupt him.

"Pardon?"

"My bride price. I am not poor. You should know that."

Thoren's brows drew together like the walls of a canyon. "What is a bride price?"

How could he not know that? Didn't all women everywhere have a bride price?

Did his lack of knowledge bode good or bad for her?

"It is customary for the bride's father to bring her groom an amount of money or goods so he will protect her, but as I have no father, I'll give you the bride price myself."

"Wait a minute. What do you mean bride and groom?"

How could he not realize what just happened? Then again, he didn't know what a bride price was.

"When you beat Lord Simon, you took me for your wife."

"I did no such thing! I rescued you from him."

How sad. Tall, handsome and possibly evil clearly didn't function on all four wagon wheels.

Ignoring a snickering Enar, Keara shut her gaping mouth and tried to explain. Slowly. So he understood.

"As in every town, the town square is where you get married. Lord Simon was trying to marry me against my will. When you stepped in, you took me as your own. As your wife. Therefore we're married and you get my bride price."

He uttered a curse that curled her toes.

And didn't that make a woman feel good about herself. If he didn't mean to marry her, then what did he want from her? Did he even want the obvious benefit to being married? He was the best-looking man she'd ever seen, but the whole thought of sleeping with a stranger gave her chills.

Enar slapped Thoren on the back. "Fates, my

friend, Fates."

Thoren glared at Enar. "That was not a marriage. Where were the rituals? The priestess?"

Keara tried to swallow and got nowhere. If he didn't think they were married, did that mean he'd return her to Lord Simon? What would happen to her then? Her vision wavered, going fuzzy at the periphery.

Thoren grabbed her arm.

"What's wrong, Little One?"

Keara shook her head. Maybe it would be better if she stayed. After all, what did she know about these strangers? Besides their complete cluelessness about marriage?

"Do you doubt I would protect you?" One hand beat twice over his heart. "I vow on the bones of my ancestors to protect you."

Keara looked into those green eyes that stared intently at her. She had just met him, couldn't know if he was an honest man or not, but in this she believed him. His face remained impassive though his eyes spoke volumes. She saw something in them that she'd only dreamed of seeing. He did not fear her.

Even her grandmother had feared her.

Her lungs remembered their purpose, wheezing in air, clearing the fuzziness from her vision.

"But what will I do with my store if you will not accept my bride price?" Or Jamie? By the Goddess, what would she do with Jamie? She couldn't leave him, but would these men take him? Her lungs stalled.

"Why don't you take us there and we'll see?" One of his long fingers rubbed against her mark, and her muscles wobbled. His touch felt good, like a warm bath on a cold day. Why had she been so upset? Thoren gave his protection to her. Nothing would harm her again.

And wasn't that a good thing? For the first time since childhood, she felt safe.

"My store is this way."

****

His finger stroked across her mark, his will forcing her to relax, to breathe deeply. He liked the way her skin brushed against his finger, the silky smoothness, the scent of fresh grass and sunlight. Wanting to touch her more, he continued the soft strokes over her mark.

What about her affected him so?

Must be the shock of finding a Draconi female in this backward town. How could the Council not know about her? With her red hair and green eyes, she was an obvious Halfling that should have attracted plenty of attention from visitors. And yet, no one knew about her. Her own townsmen clearly didn't care for her, so one would think some word of her would have reached the ears of Draconi spies.

Speaking of spying. His job sent him to this town to find a Halfling boy. Finding Keara was a stroke of luck, but no matter what he felt toward her it should not distract him from his goal.

Her hips swayed, her black trousers hugging skin that begged for his touch. Long red hair curled loosely around her oval face where strands escaped her braid. Pale skin with a spattering of light freckles bridged her nose and drew attention to long lashes that began black and faded to the same red of her hair at the tips.

Her large green eyes expressed her feelings, peace shining in their depths, thanks to his relaxing touch on her mark. She needed him. He needed her. There was nothing to stop him from taking her, from making her his.

Nothing but his job and the fact that he didn't want a mate. No more adventure once bonded.

He needed to stop thinking about her. Which

21

was rather hard to do while touching her.

But if he didn't touch her then she would panic again and he couldn't allow that to happen. He needed to touch her.

Concentrate, Thoren, concentrate. Think about pain, yes, pain and how mad Alviss will be if you don't find that Halfling boy.

Maybe Keara could help him with his mission. Thinking about his job might distract him enough to forget about how much he enjoyed the feel of her skin against his.

"Perhaps you can help us."

"I can try." A half-smile.

"We're looking for a boy who looks like you, red hair and green eyes. He wouldn't have a father and he probably has some unusual abilities. And he'd have a matching mark to yours on his forearm."

She shook her head. "I'm sorry. I'm the only one that has red hair and green eyes. Plenty of boys don't have fathers. Roam the streets and you'll find a few."

"Are you sure?" Enar asked.

"Yes. No one with red hair but me. It's forbidden."

"To have red hair?" What kind of craziness was that?

"If it's not brown or black then it's evil. Isn't it that way where you are from?"

Thoren hissed, his lip pulling back in a snarl as he realized what life must have been like for her. Tamping down the dragon that wanted to roar in protection, he forced his lip into some semblance of normal. She tried to pull away, her face a mask of terror.

He cursed. He hadn't meant to scare her.

Why did his dragon react ferociously to her? The beast clamored to be released, to destroy the town, to protect Keara.

What was with him today? *Pull it together, Thoren. Calm thoughts, calm thoughts.* The dragon returned to its rest and Thoren took a deep breath.

"I apologize for scaring you." Her face froze, her body poised for a strike. His heart twisted. "You shouldn't have been treated that way. Where we're from," he gestured between him and Enar, "females like you are cherished. As a Halfling your magic sometimes runs stronger than full-breeds."

Something he said caused her to shiver with apparent fear. She shook her head hard enough to bounce her braid, her eyes wide, freckles popping out in a pale face.

"Magic is evil. I have no magic."

Thoren kept up the finger-stroking-over-her-mark routine until she relaxed. How could anyone say she was evil? What kind of superstitious backward people lived in this village? No other village he visited believed those kinds of things.

"Magic is not evil, Little One. Magic is in all things, but not everyone can control it. Only those with special abilities can wield magic."

She blinked and pressed her lips together. A deep breath in. "So I'm not evil?" she whispered.

Something twisted in his chest at her words and the dragon tried to raise its head. *Not again.* He took a deep breath.

"Of course you're not evil. You belong to my race. We're Draconi. We work magic." Plus many other things, but he needed to explain slowly. By the time he returned her to Draconia, she would know about her race and her abilities. "Haven't you ever done something you couldn't explain and yet it was a part of you?"

Keara sucked in her lip, her shoulders rising and falling. "Maybe."

"The middle of the street is not the place to discuss this. My spell to move the people out of our

23

way will break any minute. Why don't you show us to your store?" The last thing he needed was a bunch of superstitious folk blocking their path.

With the odd way his beast acted today the thing might come out for a destroy-everyone visit. The first thing he learned about reconnaissance missions was to never show the dragon, never use it in a fight.

Today, for the first time ever, that had been a challenge.

"My store is this way."

She took a turn at the next alley, leading them along the backside of town. The alley scenery showed no improvement over the streets, but avoiding unidentified brown globs leashed his inner dragon. How a town could be so filthy confounded him. He stepped over rubbish and sewage and tried not to take deep breaths as he followed Keara.

A couple of turns, three alleys and numerous brown globs later they came to a wooden gate set in a tall fence. Keara pushed the gate open and a whiff of clean air infused with the scent of herbs drifted through the opening.

Ah, relief.

"My store is on the other side." Disappearing through the opening, she let out a cry. "Jamie!"

Thoren shoved at the gate, slamming it against the fence. What if someone else had grabbed her? Instead, he saw Keara holding the same boy who had tried to defend her in the town square. Scrawny arms tightened about her waist as his head popped around her arm. Steel gray eyes narrowed at Thoren and Enar. He took a step away from Keara, standing in front of her, hands on his hips.

"Don't you hurt her."

Tough little guy. One had to admire a lad that stood up to two grown males.

"Jamie! What has gotten into you? He's our

master now." Keara pushed Jamie behind her. "I'm sorry. He's not normally like that."

"He's brave. Who is he?"

"This is Jamie. I found him, took him to the town square and claimed him as mine and since no one refuted the claim, he's now my apprentice." She took a deep breath, looked at the sky and then met his gaze. "He's part of my bride price."

Thoren didn't need a translation to know she wanted the boy to come with them. The Council might not like it, but keeping Jamie would make Keara happy and that was all that mattered.

By the Goddess, he was turning into a lovesick fool.

"He can stay with you."

****

Keara smiled and draped an arm around Jamie. Thank the Goddess Thoren was clueless about bride prices or else he would never have agreed to Jamie coming. Everyone knew a bride price didn't include apprentices, only coins and goods.

Despite their size, these men seemed harmless enough. Or harmless toward her. But what did Thoren mean about magic? Was he suggesting he worked magic and she could too? Was he evil? Her grandmother would have insisted on it, but Keara knew better. Thoren could have worked some sort of evil spell after he rescued her and nothing had happened.

Instead, his touch brought feelings of peace and relaxation. He wouldn't harm her. *Hopefully*. No use in dwelling on if he would or would not. Her lot was cast. She belonged to him now.

"Is that one part of your bride price, too?" Enar pointed to the back door.

Keara whirled around, surprised to see Lily standing against the shop's door, frozen in place. In her rush to see to Jamie, she hadn't even noticed her friend. Mouth agape, Lily stared at Enar, her face flushed.

"What?" Keara whipped her head around to glare at Enar, who paid her no heed as he stared at Lily like a thirsty man would a glass of cool water. "No, she's my friend, Lily."

"I see." He proceeded to turn to Thoren, mumbling something under his breath that sounded to Keara like "claim her." While they whispered, Keara inched her way toward Lily, who remained frozen at the door.

"What are they like?" Lily asked, staring at the men.

Keara kept her hand on Jamie's shoulder, in case he tried to get into a fight with men three times his size. Twice in a day, her normally quiet and shy apprentice tried to defend her. Who knew such protectiveness resided inside the boy?

"Clueless about bride prices. But otherwise, nice enough. At least he doesn't mind my mark. He saw it, but he doesn't fear me."

"Finally, a smart one." Lily smiled, but it didn't reach her eyes. "What will happen to me once you're gone? I'm assuming you're leaving?"

"They said they're taking me away, but I'm not sure when."

"I'm scared, Keara. All my family is dead. You're all I have left. You've seen how bare the store's shelves are. These crazy townsfolk will probably lynch me once you're gone." Lily gulped, trembling slightly. Her blue eyes met Keara's gaze. "I'd rather go with you. If you think they won't kill me."

"I—"

"Woman of the exquisite coloring." Both Keara and Lily jumped, as Enar's voice boomed across the yard. Lily's eyes widened as she took a step back. Keara turned to face Enar, who strode across the yard in five steps.

From the corner of her eye, she saw Lily fumbling with the doorknob, apparently deciding facing a lynch mob would be safer than facing Enar. He grabbed her arm before she could open the door. Lily squeaked, craning her neck to meet his eyes.

Holding her gaze, Enar pulled a string of round beads from a pouch hanging from his belt. "Lily of the exquisite coloring, I claim you for my woman." With a quick flick of his wrist, the beads fell around her neck, snapping in place. Lily's eyes widened. Keara grabbed Enar's arm, trying unsuccessfully to pull him away from her friend.

"Leave her alone!" Keara screeched.

"What? You do what with me?" Lily gasped.

"Claim you. Same as Keara did with the lad."

"But...but you can't do that anyplace but the town square," Lily insisted.

"No, I just did it. With this necklace. You belong to me. It cannot be removed. It cannot be broken until I die. And I don't plan to do that anytime soon. Therefore, you are mine. But do not fear. I won't be a hard master to please. I will even allow you to bring some of your things with you." His mouth curved into a grin.

"Ouch. What—" Lily scratched at her neck before her eyes rolled into the back of her head and she fainted into Enar's arms.

"What did you do to her?" Keara shrieked, reaching for her friend.

Enar picked Lily up, cradling her close to him. "I didn't hurt her. The necklace merely caused her to fall asleep. It does that when a woman first puts it on. Don't worry. She will wake shortly."

Keara whirled on Thoren, who had moved closer to them. "He can't do that. Just take her like that without proper ceremony. It's not done!"

White lines formed around Thoren's mouth as he raked a hand through his hair. "He's a Watcher, not a Draconi. This is their ceremony for claiming women. Nothing can be done, once he has his mind made up. Trust me, I tried."

He obviously didn't try hard enough because her poor friend was draped over a giant's arm like a sack of flour. Her eyes narrowed on Enar. He had another thing coming if he thought he could claim her friend. She felt steam gather in the back of her throat, leaking in wisps out her ears. Before she could take a step toward Enar, Thoren put his hand next to her ear.

Just like that, the steam vanished. Probably because she could no longer draw in air. He knew. He felt the steam and knew her difference. Despite all his talk about how she belonged to his race, how magic flowed in her veins, her confidence he meant her no harm withered like a twig cut off from a branch.

Would he insist on a lynching? Even her grandmother had threatened the rope when she saw the steam.

But Thoren only stood there, his face curious as to what ailed her. No fear, no hate, only concern crossed his features.

Maybe as an evil being, he didn't care about physical flaws such as ears releasing steam.

Thoren touched her cheek with his fingertips. "Is something wrong, Little One?"

Yes, where do I start? "No. I mean, yes. He has my friend."

"She'll come with us. How's that?"

His hand circled her wrist, his thumb tracing the dark lines on her forearm. One moment fear coursed through her veins, drying her mouth, stilling her lungs, and the next she felt relaxed and happy, like she had smoked some of the herbs her grandmother kept hidden.

What was happening to her? Normally even-tempered, today her mood swings mirrored those of a middle-aged woman.

"All right." *Shouldn't she be fighting for Lily? Doing something besides wearing a goofy grin?*

Probably, but for the life of her, she didn't care. Nothing mattered except Thoren and his touch. Everything would be fine. Nothing would harm her.

"Why don't you and Jamie pack your things? I need to talk to Enar."

Sounded like a great idea. He didn't fear her, he wouldn't harm her, which was a lot better than what she'd get staying in River's Run. And he made her feel peaceful, although she had a sneaking suspicion his touch worked some sort of a spell.

She, Jamie and Lily were on their way to what she hoped was a better life. It couldn't be any worse than what they experienced here.

"Come on Jamie. Let's pack."

Chapter 3

Thoren sat at Keara's table, watching Enar rock Lily. What a contradiction, a hard-as-stone Watcher gently holding a petite woman. Just as he wanted to do with Keara. He gave himself a mental smack. What was wrong with him today? Since when did he want to hold and act a lovesick fool toward a female?

Mate.

Oh, no. It couldn't be. Forget that thought. Think of something else. Like why did Enar decide now was a good time to claim a woman. Or how they were going to get everyone home on two horses. Any thought but why he had such strong feelings for Keara.

Those weren't really feelings. Not of the bonding she's-my-mate kind. No, he only cared since she was a Draconi female, and females should be protected. Since she obviously wasn't protected, his dragon half demanded he do so. That was all. No mate business for him.

Now that he had his feelings settled, he could move on to the other matter: *Lily.* Why did Enar pick this mission to choose a claim? Why couldn't he pick a mission where they didn't have to put five people and their belongings on two horses?

Which led to the next question he always wondered about and never got a straight answer: Why did Watchers claim women? Didn't they have their own stock to choose from? Whatever the answer, Enar refused to say and Thoren had never seen one of their women. Which led to a completely different question: what did they do with all those Claims?

A toughened race of warriors sworn to protect the Draconi, Watchers made him wary. All but Enar. His best friend was the only one Thoren had met who seemed normal. Until he claimed Lily, that is.

Although in fairness to Enar, claiming women seemed to be the norm for Watchers. And his friend seemed to care for the woman, if cradling her like a baby meant anything.

What did he really know about Watchers? Nothing much.

He'd been told that many generations ago, they needed a place to settle, and in return for the generosity of donated land, the Watchers used their warrior skills to guard the Draconi.

Why a powerful magical race needed guardians was over his head. His questions on that matter had received shrugs from all he asked. Even Enar responded that Watchers had lived among the Draconi for generations and planned to for generations more.

Which told him nothing. Including why his friend insisted on claiming a woman from this backward town.

Thoren ran a hand through his hair and glanced at Enar. "Promise me you won't hurt her." If Lily hurt, he knew Keara would too and keeping her pain-free seemed to be his new goal in life.

"I don't hurt women." Enar glared. "So, you think Keara is the trace of magic you sensed, or do you think the Halfling boy is?"

Way to change the topic, Enar. "I don't know. I definitely sensed magic in this town, but it might have been Keara. Maybe we should search the town for the boy."

"Or not. That crowd was pretty riled up and might come back. And since the Council rules forbid you from turning into a dragon while on a mission and razing this town to the ground, we need to leave. The sooner the better. We're returning with a Halfling female, so the Council will be pleased."

"As much as I hate to say it, you're right. Keara's safety comes first. We'll leave as soon as she gets packed."

A creak of the stairs, the whisper of shoes on wood. Thoren turned his head and saw Keara creeping down the stairs. Her gaze caught his, dropped to her feet and rose slowly. That look shot through him like a punch to the gut, piercing through his resistance. Was she ill? Did she need his help? He needed to touch her, to calm her fears, to soothe the hurt her pain caused him.

"What will you do with my bride price?" Her voice cracked.

Leave it here? "We can't take it. I'm sorry. We only have two horses."

"Then what can I take?" Her hands clasped in front of her waist.

"One bag."

"One bag!" Fists slammed into her hips. "Are you crazy? How am I supposed to get all this," she gestured around the room, "into one bag?"

Was it too much to ask for a female to take one bag? He had sisters; he knew the request was outrageous. But they had no other choice. How was he supposed to get an entire store on a horse?

"What about one bag for my personal items and one bag for store items?"

Thoren glanced at Enar who shrugged. "All right. Two bags. How much of the store are you planning on taking?" On the other hand, the store was valuable. Even he, who knew next to nothing about herb craft, realized the value of the vials and potions lying on the shelves and cabinets.

"As much as can fit in two bags. This is my life.

I'm an apothecary." Her forefinger circled her thumbnail, over and over. "What will I do in your land?"

"You may do whatever you like. The priestesses have herb lore. You could talk to them."

"I would be allowed to do that?"

"Of course. Why wouldn't you?"

She shrugged, her lips turning down.

"Why don't you go pack your things?"

She took a deep breath and released the air with a sigh. "All right. But I'll come back down and you can help me pack up the store."

"It's a deal."

He watched the alluring swish of her hips as she climbed the stairs. Keara had the power to keep him from his mission, to keep him rooted in Draconia and enjoying every moment of it.

Bugger it. The sooner he could drop her off, the quicker he could return to his love: his work as a spy.

But with Keara in the picture, spying no longer seemed as pleasing.

****

Keara paced the floor of her bedroom, running her hands through her hair, pulling the strands loose from her braid. Jamie sat on his pallet, his gray eyes watching her movements. Thoren wanted her to leave her home, her shop, the only place she knew. The town might not be welcoming to her, but the shop held memories of her life. How would she be able to pack that?

And Lily. What would become of her friend? Enar frightened her, although she doubted he meant Lily harm. Would going with Enar be better for her friend or worse?

She should be thankful that although Thoren didn't consider them married, he still wanted her to go back with him to his land. Her land. Her people.

33

What an odd thought.

An even stranger thought was his insistence she possessed magic.

Did she? Was that why she healed the sick by placing her hands on them? Why her ears smoked? What did she really know about herself? About her newly discovered race?

Nothing. Nothing at all.

She should be thankful Thoren wanted to take her back. Provided he told the truth.

A shudder ran through her. Of course he told the truth. Because if he didn't...she didn't want to think about it. Since he told the truth—she refused to think otherwise—the Goddess watched over her when She sent the men to find some boy.

Speaking of. "Jamie, have you seen a red-headed boy? The men were looking for one."

Jamie shook his head, his talkative streak obviously at an end.

"They said he might not have red hair, but would have unusual abilities. Oh, and he'd have the same mark I do." She raised her sleeve and pointed to the spindly lines shaped like a dragon.

Jamie's eyes widened, his head shaking like insects' wings.

"No? Never seen that on anyone else? All right."

Now that her braid was completely undone and hanging in strands, she might as well do something productive. Like try to cram an entire life into two bags. Unbelievable her life had come to this, to being married to a stranger that didn't consider them married.

But what a choice. She'd take mister jaw-dropping gorgeous over Lord Simon any day. How could she have considered the thought that Lord Simon would be an acceptable match? What had she been thinking?

Keara dropped her hairbrush and comb into the

open bag. She had made the correct decision. If she told herself that enough times, it might stop the fear she felt when Thoren stopped touching her mark. With his hand on her, all she wanted was him, his touch, his acceptance.

From his raven's-wing-black hair to his thick, leather-covered thighs, he exuded a sensuality any normal woman would want to taste, touch, and claim. And in that regard, she was normal.

She wouldn't mind this marriage, sham or not. Having him care about her, to find her pleasing to his eye, might never happen, but she would enjoy this time with him and the new feelings he awakened within her.

"We have to pack, Jamie. We're going someplace new." *And I hope they like us better there than they do here.*

Chapter 4

By the time Keara and Jamie finished packing and made their way downstairs, Enar and Lily had left.

"Where are they?" Her voice sounded panicked and she hoped Thoren didn't notice.

"Don't worry. They went to get Lily's things, stop by the inn where we were staying, pick up our gear and horses, and return here. We'll leave before dawn."

Dawn. She had until dawn and then her life would change, hopefully for the better. Dawn, and she'd never see this shop, her life's memories, again.

Keara looked at the cabinets where her grandmother's potions—formerly bestsellers—sat in colored vials, unsold and unwanted. Business had all but disappeared in the last three months, since her grandmother's death. The store smelled the same, the fragrant scent of herbs hung heavily in the air, but townsfolk no longer shopped here.

Keara shoved her hands through her hair, and stared at the shop, remembering what it once was, what it would never be again. She knew in her heart, they would never return, that this was the last day she'd see her store.

What should she take? "Are there places to gather herbs where we're going?" She turned to look at Thoren, who stood by the table with Jamie, both sets of eyes focused on her.

"There are. But you might find other things besides herbs to sate your healing abilities."

Her head cocked to the side. "What other things?"

He smiled. "Magic."

A chill ran down her spine. "You said that earlier. And it's not evil?"

"No. This is the only place I've heard of that insists magic is evil."

"Are you sure?"

"Do you really think you're evil?"

She circled the nail of her thumb with her forefinger. "Grandmother used to say those with green eyes were evil."

"What do you mean by evil? Do you kill? Do you want to hurt people?"

"Of course not! But all that are not like the others are evil." *Did she really believe that*?

Thoren took a step toward her, locking her gaze to his. "Evil is not how you look. Evil is how you act. The man in the square looked like the others, but he was evil."

"You got that right," Jamie chimed in, breaking the connection Thoren's eyes held over her when he glanced at the boy.

"Do you know how I know that man...what was his name?"

"Lord Simon," she whispered.

"Do you know how I know Lord Simon is evil?"

No, she didn't, and as long as Thoren looked at her, she didn't really care either. What was it about this stranger that sent coils of pleasure racing through her veins straight to her core? And his touch. The only thing better than him looking her in the eye was his touch upon her arm. She'd do anything he wanted as long as he touched her.

Maybe she should avoid his touch.

It was a little hard to do when his hand circled her forearm, one finger rubbing across the spindly dragon imprinted on her skin. *Ah, that felt good*. At least her new husband-who-claimed-he-wasn't-her-husband no longer scared her.

Even all his talk about magic no longer frightened her. All her life she knew her differences. She hid them well, but they still existed. More than anything, she wanted his belief to be correct. Who wants to be thought evil?

His finger rubbed across her mark and shivers ran down her spine, lodging in her core. So much for worrying about sleeping with a stranger. If he wanted her, she was more than happy to accommodate. The kitchen table would do nicely, thank-you very much.

"I know he meant evil because his touch gave you pain. When touched by one that means harm, the mark will hurt. But you don't have that reaction when I touch you, do you?"

No. Definitely not. Was it her imagination or were his lips moving closer to hers? Oh yes, she felt his breath on her face. Her eyes closed.

"Does that touch work on men too or only women?" Jamie asked.

Imp. Thoren took a step back, dropping her arm, red coloring his ears. Keara grabbed the spot his fingers vacated, the absence of his touch leaving her cold. She really needed to have a discussion with Jamie about when to leave the room.

"It works on anyone with a mark. Draconi can tell a person's intentions when their mark is touched." Thoren smiled at Jamie.

Jamie pointed a finger at Thoren. "You're a Draconi?"

"That's right."

"So what's a Draconi?" Keara asked.

"Didn't your mother or father explain to you what a Draconi was?" One black brow rose.

"My mother died when I was still a babe and my grandmother never knew who my father was. He left before I was born."

"So no one told you what a Draconi is?"

"No. Tell me, what is a Draconi?"

"We're a race of shape-shifting sorcerers."

Did she hear him right? *Shape-shifting sorcerers*? Since when did tales told to give children night terrors come to life?

"Don't be frightened, Keara."

Forcing her lips into a grin, she tried to breathe normally. *Or breathe at all.*

"It's a part of who we are. And only the males change, you don't have to worry about changing shapes."

Thank the Goddess. If she had changed while she lived here, she would've been lynched for sure.

"Why don't the women change?" Jamie asked.

Her usually quiet and shy apprentice was all about talking today. Perhaps he wanted to know more about the land they were traveling to, but he had never been this inquisitive about anything she tried to explain to him. Maybe for a boy, shape-shifters held more interest than herbal lore and the running of an apothecary shop.

"Good question. Why don't we change?"

"I'm not sure. It's exceedingly rare and hasn't been reported in many generations. No one understands why females don't change like males. But females have their own powers that the males don't."

"What kinds of powers?"

Enar slammed the back door open, halting the conversation.

"Hey, the horses are out back and it looks like we have company."

So much for learning what powers Draconi females possessed.

Enar strode into the room, holding hands with a wide-eyed, paler-than-normal Lily.

"Company?" Thoren stepped toward Enar.

"A group of men-at-arms heading this way. And they aren't being too quiet about it."

"Lord Simon!" Keara whispered, her heart racing. She should have known he would never leave her be. Once he made a decision, he followed through like a flood bursting a dam. Instead of fretting over what to take and leave, she should have grabbed Thoren and ran.

Too late now. Lord Simon would kill them all and take her for a wife.

"We've got to leave before he gets here! He'll kill you!" Keara motioned toward the back door.

"I said I would protect you." Thoren glared at her, forehead furrowed into rows.

True, but she heard the noise of footsteps in the alley closing in on the yard, more murmurs from the front of the shop. Keara smelled fury drifting in from the street, harmful intent washing in through the cracks in the walls, threatening to suffocate them. How would Thoren protect her? Fly them away?

Reaching into his pocket, he pitched Enar an iridescent ball. "Take the boy!"

Holding Lily with one arm, Enar grabbed Jamie against him as he squeezed the ball, disappearing from view. Keara screamed. Thoren lunged for her, clasping a hand over her mouth, his fingers pressed firmly against her skin.

"Hush." He wrapped an arm around her waist, muttering words she didn't understand, causing the air around them to shimmer.

Keara's heart pounded an erratic beat, her breathing quickened. The front and back doors burst open with a bang, spilling rays of evening sun and soldiers from Lord Simon's regiment.

Thoren's arm tightened around her waist, pinning her arms against her sides. His other hand clamped over her mouth, his mouth next to her ear.

"I cast an invisibility spell. They can't see us, but they can hear," he whispered, his breath tickling the sensitive skin of her ear. "Nod if you understand to be quiet."

Keara nodded and Thoren dropped his hand from her mouth. She shivered as her eyes tracked the last spot she saw Enar.

The air opposite her shimmered slightly, showing glimpses of the three pressed against the wall. Enar held Jamie with one arm, the boy hugging his legs, while Lily hid her face in his chest.

Lord Simon stormed in, his eyes filled with malice as he directed his men to search upstairs before flopping in a chair at the table beside Keara and Thoren's hiding place. How had she ever thought this man a socially acceptable choice? She must be as addled as Lord Simon's father in his last days.

Blood pounded through her veins, beating in her ears and she wondered if Lord Simon could hear it too. Thoren's hand found her left forearm, his fingers slowly stroking from her mark down to her wrist and back again.

Her heart slowed, the blood racing through her ears becoming a mere trickle as pleasurable feelings flowed from his touch to her lower belly, pooling warmth in her core.

Her body relaxed, the tension fleeing, as she realized despite the danger surrounding her, she remained safe in Thoren's arms. He meant what he said about protecting her.

And about magic. If she wasn't so frightened, she'd think the whole invisibility thing pretty exciting.

"Sir, we checked outside, there're horses. Look like they've been ridden, but we don't find evidence of people. They ain't outside, sir."

"Sir, they ain't upstairs either." Boots clomped

against wood as the soldiers strode downstairs.

"They were just here, you lily-livered sons of goats, I heard them! Now search again. Tear up the floors if you have to. They have to be someplace!" Lord Simon jumped to his feet from where he lounged at the table, gesturing at something on the floor. "See here. It's a bag, packed and ready to go. They have to be here, search again!"

The men hustled, kicking the rugs around until they located the trap door to the cellar.

Why had she dropped her bag smack dab in the middle of the floor? Why hadn't she placed it against the wall? Or left it in the bedroom? Due to her carelessness, the soldiers would tear up the shop looking for her.

At least Thoren had a spell. Of...magic. Nice to know magic could be used for good. Which went a long way in convincing her Thoren spoke the truth about evil and magic not necessarily being related.

She watched as Lord Simon stood at the entrance to the cellar, allowing his men to creep down the ladder into the darkness below, while he stayed in the light. It figured he refused to sully himself with trivialities like searching the premises. Goddess forbid he actually scuff a boot. Or run into men who with a small flick of the wrist could hurt him.

Frightened horses nickered as the soldiers grabbed their reins. If they took the bags, then neither Lily nor the men would have extra clothing to wear on the journey. And if the soldiers took the horses, they'd all be walking.

Provided they even got to leave.

"Nothing down here, sir."

"Well, search again. They have to be somewhere."

"Maybe, sir, they left some other way. Because, no offense sir, but they ain't here."

Lord Simon glared at the soldiers, shoving a lock of brown hair behind his ear. "They couldn't be far, their horses are still outside. Peter and Markus, take your men and search the area. Hun and Geo, guard the front with me. The rest of you hide in the yard. If they come back for the horses, take them. I only want the apothecary. The rest are expendable."

Had she actually considered this man might not mean her harm? Praise the Goddess Thoren came along when he did. Who knows what would have happened to her otherwise.

Steam circled around her face and she craned her neck to see it coming from Thoren's ears. His ears smoked just like hers. No wonder he hadn't insisted on lynching her when he saw steam rising from her ears. Keara closed her mouth. Maybe what she considered odd, a Draconi considered normal.

His arm clenched around her waist, his lip turning in a snarl as he glared at Lord Simon. If only looks could kill. Wait, maybe they could.

Or not. Lord Simon remained upright and alive.

Oh well.

The lord walked out of the shop, stopping to stand with legs wide and arms crossed in the doorway. His men took up a post on either side, generating stares from the people walking in the street.

She took as deep a breath as possible considering the vise grip of Thoren's arm around her waist. For the moment they were alone in the shop.

"Anything in the shop you can't do without?" Thoren whispered in her ear. The man needed to stop doing that. Breathing in her ear, making chills shoot through her body when she should feel scared instead.

Her head turned to shelving behind the counter in the front room. "I would like to take my books. But I don't see how we can get them with him standing in the doorway."

"Leave that to me. Will they fit in your bag?" He gestured to the bag on the floor in front of them.

She shook her head. "There's a satchel under the counter that most of them would fit in. But that would be another pack for the horses."

"We're leaving the horses."

Was he crazy? The thought of walking, who knew how far while carrying a couple of bags, made her body ache. But it beat the alternative.

"Keep close to me and we'll walk to the shelf."

Her eyes darted to Lord Simon's back. "Won't he hear?"

"Not if we're quiet."

She nodded, the movement jerky as adrenaline pumped through her muscles. Thoren kept his arm around her waist, moving her toward the shelves, watching Lord Simon and his minions through the storefront window. They paused by the counter for her to grab the satchel.

"Keep it under the counter. It's not protected by the invisibility spell."

Lord Simon would come running if he saw a satchel floating across the room. Keara watched with trepidation as Simon twitched, rising onto his toes, bouncing off the ground to do the motion again. Sounds from the street floated through the open door, covering the noise she made putting the books into the bag.

"Anything else?"

Keara looked around the shop, memories passing over her. She mixed her first potion here, treated her first patient over there at the table by the door, mixed herbs at the counter. Twilight bathed the shop, drifting through the windows, casting long shadows of the men guarding the place. She took one last look, knowing she'd never see the place again, trying to remember the pleasant times and forget about the bad.

Taking a deep breath, she turned toward Thoren, whispering in his ear. "I'm ready."

He flicked a hand at the satchel and it vanished. Keara gasped, unable to help herself. Lord Simon whirled, stepping into the shop, obviously looking for the source of the sound.

"Did you hear that?" he asked his men.

"No, sir."

"Didn't hear nothing, sir."

He looked right at Keara, his eyes narrowing. She felt Thoren tense behind her as a trickle of sweat ran down her spine. Her surprise at the satchel's vanishing act almost caused their capture. If Lord Simon saw them, it would surely mean Thoren's death. Would Thoren dole out a punishment for her almost getting them caught?

She glanced over at him. His jaw thrust forward. This close she saw the stubble from where he needed to shave. His eyes locked onto Lord Simon, staring at him as a hunter would prey. Thoren remained motionless, if Keara hadn't felt his heart beat from where her back pressed against his chest, she would have thought him a statue. How a person could remain so still confounded her.

After what seemed like an eternity, Lord Simon turned around, returning to his post by the door. Keara exhaled a breath she didn't realize she held.

Thoren led her back into the room behind the shop where Enar, Lily and Jamie hid.

"Is everything in the bags on the horses?"

"Yes. Packed and ready to go." Enar's voice whispered across the room, although Keara still couldn't see him clearly.

Why could she see him at all?

Thoren moved her so they stood in sight of the horses, which stood by the back door. He flicked his hand and the horses' packs disappeared. Wasn't she good for keeping her gasp internal? Thoren motioned toward the bag on the floor and it also vanished.

She needed to learn that vanishing trick. Then the next time Jamie interrupted her and Thoren she could transport him to another room. Better yet, she could make Lord Simon disappear right off her property. Or maybe only small things could vanish since Thoren hadn't made the lord disappear.

And since Lord Simon remained standing, the potential remained for her to be caught and the others killed. Good thing she didn't need to speak, she couldn't even swallow.

"Is there any way out of here besides the front or the back door?" Thoren turned to Keara.

She shook her head.

"There're the sewers in the cellar." She was surprised to hear Jamie say. "Leads to the south river."

Keara gaped in the direction of her apprentice, too shocked to say anything. How had he known that? She didn't even know and she had lived here her entire life. Of course, she had heard of—and smelled—the sewers, but didn't realize anyone but the thieves and lazy, non-working maintenance men knew their location. Maybe she wouldn't ask Jamie; she might not want to know the answer.

"To the cellar then. Jamie, you'll lead once we're at the bottom."

Once down the stairs and out of sight of the open trapdoor, Enar handed the ball back to Thoren, appearing suddenly in front of Keara, Lily still attached to his arm. Her friend's hair stood out in the darkness, a pale shine against the almost complete blackness. Keara reached for Lily, grabbing her ice-cold hand with all her strength.

At least they were together. For now.

Keara clung to Thoren's hand as he led them into the darkness, away from her shop, away from her old life and into a new one.

May the Goddess go with her.

****

Thoren led Keara toward Jamie, who stood against the far side of the room. His night vision allowed him to see clearly, but he doubted anyone else could, if the stumbles and grunted curses meant anything. He didn't dare use his magic to light the room, fearing the men above might notice.

Kill and protect. The dragon in him roared, wanting to kill the one that meant harm to Keara, finding running away unacceptable. It took all his will to tamp the beast down, and despite his efforts, his ears smoked.

What in the name of the Goddess was wrong with him? No other Draconi female had ever affected him like this. Of course, no other Draconi female had ever been threatened in his presence, so maybe this was just the way males reacted when females were in danger.

That must be it. Females should be protected, cherished, not chased through cellars and sewers by a regiment of scurrilous soldiers. No wonder his inner dragon was upset.

Focus on the situation at hand. Focus, focus, Thoren.

Jamie stood in front of a small iron door built into the stone wall. Thoren placed his hand on the dampness of the wall and leaned into the opening, taking a deep breath. Big mistake. He choked on the rank smell of human excrement, mixed with dead animal. He pulled his head back, trying to smother his cough, eyes tearing from the effort. Jamie made a face as he breathed in the rank air.

"You'll get used to it. Come on!" The boy ducked through the opening, standing in the smelly, rock-lined tube.

Jamie had a point about leaving. Thoren tried

47

breathing through his mouth, which didn't help much, as he walked through the small door, bending over double in the sewer in order not to bump his head. Enar cursed, bending his legs in a duck walk.

"Warriors are not meant to crawl around sewers."

"Nothing besides rats and small boys are designed for it, my friend."

Enar snorted. A small click echoed through the tunnels as Jamie pulled the iron door shut. Darkness settled, broken by the trickle of water under their feet and the thick scent of sewage in the air around them.

"Jamie, in front."

Jamie splashed by the others, unimpeded by raw sewage, to stand in front of Thoren. Thoren focused on his hand, drawing his magic until a blue flame danced in his palm, illuminating the dank walls of the tunnel. Keara's hand touched his back, causing a shiver up his spine. The light flickered before growing brighter.

"Best keep it down, Draconi. I have no desire to burn in this tunnel." Enar chuckled.

A splash, followed by scurrying feet, heralded the movement of a rodent. Keara's grip tightened on his shirt. His beast roared. She trusted him to protect her, to save her.

What was wrong with him today? Where were all these emotions coming from? Talk about channeling one's inner demon.

What if she was his mate? What if all these emotions of protect and kill meant she belonged to him? Just what he needed. He didn't want a mate. He wanted to remain a spy. Maybe in another twenty years or so he'd want to settle down, but not now. All he had to do was convince his dragon Keara was not his mate.

Something told him the beast wasn't believing

it.

Water dripped into the small stream they straddled. Thoren focused on the steady drip, gaining control over his emotions. He needed to stay focused on the task at hand, and get them all to safety. Trying to decide whether Keara was his mate had no bearing on the fact that she needed to be protected. And the only way to do that was to leave this town.

Unfortunately, leaving the town meant crawling through the sewers, but nothing was perfect. At least no one followed them.

"Almost there," Jamie said.

Goddess be praised. Fresh air directly ahead.

The tunnel burst open into the side of the town's wall, the sewage stream falling over the edge into the river below. Thoren closed his hand, extinguishing the flame, before standing next to the opening. Using his magic, he reached out, feeling up along the wall and out across the ground, checking for the presence of humans.

"All clear. Enar, the bags are on the ridge where we first entered this valley. I'll lead if you'll guard the rear. They weren't following us, but they might have figured out where we went." And with the way his dragon wanted to fight Lord Simon, the last thing he needed was for the men-at-arms to have followed them. The Council would have kittens if he changed into a dragon and fought a group of humans.

Once out of the tunnel, they all breathed easier. Dragons were not created to traverse odiferous tunnels. Soon they would be at the campsite and then tomorrow would begin the long journey home. On foot. Because Goddess forbid he change into a dragon and fly them home. Oh no. The Council frowned on that. No changing into a dragon unless an emergency arose.

And walking for two weeks did not qualify as an emergency. He hated this part of the job. Why should he walk when he had a set of wings and could make it home in a couple of days? But rules had to be followed. Even if it meant walking home.

Keara touched his arm and his dragon purred. "Where are we going?"

"We had a site before we came into town. We're going there for the night. We'll begin the journey home tomorrow at first light."

She nodded. "All right."

Twilight caught sparks in her hair, shimmering in glowing haloes about her face. His heart leapt in his chest as he watched her move, watched her tuck a strand of hair behind her ear. He'd seen plenty of beauties in his journey around Draconia, but Keara's beauty surpassed them all.

Maybe once he returned her to Draconia, all these protective feelings would subside. If not, he had a whole new problem. Males reacted this way toward their mate.

Keara smiled at him and his dragon roared in triumph.

He cursed.

Chapter 5

Keara sat on a log beside Lily, Jamie at her feet, watching as Thoren and Enar laid wards to keep Lord Simon, or anyone else looking for them, at bay. She shivered as Thoren laid another ward. The magic thrummed through her veins, speaking to her in a language she didn't understand.

"Do you feel that?" Keara asked Lily.

"Feel what?"

"That." She shivered as Thoren spoke another magic word. "Every time he lays a ward I feel it in my bones."

"I don't feel anything." Lily continued to stare at Enar.

Her poor friend. Keara placed a hand over Lily's. Although Thoren's ways seemed strange, she was gaining confidence he meant her no harm. With Enar though, she wasn't as confident. At least not where Lily was concerned.

Keara glanced at Jamie when Thoren placed the next ward. Her apprentice stared at Thoren, watching his every move, but didn't seem to react to the magic. Of course he wouldn't, he had no magic, unlike her. But what did she really know about him? She knew nothing of his life before she found him and as evidenced by his knowledge about the sewers, little of his life since then. How did he know about the sewer tunnels?

Boys.

When Thoren returned she'd ask him about the wards and why she felt the magic. He wouldn't think her strange for asking. At least she hoped he wouldn't. After all, he worked magic around the periphery of their campsite, how upset could he be if she felt the magic in her bones?

Funny how over the course of the evening she felt more comfortable and relaxed around him. He didn't mind the steam coming out her ears, he worked magic and his eyes held no fear when he looked upon her. Even her grandmother's eyes had held fear. Maybe she would talk to him about his magic.

Thoren glanced over at her and grinned. She felt the heat rise to her cheeks and lowered her eyes. It was night and technically she was his wife. Would he want to claim her? Her heart raced, thumping like a bass drum in her chest. Being close to him made her blood sing and as long as he touched her she liked the idea. But with him on the other side of the campsite, the whole thought of bedding him made her stomach churn.

If her luck held, he'd be more interested in talking to her about magic than removing her clothes.

Right. He was a man and everyone knew what they'd rather do. Deep breath in, slow breath out. No hyperventilating tonight. *Slow, deep breaths, Keara.* And what about Lily? Thoren might rather talk magic with her, but Lily wouldn't be so lucky with Enar. Yet outside of sitting straighter than a ruler, her friend didn't look nervous.

Keara lengthened her spine and mirrored Lily's posture. Pretend; pretend until the state of mind becomes reality. A nervous giggle escaped her lips. Great, she was completely losing it.

Thoren must have finished placing wards around the campsite since he headed her way, Enar following. Lily froze and Keara tightened her grip on her friend's hand. Lily squeezed back with the strength of a giant, her body becoming still. Enar stopped in front of Lily, holding out a hand, his blond hair brushing against his cheeks.

"Come, Lily. You will sleep with me."

Lily's hand shook as she gulped. She took a deep breath and with one last squeeze dropped Keara's hand. Looking Enar in the eyes, she placed her hand in his and allowed him to lead her to the bedroll to the right of the log they sat on. Keara watched, unable to move, as Enar threw a blanket over them, hiding them from view, the blanket blending in with the scenery, making them part of the ground.

The blanket hitting the ground unfroze Keara and she leapt at Thoren, grabbing his arm. He dropped the blanket he'd been offering to Jamie on the boy's lap, blinking in surprise at her sudden movement.

"Don't let him rape her. He's going to hurt her!"

"He's not going to hurt her." Thoren touched her arm, but she took a step back until he dropped his hand.

Did he really know that? No. She started toward where she last saw Lily, but Thoren grabbed her by the arms, halting her in her tracks. "Calm down. He's not hurting her."

"How do you know?"

"I can see them. It's all right, Keara. No one is hurting anyone this night." He turned to Jamie. "Jamie, pull the blanket over you when you sleep and no one will be able to see you. Don't remove it until we tell you to. Understand?"

Jamie nodded at him, unfolding the blanket. Holding a section of it over the ground, he peered intently at it and then held it up in front of his face.

"Hey, check this out! You can see through it, but it disappears when you hold it over the ground." Jamie waved the edge of the blanket over the ground and in front of his face.

"It's an invisibility blanket. It blends into the surroundings to keep you hidden, but you can see through it. It's also a real blanket and will keep you warm on a chilly night."

"Magic?" Keara wondered.

"Yes. See, magic is not evil."

"Of course it's not," Jamie chimed in and Keara looked at him in shock. Today was the day for learning interesting things about her apprentice.

"You can pull that blanket over your head and go to sleep. I've set the wards so no one can get in and no one but a Draconi can get out. So don't worry about people getting in and hurting you or Keara, all right?"

"You sure?"

"Yes. And I promised to protect her. You can rest easy."

Jamie threw his arms around Keara's waist, burying his head in her chest. She stroked his back, amazed at his protectiveness toward her. Today was the first day he showed that side. Who knew what other interesting tidbits she'd learn about her apprentice if given enough time?

"Good night, Jamie."

"'Night, Keara." Jamie lay down, yanking the blanket over his head, blending into the ground.

Her turn. Placing her hand in Thoren's outstretched one, she straightened her spine and followed him to their bedroll. Glancing back to where her friends lay, she could see nothing but rocks spread on the ground despite the bright moonlight. Staring hard enough produced a shimmer of energy, allowing her to see glimpses of Enar's back where he lay on his side. Her shoulders relaxed as she realized Thoren spoke the truth. Enar was not hurting her friend.

"Satisfied?" Thoren's voice broke through her thoughts, her head jerking around to meet his eyes.

"I can see through the blankets. If I can see through them so can others. Are you sure we're safe?" How embarrassing. If her voice got any higher, she could sing soprano. Taking a deep breath, she tried to calm her heartbeat.

"You can see them?" His voice sounded surprised, pleased. "Your powers are strong then. That will make it easier for you when you have your unlocking ceremony."

"What's that?"

"Lie down and I'll explain." He gestured to his bedroll.

Keara looked up at him, down at the bedroll and back up at him. Heat seared her cheeks as she stared at him. Her husband. In the dark. Gesturing toward the bedroll. She knelt, facing the lumps of darkness that were her friend and apprentice, before lying on her side.

She felt Thoren lie behind her and then the blanket settled over her, never quite touching her body, the transparent material caressing her with a lover's touch. Hard to believe this would keep them safe from prying eyes, but since the others were hidden, she supposed it worked.

Where to start with all her questions? Thankfully, Thoren seemed happy to stay on his side of the bedroll. If she talked enough, maybe he'd stay put.

"What is an unlocking ceremony? No, wait. You said Enar wasn't a Draconi, so what is he and why did he claim Lily? No, no, no, never mind, that's not what I want to know first. First, I want to know why I felt the magic when you laid the wards." Keara rolled over to face Thoren.

This close she could see the stubble on his jaw, feel his breath on her face. If he touched her, she'd do anything he wanted. But he kept his hands to himself.

Was she relieved or upset? Relieved since sleeping with a practical stranger sent shivers down her spine and yet she wanted him to want her. Her body craved his even without his touch.

Conflicted was not a state of mind she liked.

"You felt the magic because you're a Draconi. We feel magic. Because of where you were raised, with a bunch of superstitious, magic-hating people, you never felt it before. You'll feel more of it the closer we get to Draconia."

"So it's normal to feel magic?"

"It is. Eventually you'll learn to control it."

"That's good. So what about Enar? If he's not Draconi, what is he and why did he claim Lily?"

A deep breath. "Enar is a Watcher. They guard the Draconi."

"I thought you said Draconi worked magic. Why do they need guards?"

"Good question. I've wondered that myself, but have never gotten a straight answer. All I know is that many years ago, before any Draconi alive was born—and since Draconi live for around five hundred years it was a very long time ago—Watchers needed a place to settle and in return for the Draconi generosity of donated land, the Watchers used their warrior skills to guard the Draconi. Since that time, male Watchers are assigned to male Draconi as guards. Enar is assigned to me."

"Draconi live for five hundred years?" She would live that long?

"Around about there, yes. Because we live so long we don't usually have many offspring."

Five hundred years? Keara's mind stuttered trying to think of that many years. Might as well give the poor brain a break and ask what will happen to Lily.

"I'm sorry. That's going to take me some time to

get used to. Five hundred years? Back to Lily. Why did Enar claim her? What's going to become of her?"

"I don't know. Enar won't hurt her, he's my best friend and I know he loves females almost as much as he loves a good fight, but although I know Watchers claim women, I have never seen a claimed woman and Enar changes the topic every time I go near it. There's a lot about Watchers I don't know."

Judging by the hard set of his lips, there was a lot about Watchers he knew and didn't care to tell her. Hopefully his lack of knowledge didn't bode ill for her friend.

Back to more questions. If she filled her head full of new information, she wouldn't have to dwell on whether or not the Draconi would accept her.

"And the what-did-you-call-it ceremony?"

"Unlocking?"

"Yes, that one. What's that?"

"All female Draconi have limited powers until they reach puberty. After puberty, they undergo a ceremony to unlock their powers. You must have strong powers because you can see through the invisibility blanket with your powers locked."

"And that's good?"

"Oh, yes. That's very good. Females usually have the strongest powers, but the males change into dragons."

"Dragons?" Big scary mythical creatures? That was what he shape-shifted into? Until his hand clamped on her forearm, she hadn't realized she'd scooted backward.

"Like the shape of your mark. Don't be frightened."

Relaxation coursed through her veins. Why was she backing away from Thoren? She should be trying to get closer to him, to join with him as one being, to become his.

What on earth was she thinking?

"You're casting a spell on me."

A hint of white gleamed as he smiled. "No spell. Just my touch."

"It puts me at a disadvantage because whenever you touch me I want to do whatever you want me to."

"I'll have to remember that." His grin widened, showing even white teeth, but he stopped touching her.

Keara blushed, thinking about what she'd like to do with him. About how she wanted to start with kissing his lips, then work her way down his body, licking and stroking every inch. But she felt that way only because he touched her. Wait, he wasn't touching her now and she still wanted him, wanted his touch.

Talk, Keara, talk.

"Uh-huh. What's your home like?"

"That will take all night to describe. Suffice it to say, you'll fit in fine. There are other Halflings like you..."

"How do you know I'm a Halfling?"

"Draconi have green eyes. We look for green eyes coupled with red hair since all Halflings have red hair. Well, almost all, very rarely there's one that doesn't. It hasn't happened in some time, but the last time a Halfling didn't have red hair, they had incredible powers."

"What happened to him?"

"It was a female and it's a long story. We need to go to sleep."

"Oh. So Halflings like me are common?"

His face tensed. "Lately they are."

"And this makes you unhappy?" Did he resent her?

"No, no. It's complicated. But it has nothing to do with you. Don't worry. You'll be welcomed in Draconia. Draconi are friendly to those with Draconi blood. Enough talking. You should try to get some sleep. We'll be leaving at first light and it's a long journey."

"How long?"

"About two weeks."

Ouch. Her feet already hurt and they hadn't even started walking.

"All right. Good night."

She rolled over into her original position, turning her back to him. Luck walked with her. He didn't want to bed her. But if she was so lucky, why did she feel so disappointed?

****

Thoren watched Keara's ribs rise and fall with her breathing. He doubted she slept as her body still held tension. How difficult this must be for her. Learning who she was, discovering an entirely different race she never knew existed. He could tell it made her nervous, all the new discoveries, but she possessed a bravery he admired.

Glints of moonlight sparked red rubies in her hair. One hand hovered over her head, wanting to touch, wanting to comfort. Thoren yanked his hand back. What was it about Keara that made him want to touch her? Made his blood thrum when she smiled? Laying this close to her, his body demanded he touch her, turn her toward him, stake his claim on her.

He stuck one hand between his knees. Maybe the knee crunch would stop him from grabbing Keara.

What in the name of the Goddess was wrong with him?

Unfortunately, he suspected he knew. But if he took her for his mate, he'd have to stop his work, the work that gave him a purpose. And where would that leave him? Without a job, sitting around mindlessly watching his female and wishing he was out spying in another land.

Time was on his side. Only one female existed per male. Only one. And if fate decreed Keara his, and he wasn't completely sure it did, then she wouldn't find a mate until he was ready to quit his job.

He gritted his teeth as his imagination saw other males touching her, covering her with their bodies. Steam leaked out his ears and he rolled onto his back, hands pressed against his ears.

"Are you all right?" Keara mumbled, starting to turn over.

No. "I'm fine. I have a hard time falling asleep." *When I'm in pain from wanting you.*

She rolled back onto her side, facing away from him. Praise the Goddess. If she had continued rolling over, he might have acted on instinct. He moved onto his side, facing away from Keara's back. Maybe that position would help.

Or not. Only one thing would help his below-the-belt ache and it wasn't staring at tree branches. *Think about pain, catching your finger in a door, getting into a fight.*

He cursed. It was going to be a long night.

Chapter 6

"Thoren!" Enar's bellow woke Thoren with a start.

Blinking his eyes for good measure, he stretched before throwing the blanket off. The rising sun meant he had somehow managed to fall asleep the night before. Shame he didn't feel like he'd slept. Being in proximity to Keara fired his blood.

But, outside of whatever caused Enar to bellow like a bull in heat, today would be better than how he felt lying next to her last night, burning with desire. If he repeated those words long enough, they would come true. Keara rolled over and stared out of sleep-swollen eyes, a puzzled look on her face as she glanced between him and Enar.

So much for high ambitions. One look and he turned into a simpering idiot.

So stop looking.

Pushing himself to a sitting position, he glared at Enar. "What is worth bellowing about this early in the morning?"

"The lad is missing."

"Missing? Are you sure?" Thoren hopped to his feet and immediately wished he hadn't. He didn't need to glance down to see the cause of Enar's grin.

Hopefully Keara wouldn't notice.

At least Enar refrained from being a wit.

"Yes. He's nowhere in the warded area."

"I saw him head that way." Keara pointed toward the woods. "It looked like he needed to relieve himself."

61

How could a non-magical child get over there? The wards were at least six feet from the woods.

"Are you sure?"

Keara huffed. "I know what I saw and he walked over there." She pointed again at the woods, head tilted, eyes glaring at him.

Then that would mean...

Cursing, Thoren mentally smacked himself on the head. Why hadn't he seen what Jamie was? What kind of a reconnaissance expert can't tell when his prey is sitting under his nose?

Because he looked for red hair and green eyes, not brown locks and gray peepers.

His first mistake. The number one rule of reconnaissance was things were not always as they appeared. That rule saved him on many occasions. And then he obviously forgot all about it once he saw Keara.

"Goddess's teeth."

"That about sums it up," Enar said.

"We have to go after him, you know."

"Of course. Pretty amazing, no red hair. That's awfully rare, right?"

"You have no idea."

The last time a Draconi Halfling had brown hair her powers had been greater than those of the High Priestess, or so the stories said. No other Halfling had been found with brown hair since.

Until now.

Goddess's teeth.

"Can you walk through the wards?" Thoren gestured to Lily. Maybe she possessed some powers too. Oddities seemed to abound in this village in the middle of nowhere.

Lily came to a halt when she started to cross the ward line. She put her hands up, feeling the invisible wall, before turning to him with her mouth gaped, eyes wide.

"It's a solid wall! Amazing!"

Praise the Goddess. Something went right. Only magical beings could walk through wards.

"How long have you known Jamie?" Thoren ignored Lily, who continued to run her hands over the "wall," and focused on Keara.

"Three months. He's going to be all right, isn't he?"

"Where did you find him?"

"The woods outside the town. I told you he said his parents were dead and I claimed him. Shouldn't we be out looking for him?"

"Does he have any...special abilities?"

"Special abilities?" Keara tilted her head and cocked an eyebrow at Thoren.

"Like yours. He's the Halfling we've been looking for."

"Are you sure?" Keara stared wide-eyed at Thoren.

"There is no other explanation for how he got through the wards. Only Draconi can get through wards. Notice how Lily was stopped by them?"

"But Jamie? He's just a boy. And he's lost. You need to do something about that."

"We're going. Don't worry. You and Lily stay put."

"No! I'm going with you. He's my apprentice."

"Simon could get his hands on you again, so you're staying here and that's that."

Keara crossed her arms, eyes narrowed, steam curling from her ears. "You can't tell me what to do."

"I don't want you to get hurt and you won't get hurt if you stay inside the wards."

Two heartbeats and her glare narrowed. "Fine. Just bring him back."

"We plan on it. Stay here."

She nodded, lips pressed together.

They found missing Halflings for a living. It

shouldn't take long to track down one small boy.

An hour or so later it became obvious that finding Jamie was harder than he imagined. Despite searching the clump of bushes Keara directed them to, they found no signs of the boy.

A vague scent, similar to the one Thoren had smelled about the town, led a trail away from the campsite. Why would Jamie wander away from safety? Probably for the same reason he and Enar got into trouble as children. Things needed exploring. Although what in the name of the Goddess needed exploring in the middle of the night in hostile territory, he didn't know.

Thoren started walking in the direction of Jamie's scent, head up, sniffing the air. Enar walked in front of him, staring at the ground, looking for tracks. So much for getting an early start home. The day was rapidly heading downhill. Jamie's scent led back to town. The lad either forgot something or was captured. Just his luck. Draconi boys were trouble.

He should know.

"Look at this." Enar pointed to the ground.

"What?" Thoren walked to where Enar stood, looking at a patch of grass.

"It's trampled. Jamie's tracks lead here, where they are joined by several others. Then his tracks disappear and the larger ones move off in that direction." Enar pointed toward the town.

Thoren looked at the trampled grass, barely making out what Enar described. Good thing he used his nose to track. Enar, though, confirmed what Thoren scented, Jamie's trail led back to the town.

"Draconi boys are too curious for their own good."

"And they get their friends in trouble too. I remember." Enar laughed.

"We'll use the invisibility balls..."

"No. I can't fight holding one of those things.

Cast a spell, sorcerer."

"Good point." Thoren chuckled at the mental image of Enar trying to wave a sword while holding the invisibility ball. Funny, but not the most effective way of fighting. "I'll cast a spell rendering us invisible, we'll sneak into the town, grab Jamie and hightail it out."

"Sounds like a plan. Then you can get back to your female and continue what you started this morning."

"She's not my female and nothing was started. Things are always ready for action in the morning."

"Mmph. Especially with a pretty female around."

Thoren's lip peeled off his teeth and for the second time in his life, he snarled at his friend. He really needed to get in control of these emotions. Enar paid Keara a compliment, there was absolutely no reason to stake a claim on her.

So why was his lip still up around his cheekbone?

Enar stood, arms crossed, one eyebrow raised.

"Sorry. I seem to be a little upset right now. Maybe you have a clue why?"

Enar snorted. "I've yet to meet a Draconi who could fight the mating once he found his female."

"She's not my female." Or was she?

"Whatever, fool." Enar smacked him on the arm. "Let's go get the lad. I'd rather see *my* woman instead of chasing after imps."

****

Keara paced from one end of the warded ground to the other, ignoring Lily who sat against a tree, wrapped in a blanket. Thoren had pointed out where the ward-lines stood, telling her to stay inside them so that she would be safe from harm. For the past hour she had done just that, not daring to step outside the lines for fear of what might happen. But now her fear for Jamie overruled her fear for her own safety. She shouldn't be at the campsite, pacing uselessly, while Jamie was lost and alone. She should be out trying to find him.

She marched back to Lily, determined to find Jamie on her own.

Lily poked her head out from the blanket, eyes wide. "Don't even think about leaving me here alone."

"You have the blanket. No one can see you. Jamie needs me. The men don't know their way around these woods. What if they get lost?"

"They won't get lost. You on the other hand..."

"Don't be ridiculous. I grew up around here. Grandmother used to take me to these woods for herbs." Once, when she was little, but still. "I'm going to find Jamie. He needs me."

"And I don't?"

"You have the blanket. And you're sitting in the wards. Jamie's by himself in the woods. What if something happened to him? I can't leave him alone out there!" Keara gestured to the woods.

"Are you sure nothing can get to me?"

"Thoren said nothing non-Draconi can get through those wards. You can't get out can you?"

"No."

"Then nothing can get in to you. You're safe. Jamie needs me."

"Thoren won't be happy about it."

Keara sighed. "I know. But I have to. You understand, don't you?"

"I understand. Don't worry about me. I'll hide under this invisibility blanket." She pulled the blanket over her head, disappearing from view. "Be safe."

"Thanks, love. I won't be long."

Tracking the men wasn't as hard as she feared. Strangely enough, it seemed easier to track their scent rather than the marks left on the ground. Did dragons track by scent? She shook her head. Who would have thought she was part—dare she say it— dragon? Until yesterday, she didn't realize dragons existed outside of fables. What did a dragon look like? Thoren claimed to be one, but he looked like a man.

Maybe dragons were sexy, good-looking, raven-haired men.

A woman could get used to dragons like that. Especially one like Thoren. Over the course of a day, she went from being frightened of him to excited whenever he was near. Her entire body tingled when he touched her and she had this odd urge to throw him down and bite him on the neck.

Why was that? Maybe dragons did that type of thing. She'd have to ask. Or not. How embarrassing would that conversation be? *Hey, Thoren, I want to bite your neck.* Right. He'd think her some sort of evil night creature.

Looking up from the trail she followed, Keara saw the wall surrounding the town of River's Run. Talk about being lost in thought. Had she actually walked all the way back to town and not noticed? What a way to be careful and watch where she walked.

Was she in danger? Did Lord Simon want her enough to chase her? He wasn't that ambitious, right?

Probably not, but to be safe, she probably should return to Lily. If her nose proved correct, Jamie and the men were in town, not in the woods. And if she could scent Jamie, no doubt Thoren could too and do a better job of it. As hard as it was, she needed to trust him to return Jamie.

Taking one last look at the town, she turned, only to come to a complete stop. Her lungs stopped pumping, her heart double-timing it.

"Hello, Keara," Lord Simon leered. "Nice of you to find me. Saved me a lot of trouble."

Keara tried to scream, but someone grabbed her from behind, slapping a grimy hand across her mouth. The scent of stale sweat and overripe bodies assaulted her. Time slowed, until her awareness focused solely on her useless struggling and the frantic beat of her heart thudding in her ears. Her feet kicked against the shins of what had to be a tree. Despite her efforts, he didn't budge. What was Lord Simon going to do to her? Why did he want her badly enough to capture her?

Stalking toward Keara with the grace of a large cat, Lord Simon pulled a stained rag from his tunic. His lip curled as he came to her, his eyes flat, emotionless. He stuffed the foul tasting cloth into her mouth, almost choking her with it. She shook her head, trying to spit the gag out, trying not to have him tie it, but he slapped her, stunning her into stillness. The cloth cut into her cheeks as he pulled it tightly behind her head.

"I have plans for you." Simon shook a finger in her face. "You've been a bad girl, running off, making it hard for me to find you."

The henchman loosened his grip from her waist, grabbing onto her arms, yanking them behind her back. Simon tied her wrists together, twisting the ropes until blood pulsed in her hands, trapped there by the bindings. The gag caught her yelp of pain. When he finished tying her hands, he cinched her feet together. If his henchman hadn't been holding her arms she would have fallen over. Fear coiled in her stomach, and she swallowed the nausea that threatened to overwhelm her.

The henchman pitched her over his shoulder and blood rushed to her face, throbbing against the gag. Each step he took stabbed his shoulder into her stomach as she fought to breathe. Her shoulders ached from the tension of her tied wrists. Her hands and feet tingled as they went numb.

Would Thoren know to look for her? Would he care? How could she be so stupid as to fall into Lord Simon's clutches? Again. Would she be able to escape him this time?

Soon the man carrying her stopped. Keara raised her head to see that they stood at the side of the wall surrounding the town, an open door spilling darkness before them. The position hurt her neck, and she let her head fall against the man's back.

"Welcome to my home, Keara. You'll stay here until the hooded man decides to take you elsewhere." Lord Simon chuckled as he grabbed her braid, jerking her head up to meet his gaze. "Who knows? If you're good, he might even share you." Despite her eyes watering, she managed to fix him with a glare. Not a smart move, to antagonize one's captor, but no way would anyone be sharing her.

And who was this hooded man? A chill ran down her spine a second before Simon's palm smacked against her cheek. The pain ricocheted through her already aching head.

"You'll learn not to look at me that way. Fast or slow, you'll learn." He dropped his grip, allowing her head to bang against the man's back.

Keara ran her tongue around the inside of her mouth, feeling the cuts, trying to swallow the blood before she gagged. Her cheeks on fire, tears of pain and frustration ran from the corners of her eyes. The man walked through the opening in the wall and the door slammed shut behind them with a bang, plunging them into darkness.

Bile rose in her throat the deeper they walked through the stone tunnel. Cold fear shot through her veins when she saw the barred cells of the dungeon, chains dripping from the walls, the rank smell of damp thick in the air.

Oh, please Goddess, don't let them keep me here!

Keara raised her head, blinking away the tears. She would not cry. She would not give Simon the satisfaction of seeing her upset. Torchlight flickered against the damp stones. From one of the cells came shuffling noises, like that made by a large beast. A huge shadow appeared in the cell from which the noises came and the shuffling sound grew louder. Her heart stepped up its rhythm, a frantic thudding in her chest, echoing in her ears. Would they feed her to the beast? It took all her willpower to turn her head to the side, to stare at the beast as it came toward them.

The man carrying her gasped, almost dropping her as he took a step to the side. But Keara couldn't look away. Her gaze remained transfixed by the monster. Blood red scales glinted in the torchlight. A long snout culminating in sharp teeth and large nostrils butted against thick prison bars.

Glowing green eyes blinked at her, widened, then narrowed. It let out a roar that shook the dungeon, causing little rivulets of dirt to drop on their heads. Claws tried to grasp the bars as the thing roared again. Steam started coming from its nostrils and a small amount out its ears. Opening its mouth, gracing them with a view of sharp teeth, it let out a plume of fire, narrowly missing them.

Heat blasted against Keara as the man holding her dropped her in a panic. She landed with a thud against the dirt floor, stunned, the breath locked in her lungs. The creature bellowed its rage, letting loose another plume of fire, which raced in the air above her body, hitting full force the man who dropped her. A scream of pain lasted seconds before ending abruptly.

Keara smelled the nauseating stench of burned flesh and concentrated on not gagging. Opening her eyes, she stared in horror at the monster. It stared back, making little whimper noises, steam still pouring from its nose and ears.

Free me and I'll help you. The words in her head startled Keara. Had she hit her head hard enough to hear voices?

"I see you've met my father's pet." Lord Simon stood beside her, causing her to twitch in surprise. She missed hearing his footsteps in all the commotion. The creature started making snuffling noises, heralding another fireball. Lord Simon yanked Keara to her feet, holding her against him as a shield, dragging her body backward. A roar bellowed from the cell as the monster threw itself against the bars.

"Father claimed it was a man when he captured it, a powerful man. Not like you could believe a thing my dear father said. He captured the 'man' here right before he lost his mind."

Keara remembered her grandmother treating Lord Simon's father for dementia. The old woman had been puzzled, saying no good reason existed for a man his age to lose his mind.

"Now our little 'man' sits around, eating cattle and billowing smoke. He must really hate you though because he's never made a crispy critter out of one of the men before. I'll keep that in mind, in case you fall out of favor with the hooded man."

The creature roared again. *Free me, girl, and I'll set you free.*

How? How do I do that when I can't get free? Great, just great. I'm carrying on a conversation with that creature in my head. Maybe dementia was catching. Or maybe the thing could talk in her head. Lord Simon reached the stairs, starting to back up them. Keara's feet bumped against the steps and she caught her breath.

The keys, girl. Give me the keys.

Good thing she was gagged. If not she'd be

laughing hysterically. *I'm losing it.*

No, not losing it. Think about the keys landing in front of my cell. Think hard.

Why not? What did she have to lose? Before Lord Simon could drag her around the bend in the stairs, she sighted the keys hanging on the wall, several feet from the creature's cell. Closing her eyes, she pictured them floating off the wall and toward the creature, landing outside the bars of his cell. When she opened her eyes, the wall of the stairwell blocked her sight to the dungeon, so she couldn't tell if the keys still hung on the wall or not. But a voice floated through her head on a sigh.

Good try, girl. Good try.

Chapter 7

"He's not well guarded." Enar peered over Thoren's shoulder, keeping in close proximity with his friend, thereby ensuring he remained invisible.

Thoren cocked his head to the side, watching the two men guarding Jamie roll dice. Hiding under the spell of invisibility, he and Enar had tracked the boy back to Keara's store, where Jamie sat behind the counter tied to a chair and gagged, guarded by two not very observant men.

Through the open window, Thoren heard the dice rattling in the wooden cup before he saw them thrown onto the counter the men lounged against. One of the men let out a cheer, raking a pile of coins toward him. The other man glared at the winner, but proceeded to roll the dice again. Jamie stared at the game, dried blood frozen in rivulets from his temple to his jaw.

Crowds of people dressed in identical colors of drab brown and black cried noisily to the vendors hawking their wares in the stores lining the narrow street. Hit from behind by one of the passersby, Enar stumbled into Thoren, who fell against the window with a loud "oomph."

"What was that?" one of the guards asked.

His friend shrugged. "Nothing important."

"Dumber than rocks." Thoren shook his head.

Enar chuckled. "Lucky for us. Which one do you want?"

"The bigger one. You'd have trouble with him."

"If it makes you feel better to compensate for

what you lack..."

"You wish."

"Mmphm. Now do I use Blood Seeker, or the flimsy sword?" Enar mused.

Thoren glanced over his shoulder at the huge broadsword strapped to Enar's back. Enar reached up, fingering the hilt of Blood Seeker, before placing his hand on the smaller sword sheathed at his waist beside his dagger.

"Wouldn't be very sporting," he said to Thoren's raised brow.

"Hmm, tough and yet sporting. What have I done to deserve such a friend?"

Enar snorted. "Lucky, I guess. Ready?"

"As ready as I'm getting."

Thoren swung the door open, landing it on the wall with a bang, simultaneously dropping his spell. Enar bellowed a war whoop and the two guards jumped, paling even as they reached for their weapons. Thoren pushed the weapon of the larger man aside, landing a punch on the side of the man's jaw, knocking him into the counter. The man slipped to the floor, head lolling.

While Enar toyed with his victim, Thoren slid across the counter and pulled the gag off a wide-eyed Jamie.

"Did they hurt you?"

Jamie shook his head, mouth working like a fish, but no sound coming forth. Thoren touched the lump on the boy's head that still oozed blood. It looked like he had been hit with a sword hilt.

"You sure?"

A vigorous nod.

Guess their definitions of hurt differed.

Thoren pulled his knife, sawing through the bonds holding Jamie's arms to the chair. His knife had no sooner touched the ropes circling Jamie's ankles, when Thoren heard the back door creak open. The knife's movement froze as Thoren raised his eyes, looking for the newcomer.

"Hey, George, Hans, you can kill the boy." Footsteps sounded, carrying the voice closer. "Lord Simon has the woman. Said the dumb bitch fell right into his hands."

Keara. Cold rage spread throughout his limbs, focusing his thoughts into a single thread. Simon had Keara. Simon would die.

Dropping the knife, Thoren leapt to his feet, stretching out his hand to slam the newcomer against the wall with a blast of magic. Using magic, Thoren pinned the man against the wall, rage beating his pulse. He felt steam escaping from his ears and didn't care who saw.

Simon had Keara. Simon would die.

The man's eyes rolled, showing white as he struggled to breathe, hands flapping uselessly against the invisible grip on his throat, his feet kicking against air.

"What woman are you talking about?" Thoren snarled, his voice warped with fury.

"The...the witch...the apothecary witch," the man squeaked as wetness stained the front of his trousers.

"Where?"

"Lord Simon's house. I swear I had nothing to do with it. I'm just the messenger!"

With a roar, Thoren threw the man against the opposite wall, knocking him unconscious. Steam whipped around his head, blurring his vision. Scales rippled down his arms, his fingers changing into claws. The beast roared to escape.

What was happening to him? Why, in the name of the Goddess, was he even considering turning in a non-Draconi town? Had he completely lost his mind?

Taking a deep breath, he pushed the dragon back where it belonged. The claws shrank into fingers, scales disappearing into skin. He ran a hand through his hair and stared at the ceiling, trying to get his breathing under control. Forget the breathing, he needed to get his entire body under control. If anything happened to Keara, he became like a demented dragon, bouncing off the walls, threatening to turn into the beast.

He refused to think about what the demented dragon act meant.

"Now that you've finished playing darts out of soldiers, are you ready to go find Keara?" Enar leaned against the counter, a wide-eyed Jamie at his side.

Did the boy know he was a Halfling? There would be plenty of time to ask, but now they needed to find Keara. Thoren turned to Jamie.

"Tell me the quickest way to Lord Simon's house."

Jamie looked at the floor, then cut a sideways glance at Enar. "Umm. Well, you see, the quickest and safest way would be the sewers."

Thoren groaned.

"Sweet Goddess, not again. I doubt I could abide the stench." Enar shivered.

"And you know where his house is from the sewers?" Thoren raised a brow.

Jamie blushed. "Yes, sir."

"Thought only thieves knew where the houses were on the sewer line." Enar crossed his arms over his chest. Jamie gulped and backed away a step.

"Small boys do too. Especially when they got nothing better to do."

Thoren threw Enar a glance, remembering their youth.

"Lead the way, Little Adventurer. But stick close. You have some explaining to do once we get Keara freed." Thoren gestured toward the cellar.

****

From the dungeon, Simon carried Keara to what looked like a bedchamber, pitching her on the bed. She rolled, trying to get off the bed, but a hand stopped her. Her eyes followed the hand up the arm to the person's head. A cowl hid the face in dim shadows. A brown robe like a priest's cloaked its body. A squeak was the only sound the gag allowed her to make. Chills flowed through her skin from his touch on her shoulder and her body shook. Who was this?

Keara tried to roll the other way, but the hooded man stopped her, keeping her on her side. She felt cold steel slip between her hands and then relief as the rope around her hands released. Unfortunately the relief didn't last. Simon grabbed one arm, the hooded man the other, and despite her struggles, they tied her arms to the bedposts. Her heart pounded against her ribs. They were going to rape her, they were going to kill her and no one would be able to stop them.

She pulled against the ropes holding her, but only succeeded in tightening them.

"Quite a fighter. Hopefully her powers are as strong as her spirit," the hooded man said.

"I brought her to you. Do you have my money?"

"I said I'd pay you once she works out. Currently she's tied to a bed. Until I know how well she'll work out, you don't get paid. Understand?" His voice hardened and Simon flinched. Hooded Man pulled the cowl further over his face, the drapes of robe hanging from his arm slipping up, exposing skin. Spindly black lines danced against pale white flesh.

Her eyes popped wide and froze. Draconi. A Draconi had her captured. What did that mean? Did Thoren know this man?

As if he read her thoughts, the hooded man turned toward her. "Ah. So you know."

"Know what?" Simon asked.

"She knows who I am."

Simon glared at Keara before turning back to the hooded man. "How? I don't even know who you are and we've worked together for several weeks. A name would be nice."

The man waved a hand and Simon shrugged. He turned back to Keara. "You're wondering why you're here. Let me tell you. You, my dear, will help me get revenge on my enemies, especially that hard-nosed bitch priestess who had me banished. I've waited months, plotting a way to get back at that bitch, and then like a gift from the Goddess, I saw you. Imagine that, a female Draconi unguarded. It took little effort to convince Simon to help me capture you. I couldn't resist having you as mine and using your powers for revenge. Now, now, don't shake your head just yet. You will help me. You won't have a choice. Our friend here," he gestured toward a grinning Simon, "has a special herb he's going to feed you. It makes you quite amenable to whatever we want you to do. What's it called?"

"Zombie dust," Simon smirked.

Zombie dust? A barbed ball formed in her stomach, gnawing at her insides. Her breath caught. Zombie dust was against the apothecary code, forbidden, dangerous. Ground roots from the plant mixed with oil from the leaves and steeped into a tea made a drink so dangerous even the town's laws forbid the possession of the plant. Too much and the user could die. Just the right amount and she would do whatever the one who gave her the drink asked. Anything. Cold seeped out from her stomach, shaking her limbs like a baby's rattle.

"Ah. So she knows what zombie dust is."

"Of course she knows. She's the town's apothecary." Simon faced her. "But what you didn't know is that I have taught myself herb lore. Nothing like you, of course. My skills focus on the illegal, the dangerous. Why should I bother to learn the mundane that you practice?"

Thoren had to find her and fast. Would he even bother? And what kind of punishment would Thoren give her for wandering off and getting caught? Despite what he thought, he was her husband according to her laws. How many bruises and scrapes had she and her grandmother tended when a husband decided his wife displeased him? She shuddered. Power crept out of Thoren, along with sheer masculinity. If he turned a mind to beating her, there wouldn't be much left to clean up.

Be that as it may, she'd rather face Thoren's wrath than whatever evil these men had planned for her.

Simon moved to a table on the opposite side of the room from where she lay and started mixing what she assumed to be the zombie dust potion.

The hooded man ran a finger down her throat, between her breasts. She jerked to the side and he laughed.

"Soon you won't mind. You'll do what I want. Where did you find her?" He walked to where Simon stood mixing his potion.

"Outside of the town. Her apprentice had returned. We have him too, she obviously was chasing him down. Guess she didn't like her rescuer after all."

"Is that true, female?" The man turned to Keara, his face still hidden in shadows.

Keara glared at him, refusing to move her head.

"Did he touch you, or will I be your first?"

Oh, Goddess no. Please let Thoren come, please let Thoren come.

The Draconi laughed. "You'll find me pleasing, don't worry. I'll unlock your powers and together we'll wreak vengeance on the others. You'll even enjoy it because I said you would." He laughed again, the noise echoing in the room.

Crazy. He was crazy and Simon was one step behind him. Why her? Oh, of course. She was the only Draconi woman nearby. Guess he couldn't get one from Draconia so he had to settle for her. Great. If her heart pounded any harder, it would burst.

Simon hummed as he worked, heating the water to a boil, the hooded Draconi standing watch beside him.

"Finished! Now missy, you'll drink and do as I want." Simon held a cup in his hand as he turned toward her.

"Give that to me. I control her." The Draconi held out his hand.

Simon looked into the shadows of the cowl and his face lost all expression. Wordlessly he handed over the cup.

"Ah, my love. Drink and you shall be mine. Remove her gag."

Simon, face still blank, bent over and untied the gag. Keara ran her tongue around the inside of her dry mouth, relieved to have the gag gone. She pressed her lips together. They could think again if they thought she'd just open her mouth and let them give her that drink.

The hooded Draconi placed the cup against her lips. She turned her head, pulling her bonds as far away from him as possible. Her pulse raced in her ears, her heart thudding against her chest.

"Now, now. Don't be like that. Help me out."

Simon grabbed her jaw, squeezing until she moaned from the pain. And then he pinched her nose shut.

"Open for me, Keara. Open and breathe."

Keara shook her head, trying to dislodge his hand. She saw stars as she forced her body not to draw a breath through her mouth. She tried to retain consciousness, tried to keep her lips sealed, but it was useless. In the end, the drug spewed down the back of her throat, trickling out of her mouth.

She couldn't have been unconscious for long, for she came to her senses choking on the drink, trying to breathe. The hooded Draconi held the cup almost upside down over her mouth, draining it down her spasming throat.

"Good, my love. Now we wait." A cold hand stroked her arm.

Taking the cup, Simon walked across the room and placed it on the table. The evil hooded Draconi sat next to her, the creepy nothingness of his face staring at her. Tears streamed down her cheeks as she tried to breathe, tried to spit out some of the drug. Unfortunately, most of it had gone down into her stomach. She shivered. She would fight him, she couldn't let him control her.

The room started to spin and she shut her eyes against the dizziness that threatened. Too soon! The drug worked too quickly. She opened her eyes, her vision swimming at the edges. She didn't feel any different, only her vision changed.

"I think it's starting to work." The hooded Draconi peered into her eyes. "Her pupils are dilated."

"Good, good. That means the potion is working. Let's try a test."

Nodding to the Draconi, Simon took the knife and cut through the bonds holding Keara to the bed.

"Don't move," the Draconi said and despite her desire and her brain screaming at her to run, fight, do anything but lie still, her body refused to move.

Keara stared at the face in the shadows as the men rubbed her wrists.

"Oh, she's good. This is great. I didn't think it would work so well."

"I told you I knew how to mix it."

"Give me your knife." Simon handed over his

knife. "Now Keara, take this knife and throw it at the fireplace."

Without pause, she grabbed the knife from the Draconi, aimed and threw. At least it was the fireplace and not a person. She had no control. Not even for a second did she think of disobeying him. She wanted to scream and yet she turned back to him.

He kissed her, thrusting his tongue inside her mouth. Her mind wanted to gag, to push him away. But her body let him. Oh, Goddess.

Stroking her hair, he turned to Simon. "Get me the knife."

Simon obeyed as if he'd had a dose of zombie dust. Within seconds the knife was back in her hand.

"We have to step out. Simon and I have things to discuss that don't involve your pretty little ears, but don't fret. I'll be back. And when I do, we'll make good use of this bed. Until we return, guard the door and don't let anyone in the room. Throw the knife at them if they try to come in. Understand?"

Keara nodded. His thumb traced her lips. "That's my girl."

He arranged her so she sat on the edge of the bed, ankles still tied together, knife in hand, facing the door.

"See you soon."

"Don't go anywhere, Keara," Simon sneered, shutting the door behind them.

Finally, they were gone. Now she just had to untie her ankles and walk out. Untie her ankles...

Her brain gave the command but nothing happened. She remained sitting on the edge of the bed, staring at the door. The longer she tried to move and got nowhere, the more terrified she became. A puppet. No will. No mind. Only strings.

Dear Goddess. This was not good.

Chapter 8

Water dripped steadily from the ceiling of the sewer line, little drops reminding Thoren of each minute Keara had been captured. Was she dead? Why was the lord so interested in her? He felt the beast stirring inside and forced his mind to think of other things. How long could he go between breaths?

"Here." Jamie stopped, pointing at a wooden door crossed with metal bars.

"Praise the Goddess!" Enar muttered, holding his nose.

Thoren held his hand containing the conjured blue fire closer to the opening. Rust covered the lock, evidence of its lack of use. He raised a brow at Jamie.

"You sure?"

"Uh-huh."

"You opened this door?"

Jamie's eyes narrowed. "He wanted Keara. I had to know how to get to him in case he took her. So's I could get her out."

"And this is his?"

"I said it was." Jamie pointed to a stone with etchings. "It's written right there. Carved into that stone. That's what the thieves do, see. Carve whose house it is into the stone. Think you can get in?"

"I know I can get in. One day I'll teach you, but now..." Whispering a spell, he unlocked the door. A good thud with his shoulder and the door squeaked open on its hinges.

"You have to teach me how to do that!" Jamie

said.

Enar walked past him, short sword in hand. "Think a big bad Draconi like you can make a spell that keeps the whole town from knowing we're entering?"

"How do you know I didn't?"

"Niiiice."

Thoren stepped inside behind Enar, motioning for Jamie to remain in the sewer. The boy should be safe there. Who knew what they'd find inside?

The door opened into a storage area. A tiny room filled with dirt-covered boxes and crates. The blue light from Thoren's fire flickered against the stone walls, casting long shadows that danced like eerie spirits. Enar strode across the small room, sword at the ready, reaching the door on the opposite side with Thoren right behind him.

"Ready?" Enar's hand hovered above the latch, face turned toward Thoren.

"Ready." What would he do if Keara died? Steam brushed against his throat and red clouded his vision. *Focus on the moment, focus on the moment.* If he dwelled too much on the what-ifs, his ability to react to the current situation would diminish. *Focus, focus.* The steam dissipated and his thoughts returned to what was happening here, now.

Enar flung his weight against the door, which opened without a sound. Thoren inhaled deeply, drawing scent through his nose. The slight scent of Keara mingled with the overpowering scent of Draconi, male Draconi. What in the name of the Goddess?

A glance at Enar told him the Watcher didn't smell the scent. What did he expect? His friend, although powerful, was not a Draconi and didn't have the same tracking ability.

"Enar."

"What?"

"Do you smell what I do?"

Enar knelt by a burned corpse. "That this man's dead and burned to a crisp?"

"Huh?" Thoren looked at the charred heap of what used to be a man lying by Enar. Charred heap of man, scent of male Draconi. Thoren pivoted, turning the opposite way of where the man lay, looking toward where the fire obviously originated.

"What were you talking of then?" Leather creaked as Enar rose to his feet.

"Oh, that maybe." Thoren pointed toward the large, male Draconi trapped behind the bars, stuffed into a cell not designed for him.

Enar drew a sharp breath. "By the Goddess! How did he get there?"

Are you two going to point and stare all day or do something about me? That filthy son of a goat took a female Draconi up those stairs. The scaled dragon motioned with his head toward the small set of stairs behind the dead man. *Well, don't just stand there, move!*

Thoren jumped as the dragon's voice echoed through his mind. A Draconi male locked in a cell. Who would have thought he'd find that in Caustasia? How could a Draconi get into a cell? He shook his head, walking toward the dragon.

Stop! Not you! The Watcher must free me. The bars are titanium.

Thoren cursed. Titanium was the only thing that could stop a Draconi from working his magic. No wonder the creature stood behind the bars. But why was he in dragon form? If captured in human form he would remain as a human and it was virtually impossible to capture a Draconi in his dragon form. Unless...a shudder rippled through him.

The dragon's capture must have happened while in human form prior to going through his Change. If no female was found to help ease a male's way through the changes his body underwent, he would remain in dragon form until death. To be locked away, to never have the choice given you. Thoren shuddered again.

"How long?"

The dragon sighed. *Too long. The only thing that kept me going was the thought of what would happen to the one that put me in this cell once I was freed. Enough about me, you need to save that female, she's been upstairs too long as it is. Your Watcher can free me.*

"I can free you," a voice with enough confidence to suit a giant spoke from the storage room.

Thoren turned to Jamie who stood in the doorway to the small storage room. Was it too much to ask the lad to stay put? Apparently so. Although if given a choice between staying in a sewer and disobeying an order, he'd probably have done the same thing.

"I thought I told you to stay put."

Jamie's eyes blazed. "Thought I could help. And I was right. I can free him," he waved his hand in the direction of the dragon, "and you two can free Keara."

"You can't touch the bars either, Jamie. You're part Draconi. Same as Keara." Thoren waited for shock to pass over Jamie's face, but the boy just shrugged.

"Duh. But I'm just a kid. And titanium only works on adults."

Who told you that? the dragon asked.

"My father."

"Why didn't you tell us you were Draconi?" Thoren took a step toward the boy.

"You didn't ask. Now do you want me to help you or not?"

Had he been this exasperating as a boy?

Thoren turned to the dragon. "Is that true?"

The dragon shrugged. *It doesn't hurt to try. You two are needed upstairs.*

"All right. I'll leave him with you, but don't let him wander off. He's good at it."

The dragon nodded. *Will do.*

Thoren followed Enar toward the stone stairs. "Stay here with the Draconi, Jamie. We'll bring Keara back, don't wander off."

"As you wish." Jamie grinned.

He needed to ask his mother, but he was fairly certain he had not been this much trouble as a hatchling.

The last thing Thoren heard as he followed Enar up the twisting stairs was the dragon speaking to Jamie. *The keys are on the ground, lad, halfway between the wall and my cell.*

After climbing what felt like forever, a door stood in their path. The top. Praise the Goddess. Both men leaned against the wooden panel, their breath heaving in and out like a bellows.

"Why is it that I can practice with Blood Seeker all day and not grow tired, but walk up a flight of stairs and I pant like a half-dead pup?" Enar shook his head.

"It goes with the half-dead look," Thoren put a hand on the latch, trying to calm his breathing. Keara was close, he knew it. "Ready?"

"Go for it, dragon."

Stepping into a hallway, Thoren looked to his left, while Enar pushed the door wider and stepped to Thoren's right. A scream ripped through the hallway and Thoren stopped, turning his head toward the sound.

A wide-eyed, pale-faced servant stood staring at them as if they were the bringers of death. She took a step backward, dropping the pile of linens into a heap at her feet.

Thoren reached a hand her direction. "Shush. Rest easy."

The woman's mouth opened as if to emit another ear-piercing shriek before her eyes rolled into the back of her head and she sank gracefully to the floor.

Humans. So easy to manipulate.

"Humph. Not nearly as much fun as Blood Seeker."

"Maybe next time." Thoren patted Enar on the shoulder.

Leaning his head back, Thoren inhaled deeply, scenting Keara to the left. He led the way down the hall, Enar close behind, the only sound the rustle of their leather-clad legs as they strode toward Keara.

There. The scent of Draconi female concentrated strongly outside the last door. Keara must be trapped behind it. Thoren met Enar's eyes and nodded. Enar took a deep breath, tightening his hold on Blood Seeker and returned the gesture.

Thoren shoved his shoulder into the door, popping the latch, not bothering with stealth. Keara was on the other side of the door. He had to protect her, to save her. She was all that mattered. The door slammed into the wall with a crack and he heard the whistle of air.

He started to wave his hand to redirect whatever object hurtled at him when Enar's shoulder slammed against his, shoving him out of the way. A clatter sounded against the stone floor and he had an instant to process the fact that the object was a knife before the figure on the bed occupied his thoughts.

Keara.

She sat on a large bed, feet tied together and hanging off the side. Her arm dropped listlessly to her lap as she stared at them, her eyes a vacant mask. What happened to her? All life had disappeared, turning her into a movable statue. Why had she tried to kill him?

Her eyes blinked, her only movement as far as he could tell. She didn't acknowledge them, didn't twitch, no movement at all except for her breathing and blinking. Her stare lit something inside him. Kill and protect, save and love.

He really needed to get a handle on these emotions.

"Something's not right." Enar took a step into the room.

"You think?"

Her eyes didn't track their banter. Instead, they remained fixed, staring forward. He took in another breath and that's when he noticed it. If he hadn't been so intent on Keara's scent, it would have been obvious sooner. An aroma of crushed herbs lay heavily in the air and a table contained chopped herbs and a small cup.

He cursed. "She's been drugged."

"With what? What causes that?"

"Do I look like an apothecary?" How would he save her if he didn't even know what she'd been given? Was she even aware of their presence?

Thoren heard a faint buzzing in his head, like when he was a hatchling, first learning how to mind-speak. His eyes popped. Was she trying to speak to him? He reached out with a mental probe, foraging into her mind, trying to read her thoughts.

Her voice slammed into his brain, the equivalent of a scream.

Thoren, help me! Get me out of here before they come back. Please! He can't hear me, he can't help me, he's going to leave me. No, no, no! Don't leave, don't leave, don't leave. Help me, please, help me!

What were you drugged with?

Her body didn't move, but her mind flinched at his words and relief streamed to him from her.

You can hear me?

Draconi can mind-speak. What were you drugged with?

Zombie dust. It controls me. They told me to throw the knife at whoever walked in the door.

Will it hurt to move you?

No. Just hurry, they're coming back.

"She says we can move her." Two strides and he was at the bed, knife cutting through the bonds circling her ankles. His lip peeled off his teeth when he saw the angry red marks streaking her skin from the tightness of the ropes.

"Growling doesn't help our situation any, dragon," Enar said, placing a hand on Thoren's shoulder.

Good point. So why couldn't he stop?

Deep breaths. If he got busy breathing in then sound couldn't come out. And why was noise coming out?

He refused to think about it.

The need to take Keara to safety overrode his higher reasoning. Which was not a good thing when they were in their enemy's lair. But mates needed to be protected at all costs and, Goddess's teeth...did his brain just spit out that "m" word?

Stop thinking and focus on getting out of here, Thoren, before you get caught.

With effort, he tamped down the unwanted emotions flooding his system and focused on the here and now. Which demanded his full concentration to get them out of this mess.

Thoren gathered Keara into his arms, crushing her against him. Although her eyes still stared vacantly, he felt her mind relax, her terror receding as he held her.

Taking a deep breath, he inhaled her scent and something else, something unwanted.

Blood.

So much for gaining control of his emotions and

burying them deep inside. The unwanted feelings surged in his veins, in his mind, overriding his human half, igniting the dragon side until his vision went as red as the blood he smelled on Keara's breath. Red marks just beginning to gain a blue tinge dotted her cheeks and the corners of her mouth. From a gag.

Steam poured from his ears, out his mouth. He heard Keara gasp in his mind, her terror an acrid scent in his nose. What frightened her? He'd kill it.

"It's you that frightens her. We don't have time for this dragon-bonding nonsense. Get control of yourself." Enar stood, weight shifted to one side, hands loose at his sides. As if he was ready to fight.

Thoren? I'm all right. I'll be fine. Zombie dust wears off in a couple of hours. Don't worry about me. Just get me out of here.

Thoren looked down at Keara and back to Enar. Had he actually been about to change? What had he been thinking? That's right. He hadn't.

He threw back his head and took in the ceiling décor. Wooden beams, wooden slats. Calm thoughts.

"Are you ready?" Enar stood by the door, the fight gone out of him.

"The sooner we can get out of this place the better."

"You can say that again," Enar muttered, starting out the door.

Thoren beat his friend to the stairs, Enar's breath on his neck. Long flickering shadows danced on the wall of the stairwell, elongated shapes leading the way to their owners. Thoren's eyes followed their paths back to Jamie and the unknown male Draconi.

Jamie had freed the dragon, who now stood in the middle of the dungeon, trying to flap his wings. Little eddies of dust swirled when the wings touched the dirt floor. Jamie stood pressed against the cold, stone wall, eyes wide and shining, a grin splitting his face.

The sight of the Draconi brought Thoren to an abrupt halt, Enar plowing into him with a sharp exhale of breath. Did the dragon have the ability to transport out of the dungeon? Would his powers still work after being suppressed for so long by the titanium in his cell? If they didn't, how would Thoren manage to transport a creature that large out of ten-foot thick walls? Dear Goddess, please let the male's powers work.

"Will you be able to transport out of here?"

The Draconi blinked, disappearing only to reappear in another part of the dungeon.

Jamie's mouth formed an "O." "Wow!"

Apparently so. Point the way out and I will try.

There's a door that leads directly outside. Through that tunnel to your left. Keara's voice echoed in Thoren's head.

He turned his head to the left, noting the tunnel. Striding that direction, he peered into the darkness, barely discerning light filtering in through the cracks in the door at the end of the narrow passage. Tightening his clutch on Keara, he counted the number of steps from the dungeon to the door.

"Ten steps from there to here." He spoke over his shoulder as he unlocked the door and shoved it open enough for him to peer outside. "Looks like a stone's throw to the woods. Think you can fly?"

Doubtful. This is the first time in twenty-four years I was able to stretch my wings. But it will do me good to try.

"Our camp isn't far from here, about a mile due east. Can you locate it using our scent?"

The dragon stuck his snout against Jamie's chest, inhaling deeply. Jamie giggled as the dragon's hot breath nuzzled his torso. *Yes.*

"Good. Jamie, come to me." Jamie held a hesitant hand up, placing it on the dragon's snout and rubbing briskly before running to Thoren's side. The Draconi chuckled.

Now if their luck would hold until they all made it back to the campsite. Enar strode down the narrow passageway, pushed past Thoren and shoved the door open, letting in a stream of light.

"All clear," he said after looking around for sentinels.

Motioning with his hand, Enar beckoned Jamie closer.

"See that clump of trees?" He pointed. "Run toward them. Stop once you get to them. We'll be behind you."

Jamie took off at a sprint, disappearing into the trees. Thoren followed him, Keara clasped to his chest. He didn't need to look behind him to know that Enar closed the door, joining them at the trees. Once they gathered in the woods, Thoren cast a spell to lock the door.

Can you hear me, friend? Thoren asked of the dragon.

I can.

Good. We're outside the door. Can you make it through?

Silence greeted him broken by a loud thump. An indentation appeared in the grass before disappearing, replaced by a gust of wind generated by dragon's wings. Invisible dragon's wings. Squinting against the blue of the sky, Thoren made out the shimmering outline of the invisible Draconi flapping his wings, hovering in front of them.

Ah, friend, I am in your debt. Anything you ask, I will give, including my life.

A life debt. A solemn vow Thoren never expected to hear and yet could not deny.

And I will honor that vow until my death.

Thoren heard the beating of wings vibrating off the limbs of the trees, saw the leaves stir in the breeze.

I'll meet you back at your campsite. Stretching my wings feels good. Guess I can fly after all.

See you soon, friend.

It didn't take them long to return to the campsite, but to Thoren it felt like forever. The almost overwhelming desire to kill the one that hurt Keara mingled with self-talk aimed to convince him that what was happening was not really happening. He did not have a mate. Could not. His job came first. And yet, his emotions and lack of control over them left no doubt as to Keara's importance.

The problem was his inability to want a change in his life.

Self-talk dug up a bunch of things he didn't feel like dealing with. Better to dwell on his revenge of the one that kidnapped her. Changing into a rampaging dragon had more appeal than discovering why he'd rather have his job than a mate.

Better yet, how was he going to heal Keara? How did he get the drug to wear off faster?

He knelt, placing Keara on the ground, touching a hand to her slack cheek. How long until the effects of the drug were out of her system?

"Keara!" Lily ran to Keara, touching her friend lightly on the arm, peering into Keara's vacant staring eyes. "Dear Goddess, what happened to her?"

"She's been drugged and can't move—"

Before he could finish his sentence, a loud roar ripped through the air, dragon's song echoed off the hills. Suddenly the ground shook, grass flattening, as the invisible dragon landed with a thud, dropping his invisibility spell.

The wings might be a little underused. The dragon shook the grass off his scales, flinging it into the wall of the ward. Lily screamed, jumping behind Enar, who caught her, clamping a hand over her mouth.

"Shh, woman. It's just, um...I didn't catch your name?"

Good one, Thoren. Take a life debt and not bother to take the name of the giver. Thoren shook his head.

The dragon paused, as if he didn't know his name. A quick breath, a twitch of his lip. *Fafnir. And yours?*

"Enar. And this is my woman, Lily." Enar pulled Lily out from where she trembled behind him.

"My apologies, friend, for not asking earlier. I'm Thoren. The Halfling female is Keara, and you've already met Jamie."

Fafnir waved a front limb to and fro, dismissing the apology before he shuffled to where Thoren knelt by Keara, staring into her flaccid face. His eye-ridges popped halfway up his forehead.

How did she get to Cautasia?

Hot breath streamed across Thoren's arm. "Her father abandoned her mother before she was born. She's lived in River's Run her entire life."

Fafnir took a step back, eyes wide, mouth slack. *No.*

"What's surprising is no word got back to us. We heard about Jamie, but not her."

The dragon shook his head, looking like someone informed him of his imminent death. Thoren understood how he felt. The whole situation shocked him too. A Halfling female, who...might be...his mate and a Halfling lad with brown hair instead of red. What else did he have to look forward to? Going through the Change in the middle of nowhere?

"It's bizarre, I agree."

Fafnir looked at Thoren, blinking...was that tears?

Thoren placed a hand on Fafnir's forearm. "She'll be all right." He hoped. Either way Simon was going to die. Preferably slowly and painfully.

A small feather-like brush against Thoren's hand jerked his eyes to Keara.

Praise the Goddess, the drug seemed to be wearing off.

Chapter 9

Keara concentrated, forcing all her energy into her hand until it twitched. Not much movement, but enough for Thoren to notice. Thank the Goddess he found her, that he cared enough to come after her. She had never felt more relieved in her life than when he walked through Lord Simon's bedchamber door, deflected her knife throw and didn't punish her for it.

And he heard her thoughts! How amazing was that? What a useful trick. Although now that she thought about it, totally chilling. If he knew what she wanted to say before she spoke, how much deeper into her mind could he delve? What secrets could he uncover? She shivered at the possibility.

Would he discover the secret she held from everyone? If he did, what would he do to her? Did Draconi have those powers? She needed to learn how to keep him from tunneling around in her mind, from reading thoughts best kept hidden. He might not like what he found and she had no place else to go but with him. As soon as the drug wore off, she'd ask how to erect mental barriers to keep him out.

Thinking about her day made her face ache, each painful throb of her inner cheek reminding her of how close she came to losing her life. The drug made her vision warble like steam rising from the river on a cold day. A dull pounding in her head joined the throb in her cheek, making her long for one of her brews. But first she had to move.

Concentrating, she made her hand twitch again,

not much, but enough for him to notice.

Thoren's eyes widened as his gaze darted from her hand to her face. Hope warred with fear in his green eyes and though his face remained passive, she felt his emotions crawl over her skin like the wind, light like feathers at first, turning into a blistering gust. She wondered if he realized she knew what he felt, knew his relief that the drug was wearing off.

Small fingertips pressed into her scalp, massaging lightly, easing away the burgeoning headache. Jamie's small fingers stroked through her hair, while Thoren traced his fingers along her jaw. She became aware of someone next to her. Forcing her head to turn, she looked into blue eyes that crinkled at the corners.

"I think she'll be fine," Lily smiled at her, relief evident in her expression.

"You had us worried there for a moment." Thoren's hand fell to hers, clasping it tightly, the planes of his face still wavering in her vision.

She tried to smile, but it came out more as a grimace. Her voice had left her, since the drug still controlled her vocal chords. Forcing her lips to move, she mouthed *thank-you* to Thoren, knowing it didn't adequately describe her feelings, but unable to force her lips around anything else.

"The sun is overhead. Do we stay or go?" Enar spoke from somewhere above and to her side.

Thoren's black hair fell across his shoulder as he tilted his head to the sky. He looked back down at her and then up, presumably at Enar. "It would be better to get farther away from here, but she's still weak. I'm not sure she should be moved."

I don't want to stay here. Can you still hear me? They'll find us. If we stay here, we'll be caught. Can you still hear me? Please say yes.

"Even I can hear you, female. Tone down the

mental screams." Enar moved into her line of vision, rubbing the side of his head.

"It is a little loud," Thoren smiled at her, "but we'll work on it. You just need to be taught."

Fine. But we can't stay here. They'll find us.

"She has a point," Enar said.

"What are you talking about?" Lily looked from one face to another, wrinkles creasing her forehead.

"You can't hear her?" Enar sounded incredulous.

Lily's jaw clenched. "She's not speaking."

"Draconi can mind-speak, Lily," Thoren explained.

"Truthfully?"

"Yes. Keara is speaking to us, telling us to leave."

"Sounds good to me."

"True. But by the time she can move, it will be dark, and our campsite is warded from intruders. Only Draconi can get in and besides us, there aren't any around."

There was one working with Lord Simon. He offered Simon money to capture me. He said he needed me to get revenge on his enemies.

"What?" Thoren exploded, eyes popping wide, lips peeling off his teeth. Ripples crept beneath his skin and he shook, as if trying to cast them off.

"Who?" Enar knelt beside Thoren.

What did he look like?

I don't know. He wore a cloak pulled over his head, but he had the Draconi mark and he said he needed me to get revenge on his enemies and that he needed to unlock my powers. I thought he was going to... She couldn't finish. Thinking about what almost happened, what would have happened if Thoren hadn't appeared, made her want to shudder.

"We move. Pack the campsite and make it quick." Thoren stroked a stray piece of hair off her forehead.

"We can take him on. Finish this now," Enar said.

"Not with the females and a boy. Even a warrior has to retreat at some time. Besides, we'll be back."

"And then they won't get away."

Thoren touched her arm. "I'll be back. Lily, stay with her."

As soon as Thoren, Enar and Jamie left, Lily grabbed Keara's hand. "What happened to you?"

If she could twitch her hand, she could open her lips. Shame Lily didn't have the ability to hear her mind-speak. "Gwrph."

So much for talking.

"Sorry. I should have known. I'm so glad you're back. I was worried about you." Lily squeezed Keara's hand.

Energy to hand, energy to hand. Instead of twitching, her hand returned Lily's squeeze. Finally. The effects of the zombie dust were wearing thin.

Lily grinned. Jamie flopped beside her, out of breath, bouncing up and down.

"Guess what, guess what, guess what?"

"What?"

What? Jamie had a lot of explaining to do. Starting with an apology for wandering off in the middle of the night.

"They're going to let us ride Fafnir! It's apparently not done, and a big deal, but Fafnir insisted and we get to ride! Isn't that grand!"

"Ride? On that, that, creature?" Lily's voice rose.

"He's a dragon. Same as me. One day I can turn like that. That's grand, huh?"

Lily's face turned paler than normal. "Sure. Great. How are we supposed to stay on a...dragon?

"Duh. Hold on, silly. How're you doing Keara?"

Better. If I concentrate, I can move my hand.

We'll come back and kill them, you know.

You'll do nothing of the sort! And why did you

wander off in the middle of the night when we were being chased?

"Are you two talking again? That's rude to do that in front of me, you know."

"You're right. I think I'm needed over there." Jamie leapt to his feet and ran off.

We're not done, buddy.

Uh-huh.

Boys.

She'd deal with him later. When she felt better. Thank the Goddess they were leaving. Hopefully Simon and the hooded Draconi wouldn't bother following them. She shuddered, remembering their touches, what they wanted to do to her, the fear she felt lying bound and helpless.

The way Thoren strode in and saved her.

And said nothing about how stupid it was for her to chase after Jamie on her own.

Too bad Thoren didn't see her as his wife. Didn't see her as anything but an obligation.

"I'm a little scared about riding on the dragon."

Moving her eyes to focus on Lily's face didn't take much of an effort. Cranking her lips into a semblance of a smile did.

She didn't mind the dragon. He belonged to her race, her people. How apropos that he would be carrying her to them. If only Thoren would ride with them, then she could go about convincing him to notice her.

Did she want him to notice her?

Yes, yes she did.

How did one go about getting a man to take notice? Relationships with the opposite sex were not her thing.

But challenges? Her entire life had been a challenge. Living with her grandmother, the entire town—with the exception of Lily—fearing her, learning herb lore.

She liked a good challenge, especially when it came coupled with learning something new. According to her customs, he was her husband. And it was up to her to convince him of it.

Chapter 10

Flying, it's a good two days, day and a half if you push it, to get back home, Fafnir said as they strode away from the campsite.

The Council forbids us to turn while outside of Draconia.

You work for the Council?

I do. Thoren couldn't help the pride lacing his words.

Doesn't the Council allow for outstanding circumstances? Like a drugged Halfling with a rogue Draconi and crazed nobleman on her trail?

Did it? Thoren looked at Enar who shrugged. Enar didn't care as much about the Council as Thoren did. Who was he fooling? Enar hated the Council. But one of them should know all the rules and as he never needed to use the extenuating circumstances allowances, he forgot them. Looked like Enar had too.

His inner beast twisted, begging to be set free, to fly, to protect Keara. By the Goddess, but he was tired of feeling split in half—the rational side and the completely crazed one.

Although at the moment, he wasn't sure which was which.

Fafnir had a point. Keara was ill. The drug's effects lessened as the moments ticked by, but he worried about long-term side effects.

Everything about her worried him. The fact that Fafnir carried her instead of him. The pallor of her skin. Her feeble attempts to move.

Protect and save.

If he was punished, so be it.

You're right. We can fly until sundown and then make camp.

"Good call. The quicker we get there, the quicker we can return and put an end to this."

Thoren nodded to Enar, wondering for the umpteenth time how a Watcher understood mind-speak. As far as he knew, Enar was the only Watcher with that ability but maybe others had it and kept it hidden. More thoughts for another day.

Closing his eyes, Thoren called his beast, which didn't take long to appear since being around Keara made the dragon primed and ready to go. Turning struck him in a rush of scales and claws, bones elongating, growing bigger, flesh hardening.

As usual, turning was painless, another mind boggler as he went from two legs and seventeen stone to four legs and over a hundred and forty.

Thoren shook his head, rippling muscles and scales, his claws digging into the grass. He stood slightly taller than Fafnir and wasn't that a good thing? Females liked bigger males.

It seemed he lacked control over emotions in his dragon state. Tearing Fafnir apart for having Keara on his back sounded like a great idea. Was he actually snarling at the older dragon?

Apparently, his higher reasoning had given way to hatchling-like behavior. This mating business was for other dragons. He could do without all the crazed must-kill-what-threatens-Keara thoughts banging around in his body. If all male Draconi felt like this once they bonded to their mate it was a wonder they didn't all kill each other.

He wanted Keara to ride on his back. To soar above the ground and through the clouds with him. To know that he held her, that he protected her. He needed to stop thinking like that. Ropes tied Keara to Lily, who sat in front, and Jamie brought up the rear, wrapping his arms around her waist. Talk about protective. The boy had a tight grip on Keara, ensuring she wouldn't fall off Fafnir's back.

No, Keara would remain where she sat. Thoren knelt and Enar pitched their gear onto his back, wrapping a line of rope around the bags to hold them in place.

"Quit fidgeting, dragon."

Quit moving the rope. Are you trying to give me burns?

Enar snorted. "Uh-huh, right. Burn a dragon with a rope?"

Just get on and hey, watch where you step. Scales don't like to be bent backward. Thoren shook his leg, the flesh stinging from the bent scale.

"Whiny boy aren't we?"

Thoren turned and gave Enar a glare.

Enar straddled his back, shifting his weight from side to side, obviously trying to find a comfortable position. "I'm on, but you need to work on softening these scales. Do you have any idea how uncomfortable they are?"

Now who's the whiny boy?

He didn't have to have eyes in the back of his head to see the glare Enar gave him.

Ready? Thoren asked Fafnir.

I am.

Thoren hopped, flapping his wings, pushing against the air, rising into the sky. Nothing like flying, an activity he should do more often. Water droplets in the clouds brushed against his wings, a steady breeze whipped against his face. The ground faded away, swept by the thrumming beat of their wings. The sun journeyed across the sky and still they flew, cloaked in an invisibility spell.

Why did the Council insist on forbidding turning when on missions? Flying saved time and the view was spectacular. Rivers, forests, glades, all looked better from the air. The sharp breeze focused his thoughts, especially those regarding Keara.

She had mentioned the rogue Draconi wanting to unlock her powers. If he had unlocked her powers when he first found her, then she could have escaped Simon and the Draconi. Too bad he hadn't thought of unlocking them the night before, it might have prevented the troubles of the day.

Maybe he should unlock her powers tonight.

A tremor ran through his body at the thought. He could perform the ritual, unlock her powers and share a bedroll with Keara. Provided the drug wore off. He glanced at her, his eyes picking up movement as she flexed her arms.

Praise the Goddess she was recovering.

But he was still selfish to want to unlock her powers. Was it really for her or did he want to taste her first before he returned her to his people? Before he returned to his life of adventure? For once returning to the job didn't bring the same pleasure as normal. Flying over the hills of Draconia with his mate on his back sounded much more appealing.

He cursed. He was halfway to the kingdom of lovesick fools and falling fast.

We need to land. It's getting dark.

Thoren turned his head to Fafnir and nodded. *What about on the other side of that clump of trees? The ground looks level.*

Sounds good.

A couple of thumps later and they were down. Dropping his invisibility spell, Thoren knelt, and Enar jumped to the ground.

"We need to do that more often. I love flying," Enar said as he pulled the gear from Thoren's back.

"I don't. I thought I was going to throw up." Lily leaned against Fafnir's neck.

"It was the best!" Jamie started untying Keara

from Lily.

"I'm feeling better and think I can move." Keara pushed the rope over her head.

Relief flooding Thoren's senses, his knees going weak. Good thing he had four legs on the ground instead of two or he might have embarrassed himself by falling. Keara's coloring had returned, her eyes twinkled, although she moved slower than she had this morning.

"All off, dragon. You can turn back if you want."

He wanted. Definitely wanted. Wanted to touch Keara with his hands, wanted to ensure she was whole. Closing his eyes, he willed the beast into its cave, shrinking, pulling the scales inside, retracting the claws. The magic passed over his skin, rippling muscles, stretching skin over bones, until he stood naked before them.

Keara's eyes popped wide as she glanced down his body. *Brainless today, Thoren?* He forgot to dress. With a snap of his fingers, clothes covered his bare skin. Keara continued to stare, a blush on her cheeks.

Good thing he now had on clothes or she'd have a clear view of what was going on behind his leathers. One glance from her and his body was ready to show off its abilities to please a female. He clasped his hands together, trying to hide the bulge in his leathers. Keara's face turned the color of her hair and she twisted around, holding her arms up for Jamie.

Enar slapped Thoren in the chest. "Hey, stop staring at her arse and get to work. We need to put up camp."

"I wasn't staring." With effort, he turned to Enar. "What needs done?"

Several minutes later, they had a fire going, bedrolls slung around the heat. Night moved in with a chill on the autumn air, making the crackling flames a cheery welcome.

Thoren watched Keara eat as she tore off tiny bites, popping dried meat into her mouth. The tip of her tongue passed over her lips and his shaft twitched. He shifted and looked at Fafnir chewing on a deer carcass, effectively taking care of the growing-bulge-behind-the-leathers problem. Fafnir's teeth ripped through flesh, splattering blood on the ground. Nothing sexy about that.

And yet he still wanted Keara, the desire deepening as the evening progressed.

He needed to return her home and go back to her village to find the rogue Draconi. Maybe then, he'd be able to control these emotions threatening to overwhelm his senses.

An ache appeared in his chest at the thought of being away from her.

He cursed. And he thought unlocking her powers would make these feelings better?

Maybe not, but it would assuage the ache taking up residence below his belt. Was there a spell to make his leathers larger?

Keara smiled at him and he knew what would happen tonight. She was his.

****

Wriggling her toes gave such relief. A normal movement Keara took for granted until the drug caused all voluntary movements to cease. Tighten and release, tighten and release. Nice to know the leg muscles worked too. She fidgeted throughout their meal, happy with muscle movements.

Glancing up, she saw Thoren staring at her, lust in his gaze. Heat flooded her cheeks and she looked at her shoes, toes tapping inside.

Apparently, she could stop worrying about how to get him to notice her. He noticed all right, judging by the lustful look he gave her. She remembered the way he looked when he turned into a man, the way scales flattened into skin, limbs changing shape, the way his maleness hung heavy against his thigh. Unable not to notice that part, she had stared, and judging from the way it expanded, it noticed her too.

Still did. Thoren shifted and looked over to Fafnir. Keara pulled apart another bite of the chewy meat substance and popped it into her mouth. The leathery meat gave her jaw a workout and caused her cheek to throb. As she chewed, she watched the others, watched Thoren and Enar talk in soft tones about their escape and if anyone followed them. Fafnir ate in the shadows of the campsite, which pleased her just fine. Hearing flesh tear followed by chomping noises was bad enough, seeing them...yuck.

"I think he likes you," Lily whispered before tearing off a bite of meat with her teeth.

"Mmmph." Hard to talk when one's jaws cramped. Chew, chew, chew, swallow. "How's Enar?"

Lily blushed, her jaw tensing, relaxing. "Mmmph."

"Keara," Thoren's voice broke through the flickering flames of the fires, all power and heat. "I need to speak to you. Would you follow me?" Standing he gestured toward the woods behind the campsite.

"Definitely likes you," Lily muttered around a mouthful of leather-meat.

All right then. So much for planning a seduction.

Keara stood and placed her hand in Thoren's. Her husband. Would he claim his rights now? His hand tightened around hers. Good-bye innocence.

Following him into the shadows seemed right, like her entire life was made solely for this moment. Being kidnapped, drugged, almost raped made the desire to reaffirm life, to connect with him in the basest sense, a driving force. Thoren was here, now, and she wanted him beyond reason.

"Sit." He gestured toward a log.

Seemed an odd place to have sex, but she sat on the log anyway. He knelt before her, grasping her hands.

"I should have asked this last night, but didn't realize the need would arise. If I had done this last night, then when Simon and the Draconi captured you, you would have been able to escape. I don't think they'll come after us, but if they do, I don't want you to be vulnerable again."

The air collapsed around her, tightening, squeezing. He didn't want her.

"I ask you to allow me to unlock your powers." His eyes bored into hers, begging, pleading.

"My powers?"

"Remember last night and I explained to you about the unlocking ceremony?"

Oh, that. So much had happened since then she barely recalled Thoren's explanation. "A bit. Would you go over it again?"

"All right. All female Draconi have limited powers until they hit puberty. After puberty, they undergo a ceremony to unlock their powers. Sometimes certain powers manifest themselves earlier. Like moving objects by thinking about them—"

"What about healing abilities?" What about her secret?

"Sometimes. If the female is gifted in healing, then it will be noticed before her powers are unlocked. Are you thinking of your herbalist abilities?"

No. "Yes."

"If you have a gift for them, then it could very well be that you have healing powers. Not all Draconi have the same powers."

"So how do the powers get unlocked?"

Thoren smiled, a purely predatory grin. "All rites of passage are done by ritual."

"What other rites of passage are there?"

"Unlocking a female's power, when a male Changes—that is when he comes into his full powers, mating—you'd call it marriage, and bonding. Some are carried out with the help of a priestess and others are more private. Unlocking a female's powers can be either. Many females go to the Temple for their ritual, but not all. It's just fancier at the Temple."

"Fancier?"

"You know. Baths, perfumes, special robes, the whole bag of grain. But it doesn't have to be like that."

Her gaze held his. With her hand in his, she could feel his emotions, like a slight breeze, a ruffling of leaves. Lust, denial, lust, nervousness, lust, flowed into her, a brushing of thoughts.

So he did want her. But what did unlocking her powers have to do with his lust? Her eyes narrowed.

"What exactly does this unlocking ritual involve?"

Thoren cleared his throat. "For our people, rituals bring one closer to the Goddess and in order to reach that pinnacle, the orgasmic experience is used. Besides, the Goddess gave us sex as pleasure and passion, what higher way to serve Her than to use sex in our rituals?"

Close your mouth, Keara. He doesn't want to view the back of your throat. "Truthfully?" Talk about a complete head turn from her town's beliefs.

"Yes. In order for me to unlock your powers, I have to lie with you."

"Don't sound so nervous. Despite what you say, you married me in that square. I'm your wife. You can do with me as you will." Maybe he didn't want her, but she'd still get to experience what the whole

111

sex thing was like.

"I disagree, but let's not argue. Will you allow me to unlock your powers, to join my body with yours?"

He sounded so formal, like the words were part of a ritual. To borrow a word from Jamie—duh. Of course the words were ritualistic, they were undertaking a ritual. An odd ritual, but it didn't matter. She'd take him any way she could get him.

"I do."

His eyes glowed as he ran his thumb across her mark. "I'm glad." His breath whispered against her cheek, setting off a series of shivers across her skin.

"How does this work?" She congratulated herself for managing a whisper.

"I link my energy to yours. It's hard to describe." That breath-in-the-ear thing he did sent tingles rushing through her veins, warming her soul. Good thing her butt was on the log as her knees felt as if they'd collapse.

His thumb continued to circle her mark as his other hand grasped her wrist, thumb tracing her pulse point. "Are you ready?" His fingers stilled their motion.

Definitely. "Yes."

"This might feel a little odd. Just relax."

Keara took a deep breath. Things that started with 'just relax' had a tendency not to end well. But so far, this felt good.

A pulsing started in her wrists, creeping slowly up her arm, little tingles like ants crawling over her skin. She shifted her arms, but the tingles only increased, spreading to her shoulders. Keara tried to pull her wrists from his grasp, but Thoren tightened his grip.

"Shh. It's supposed to feel like that."

"It's a creepy feeling."

"It's just my magic searching for yours. It will

feel better in a minute."

It better. Her entire body felt like she'd been immersed in a tub of creepy-crawlies, small tingles pulsing up her arms, down her legs, centering in her torso.

With an audible pop, the energy changed. Instead of tingles like ant legs, the feeling altered, intensifying, as if a thousand hands stroked her body. Her head fell back, a moan leaving her lips, her legs falling open. Thoren moved closer and she wrapped her legs around his waist.

The invisible hands stroked, touching her nipples, flaming her core. Over and over, each touch sending her higher, soaring toward a peak of pleasure. And then the sensations transformed into tongues, licking, sucking, pulling at her nipples, her core. Faster and faster, the raspy strokes a whirlwind of desire until she shattered into pieces, fragmented into pleasure.

Thoren's lips pressed against hers, his tongue licking across the seam of her lips. Opening to him, she touched her tongue to his, stroking against the velvety softness.

Her first kiss.

And she wanted more.

Running her hands across Thoren's shoulders, she pulled him closer, pressing his chest to hers. His hair brushed against the back of her hands and she drew her fingers through it, feeling the silky strands that slipped out of the leather band tied at the nape of his neck.

One hand slipped under her tunic, a light touch stroking against her skin. Up and down, each stroke bringing his fingers closer to her breast, her hip, releasing tremors where they touched.

Wrapping one arm around her waist, the other supporting her spine, he rolled backward, pulling her on top of him, cushioning her fall. She felt the tickle of his chest hairs as they pressed against her bare skin.

Bare skin? Where were her clothes?

Breaking the kiss, she pushed up until she could look him in the face. "Where are—"

"Your clothes?" Keara nodded. "They're next to us. I didn't mean to frighten you. It just seemed the quickest way."

As if she'd admit to being frightened. Or embarrassed.

"I just didn't expect it, that's all. I was busy enjoying myself."

Thoren grinned, all male and knowing. "You were now, were you? Well, I bet I can make you enjoy it even more."

"I'd like that."

"Good."

With a little bit of pressure on her nape, he pulled her lips down to his warm firm ones, his kiss full of need. Her skin became his, sensations passing from him into her and back again. Magic pulsed between them, circling around, passing through, until she didn't know where she stopped and he began.

Arching his neck, he pulled a nipple into his mouth, sucking, his tongue circling the nub. Pleasure streaked through her veins, riding on the wave of magic. Her core heated, growing wet, her hips moving back and forth across the ridge of his arousal. The tip of him caught on the folds of her core, pulling as she ground herself against him.

So good, but not enough.

Hands at her waist stilled her frantic motions. "You have to take me inside. The female controls the ritual."

She sat up, embarrassment over him seeing her breasts a fleeting emotion. Lust flared in his eyes, one hand squeezing gently, his thumb flicking over her nipple. A woman could learn to like that look, that lust in her man's eyes. She did that to him.

And the knowledge of that small power made her smile.

How else could she please him?

She stroked her fingers down his chest, brushing her thumb over his nipple, watching his jaw stiffen as his eyes closed. "How do I do that?"

His lids snapped open. "You've never done this?"

Uh-oh. He looked worried. Despite the shadows obscuring his face, she knew her virginity concerned him. After tonight, it wouldn't be a problem. There was no way she was stopping now. No way. He was hers.

"I haven't done it in this position." Or any position, but he didn't need to know that.

"Gently grasp my shaft and put it inside you. Just be careful not to bend it."

Of course. She knew that. Innocence did not equal naiveté. She could do this. He was her husband. He rescued her twice. He wanted her.

Dragging her nails down his chest, listening to his sighs, power coursed through her limbs, slamming into her core. Wetness from her folds flowed over his staff as she grasped him in her hand, centering him against her. Rising up on her knees, she lowered herself onto him, eyes flaring as he penetrated her untried channel.

Inch by inch she lowered herself onto him until he filled her. Invasion, penetration, oneness. His hands locked on her waist, raising and lowering her, his staff pulling inside, rubbing over sensitive places she didn't know she had. Leaning forward and shifting her hips brought a rush of pleasure, focusing on one spot.

She rubbed that spot against him, faster, faster, until she shattered, floating on a wave of bliss. He grasped her hips, slowing the motion, increasing the pressure. Long strokes that pulled against her sensitive tissues, that brought her to the edge again. He joined her in pleasure, crying out as she felt his staff jerk inside her.

She collapsed on top of him, his arms wrapping around her waist.

"How do you feel?" he whispered against her ear.

"Mmm." Wonderful. Sore.

"Do you feel your magic?"

How could he think about magic after what happened between them? "No."

"Sometimes it takes awhile." He rolled them to their sides, slipping out of her, but keeping his arm about her waist.

"What does it feel like?"

"Like—" Thoren inhaled, nostrils flaring. "Why do I smell blood? Did I hurt you?"

Heat bloomed in her cheeks. She hadn't thought he'd be able to smell the remnants of her virginity. Shaking her head, she ducked, pressing her face into his chest.

"Are you not telling me something?"

"I'm all right. I'd tell you if I wasn't."

A long pause. "If you say so."

She started to nod, when her hair stuck straight out, as if a bolt of lightning landed nearby. "What—"

Waves of electricity crashed through her arms, her legs, jerking her onto her back, a cry breaking through her lips. Thoren placed a hand over her heart, pressing her into the ground, stilling the tremors shaking her limbs.

"This is the magic. Center it in you, gather it into a ball. Hold the magic in the ball."

Was he daft? How was she supposed to do that when it felt like electric snakes slithered through her veins? Closing her eyes, she pictured the strands of electricity as snakes, slithering, sliding and she reached out her arms, gathering them to her. They came, crawling into her arms, circling around her, until she managed to push them into a ball. A writhing ball.

Good thing snakes didn't bother her.

"All right. I have the ball."

"Don't let it get away from you. Think of the ball as your magic. If you let it escape, then it can cause damage. You'll learn to control it so that you determine how much energy escapes at once."

"Umm...the ball is coming apart."

"Hold it together! Find a way to hold it together."

What held snakes in place? Keara imagined a net surrounding the snakes, a tightly woven net, too small for the snakes to escape. Ah. That worked. She opened her eyes.

A burst of energy shot from her hand, singing Thoren's shoulder before slamming into a tree. The smell of burning flesh saturated her nostrils. Without thinking, she placed her other hand over the seared skin on his shoulder, healing the burn.

Unlike the other times she'd healed, this one didn't leave her drained. Tired, but that could be from the sex. Or the ritual. Or the day.

"How did you do that?" Thoren rubbed where her energy singed him.

If he only knew. "I just can. I've always been able to. And I'm really sorry about the burn. I'm not sure what happened."

"Don't feel bad, it's normal. I expected that. I didn't expect you to heal it. Thank you."

"It's normal to singe skin and burn trees?"

"It's expected when a female's powers are first unlocked. It won't last long. You'll figure out how to hold the energy in unless you need it to work magic."

"Do males go through this ritual too?"

Thoren brushed a piece of hair out of her face, tucking it behind her ear. "Males go through the

Change when they are in their mid-thirties. There is a ritual for the Change but not to unlock their powers."

"So, how do males have their powers unlocked?"

"Not in the same way females do. Males usually start working magic when they are young. When they go through puberty, they have almost all of their powers. When a male goes through the Change, then he gains his full powers."

"Have you gone through the Change?"

"No. Not yet."

"So males have powers when they hit puberty but females don't?"

"Females have some powers. As you do with healing. But until their powers can be unlocked, they don't have their full abilities. However, females typically have stronger magic than do males. Not always, though."

"So my magic is stronger than yours?"

Teeth flashed white in the darkness as Thoren grinned. "At the moment your magic is more electrifying than powerful. Maybe when you learn to control it."

"Smarty-pants." A strand of magic flew out of her fingers, cutting into another tree. Luckily, the tree remained standing. "Aargh! How am I supposed to sleep if I keep blowing things up?"

Thoren looked at the tree. "It's not blown up."

"You know what I mean." Keara pinched him.

He snorted. "Sorry. Couldn't help it. But you don't need to worry about sleep. Nothing has ever happened to a female when she sleeps. No escaping powers, no magical death blows. Don't worry."

"Thanks." She thought. What if he was wrong? What if she burned him to death in her sleep? Or set the woods on fire, killing everyone?

"Really. Trust me. Besides, I'm here. I'll make sure nothing happens."

"But the tree is burned."

"I wasn't focusing then. I am now. Trust me, Little One. Sleep."

Tiredness flooded her body, making her eyelids heavy, her mouth opening in a yawn. She snuggled her head on his shoulder, letting the heat of his body and the steady thumping of his heart lull her to sleep.

****

Thoren watched Keara sleep, the curve of her breast resting against his chest, her skin prickling in the chill night air. Instead of watching her sleep, he needed to ensure her warmth. What was he thinking?

He wasn't.

Holding out his hand, he used his magic to pull the invisibility blanket out of his bag and float it to him. With a flick of his wrist, he draped the blanket over Keara and himself. Warmth.

Not like he needed more heat. He had enough lying next to Keara.

For once, he understood why a male would do anything to be with his female. Why had he wanted to leave her? Was his job that important?

He pictured them together, her working with the healing priestesses at the Temple and him...staying home.

What did mated males do all day?

He could teach the hatchlings how to control their magic. That was an acceptable position for a mated male to have. But where was the excitement, the adrenaline rush, the joy of outmaneuvering one's enemies?

It didn't exist in teaching.

Could he live with that? He looked down at Keara, felt her breath tickle the skin of his chest. She belonged to him, of that he was sure. It took all his will not to lock inside her during sex, to mark her inside and out as his mate.

Could he give up his livelihood for her? A shiver shook him. He hadn't planned for this. Hadn't meant to find his mate this early in his life. His head pounded. Undoubtedly from too much thinking.

Thoren rubbed his forehead. What was up with his aching head? Since when did he have head pains? The brushing of Keara's soft skin against his chest, her breasts rising and falling as she slept soothed the headache into a dull throb, a background noise.

A wave of tiredness swept over him, trying to push him under. Keara had the right idea. Sleep sounded wonderful. Enar and Fafnir could watch the camp. Maybe a little shut-eye would get rid of the head pains. Taking a deep breath, he closed his eyes and let the pain beating in his skull pull him into a fitful darkness.

Chapter 11

Thoren woke with a gasp, blood pounding in his ears, sweat covering his body. Creeping shadows rustled through the trees with the wind as his wide-eyed gaze frantically roved their branches. He sat up, shaking his head, trying to remember the dream that disturbed him, to no avail. Glancing down at Keara sleeping by his side, he started to run fingers through his hair, stopping when he saw his hand.

Shadows from the moving branches flickered across his hand as he turned it to and fro. Not even shadows could play a trick like this. Concentrating, he willed the dragon's talon back into a human hand.

This couldn't be happening. He still had several years left.

A dream. That's what it must be. He'll open his eyes and everything will be fine. The hand will still be a hand. No claw.

Thoren opened his eyes and stared at the claw formerly known as his hand. Closed them. Opened again. Tried to get his heart to stop pounding like a hammer on an anvil.

Goddess's bones.

The Change. That time in a male's life where he was brought into his full powers or left forever in dragon's form. Only a female could bring a man into his powers, no female and he was stuck with scales. Same as Fafnir.

Dear Goddess, no!

Unfortunately for him, all he had available was

a female who had just been brought into her powers and had no idea what the ritual involved. He could fly home—according to Fafnir it was a little over half a day away—but to turn willingly into the dragon while Changing meant he might never return to his human form.

He shuddered. If Keara couldn't help him, he would become like Fafnir, stuck in dragon form until his death. Dear gods, he hoped not.

Keara lay on her back, one arm thrown over her head, her braid tumbling across her bare breasts. Would she be able to help him? He could explain the ritual to her, but it would be up to her to perform it. Closing his eyes, Thoren took deep breaths, trying to reduce the pounding in his veins.

He had no choice. He would try to explain the ritual and pray her fluctuating powers didn't blast him in the middle of it.

May the Goddess shine Her light on him.

She might be more amenable to doing so if he'd bother to pray on occasion. When was the last time? Obviously too long if he couldn't remember.

Slipping out from under the blanket, Thoren pulled it around Keara with his one non-clawed hand. That was starting to change into a claw.

Curse it.

In the manner of his race, he stood facing the wind to pray, feeling the touch of the Goddess as the wind caressed his hair. If he closed his eyes, he could imagine Her arms wrapped tightly around him, protecting him from the uncertainties of the Change. Standing quietly, he raised his hands to the sky, feeling Her breath on his skin, Her touch through his hair, and slowly the tension eased from his muscles.

****

Keara opened her eyes, expecting to see Thoren lying beside her. Only empty air greeted her. Where was Thoren? She started to push up on her elbow when she noticed him standing by her feet, arms raised above his head. She had to stare hard to see his chest rise and fall. Not that she minded watching his chest.

Or the muscles of his body. Or the heavy length of him which unfortunately was hidden in the shadows. Shame that.

She was definitely over her fear of him and moving down the road of serious liking.

The wind whipped his hair back from his face, dim shafts of moonlight speckling the sweat pouring down his face. Sweat? She sat up, letting the blanket pool about her waist, and focused on his face. Sweat dripped off his chin; even in the dim light she saw it. Was he sick? Maybe she should disturb him and ask, but he seemed to be praying.

His eyes opened, focusing on her. Guess he wasn't praying after all. But something was wrong as his energy field danced erratically around his upper body. Turquoise blue intermingled with apple green and yellow spikes collided with a bright scarlet that appeared to be trying to overrun the other colors. What illness caused an aura like that?

And his hands. Claws spurted from the ends of his arms.

"It's the Change."

"Your hands."

He raised a claw to eye level, turning it back and forth, a shudder running through his body. "I need your help."

"I don't know where my herb bag is."

"Herbs won't help." He knelt at her feet. "I need your magic."

"My magic?" Oh yes, that writhing ball of snakes she was supposed to control.

A burst of energy shot from her hand, striking the ground, a geyser of dirt spraying over them.

"You sure you want my magic? Because it doesn't seem to be controlled."

Thoren wiped dirt off his face with the back of his arm. "I don't have a choice. If you don't help me, I'll turn into a dragon and will never be able to turn back."

"Is that why Fafnir stays as a dragon?"

"Yes. Let me explain to you what you need to do. Please."

If he wanted to use her uncontrolled magic to help him, who was she to argue? "All right. Tell me what I need to do."

Two minutes later Keara raised a brow at Thoren. "That's all I have to do? I thought this was some complicated task."

"It's not complicated. Just new to you. Do you think you can do it?"

What he described wasn't much different than when she healed injuries. Same concept. No problem, right?

"Of course. Do you want to sit beside me?"

Thoren lowered himself to the ground, his face tensing with obvious pain.

Keara watched as the colors of his aura flickered, the red fighting for dominance. Thoren drew in a breath, sweat breaking on his brow. He wiped his forehead with his arm, while she reached a hand toward the colors, trying to still their fight. When her hand passed through the red light, it ceased its struggle, streaming instead toward her palm.

Instinct kept her hand still as the red light from Thoren's aura flowed into it, pouring into her body. She gasped as the magic streamed through her veins, heating her palms. Should she absorb it, make it a part of her, or throw it away?

Too mesmerized by the colors dancing before her to decide, Keara continued to stroke her hands down the aura surrounding Thoren's body, each stroke calming the clash of colors, easing the tension on his face. Thoren shuddered as she drew more of the scarlet into her hand. Her palms blistered, but the compulsion to continue overwhelmed the reaction to pull her hands away.

What should she do with all this magic gathered into her hands? She didn't know how to throw it away, or what would happen to whatever object it landed on, and the trees already looked pretty sad from her own energy bursts.

Absorption it was. But how?

The magic crept through her veins, lodging in every pore of her body, filling her mind. Something inside her brain unlocked like a dam breaking as the magic spread into that previously hidden place. She noticed the colors of Thoren's aura flickering in harmony before her vision darkened. Her body felt alive, on fire, every inch inside and out burning with the pulse of Thoren's magic.

She heard a cry. What was that? Who cares? Her body was thrown backward, the breath leaving her as she hit the ground, a heavy body covering hers. She wanted this, wanted him, but the pulse of the magic soothed her, enticed her to work with it, to open to it, to ignore what was happening to her body.

He entered her, stretching her to fullness and yet the magic flowing out of him and into her took all her attention.

She reached for it, pulling it about her like a cloak, diving into its depths as he plundered her body. With each of his strokes she felt the pull of magic drag her deeper, until she no longer felt her body, no longer had consciousness. Nothing mattered but joining the scarlet magic of Thoren's to her spirit, bonding him to her.

****

Thoren opened his eyes to see Keara's pale face,

her eyes closed. He kissed her cheek and looked at his hand, which praise the Goddess was a hand and not a claw. The ritual worked. Keara saved him from being stuck in dragon form.

"Thank you."

She didn't move.

"Keara?" He placed a hand against her cheek, feeling the heat pouring off her skin, then slipped it down to where her pulse beat in her neck. It took him a couple of tries to find her pulse, which beat in an erratic barely-felt pattern.

"Keara?" He shook her shoulder, hoping to wake her, getting nothing but a floppy head.

What happened? He'd never heard of a female being injured while helping a male through his Change and yet something was clearly wrong. But what?

He pulled out of her, smelling the musk of their joining, wishing he had taken his time instead of slamming into her like a green lad with his first female.

"Keara?"

Her skin burned where he touched it. Looking at her hands, he saw small blisters glittering in the moonlight. Magic only burned when it was absorbed.

Goddess's teeth, she didn't.

Thoren felt his heart jump, pounding away like he'd flown for miles. He wiped his palms on his thighs. Why hadn't she thrown off his magic? Hadn't he told her to do that?

After racking his brain for their conversation, he knew he hadn't told her what to do with the magic. What had he been thinking to describe the ritual and forget the most important part?

Absorbing such strong magic usually resulted in death. He smacked his fist against his chest in a futile effort to stop the erratic pounding of his heart. His mate was dying.

A roar slammed through his ears and it took him a second to realize it came from him.

"Thoren?" Enar stepped into view, hair rumpled from sleep.

Thoren snarled, crouched in front of Keara and flipped the blanket to cover her naked form. Enar froze, his nose the only part of him moving.

"You Changed. I smell the magic."

Yet another odd thing about his best friend coming to light at a time he couldn't dwell on it. How could a Watcher smell magic? Only Draconi smelled magic.

"Keara's injured."

"You hurt her?"

"Yes. No. She absorbed my magic."

"And that's bad?"

"She's supposed to throw it away, not absorb it. It might kill her. I need to get her to the Temple so the priestesses can perform a healing. Where's Fafnir? We need to leave now."

"Um, about Fafnir. I don't know where he is. He disappeared when you and Keara walked back here."

Thoren cursed. "I can't carry all of you and she needs help now."

"You go. We'll come later. It'll take us awhile, but we'll get there. Still have our feet."

Thoren wrapped the blanket around Keara, covering her, before he lifted her. The trees bunched too close together for him to turn into a dragon so he strode to where Lily and Jamie slept in the clearing by the fire. He placed Keara down, took a couple of steps away from her and turned. Scales rippled as skin disappeared, muscles elongating, bones snapping in a fury of change until his dragon overwhelmed the small clearing.

Keara took shallow breaths, her face reflecting the glow of the flickering flames of fire. What if she died before he made it to the Temple?

Positive thoughts, Thoren, positive thoughts.

He would make it to the Temple and she would be all right. Everything would be all right.

If only he believed it.

See you soon, friend.

"May your journey be quick." Enar raised a hand.

As carefully as possible, Thoren gathered Keara into his talons, grasping her and the blanket. Two hops later and the wind caught his outstretched wings, lifting him into the air. With powerful strokes, he headed toward the Temple.

Hopefully he wasn't too late.

Chapter 12

Thoren landed with a thud in the courtyard of the Temple, scattering grass, white-robed acolytes and priestesses. He placed Keara on the ground, the late morning sun catching highlights in her hair. Breathing heavily, Thoren willed his body back into its human form. Red scales transformed into skin, bones popping and shortening, leaving him as naked as the day he hatched. With a snap of his fingers, clothes appeared on his body and he lifted Keara into his arms. Startled voices from the acolytes and priestesses gasped around him as he marched to the gilded doors of the Temple, clutching Keara against his chest.

Aryana, his aunt and High Priestess, came barreling out the doors, trailed by an equally tall woman, Annaliese, her second in command and star healer. Perhaps they saw him coming. More likely, they heard the shouts in the Courtyard as he landed.

"Greetings, Ari." He tried to smile at his aunt, but it came out as more of a grimace.

"What happened, Thoren?" Aryana asked, touching Keara's face. "Who is she?"

He didn't bother speaking for it took too long. Instead, he opened his mind and showed them how he found Keara and the rituals they underwent, leaving out the likelihood of her being his mate and their two joinings. Not that they didn't know how rituals ended, but they didn't need to be voyeurs.

"She absorbed your magic?" Annaliese's eyes popped wide.

"Well, don't stand around talking. Take her to the healing rooms." Aryana hurried into the Temple with Annaliese and Thoren close behind.

The room Ari led them to was sparsely decorated, a bed and nightstand the only furniture. Religious paintings of dragons frolicking in fields dotted the walls. Thoren laid Keara on the bed and took a step back, leaving space for the priestesses to perform their healing magics. He watched Keara's pale face, her only movement a chest barely rising as she struggled for breath.

Aryana and Annaliese placed crystal globes around the bed, chanting words in an ancient tongue as they touched each one, causing it to glow. Magic pulsed in the air, encircling the globes, the bed, whispering against his skin. When they completed the circle, light surrounded the bed, shimmering softly.

"We have placed the healing stones around her and can only wait now. If her magic is strong she will overcome this." Ari placed a hand on Thoren's shoulder. "Annaliese will stay with her. She has healing powers far beyond mine. Come and we'll talk." She held her arm out toward the door.

Thoren looked at Keara, her red hair in stark contrast to the pristine white sheets. He grabbed the invisibility blanket, wadded it up and tucked it under his arm. Chances were good she wouldn't need it inside the Temple.

What if she died? What would he do without her?

Go about his business as he had before she dropped into his life.

Somehow, the thought no longer pleased him.

"Thoren?" Aryana's arm had to be tired held out like that.

"I would like to stay."

"The crystals will work better without you in

here. Besides, don't you need to give a report to the Council?"

Taking one last look at Keara, he followed Ari out the door. His sitting by Keara's side would not help her recover. And he could always come back.

"I don't need to give a report until Enar arrives. We're supposed to report together."

"Oh. In that case, would you care for a room? No offense, but you look exhausted."

Really? Flying all night with his mate in his claws had a tendency to do that to a dragon. "I might be a bit tired. I flew all night to get Keara here."

"I know. You showed me."

"Oh, right. Maybe I'm more tired than I thought."

Aryana opened a door a couple of doors down from the room Keara was in. "Why don't you stay here? There's fresh water in this room and we'll bring you food later."

"Thank you." He gave her a hug.

"It's good to see you again, nephew. We'll talk later." She patted his face and walked out of the room.

Thoren flopped on the bed, sinking into the mattress, and stared at the ceiling mural. Green fields, wild flowers and streams he could almost hear tumbling over the rocks danced above his head.

Keara would be all right. She had to be. Annaliese was the best healer of all the priestesses. Which figured since she was Alviss's daughter and not only was he the eldest Draconi, he was also the most powerful. And Annaliese's mother had been a well-known healer when she lived, so healing magic ran in her family.

Keara would be fine. Annaliese would see to it, Ari would help and all would be well. It would happen. Wouldn't it?

Worrying about it got him nowhere and the

longer he lay on the soft mattress, the heavier his lids became until he drifted into an uneasy sleep.

****

A thick, red fog surrounded Keara, punctuated by seven dim lights set in a circle. How did the lights get in the middle of the fog? The fog felt like it had buffeted her body forever, but the lights were new. If only they helped her see the ground, so she could lie down and sleep. But the ground had disappeared under a mantle of red and who knew what crawled around down there.

If only she could figure out a way to make the fog disappear. At the time, absorbing Thoren's aura seemed like the best way to help him, but now that it surrounded her, pressing against her body and threatening to suffocate her, she wondered what possessed her to do so. She should have thrown it away instead of asking it to go on some sort of adventure with her.

Too late now.

Without a doubt, the fog would suffocate her. Already the simple act of breathing had become almost impossible, like weights pressed against her chest. Maybe breathing would be easier if she opened her mouth.

Or not.

As soon as her mouth opened, the red fog poured down her throat, and she instinctively swallowed. Heat darted through her veins, fueling her with power. The pressure against her chest slackened enough for her to draw a breath. Was it her imagination or had the fog lessened? Yes, it most certainly had. The lights glowed brighter. Could making the fog disappear be that easy?

Wouldn't hurt to try.

She opened her mouth, allowing the fog to stream in, swallowing it down, feeling the pressure on her body lessen with each gulp. When the fog hit her stomach it dispersed, awakening fires in her veins as it ran, leaving her hungry for more.

Mouth open, she swallowed down the fog, gulp after gulp, until she stood in a clearing surrounded by seven lights. Keara stared at her arms in shock. Her glowing red arms. She held one in front of her face, poking it with her finger.

Red. Poke. Still red.

Interesting.

Power beat under her skin, more power than the magic ball of snake-like energy she held curled in her chest. Thoren's power. And it wanted free.

Pointing a finger at one of the lights, she commanded it to shatter.

The light exploded, raining shards of glass upon her hair and skin. Keara covered her head with her arms. Maybe breaking the light hadn't been the smartest thing to do.

Keara!

The voice screamed across the clearing. Keara raised her head, looking around. Nothing. Maybe she imagined it. But the voice screamed her name again. Perhaps the Goddess talked to her. She tilted her head back, looking toward the sky.

"I'm here, Most Holy One, what do you want of me?"

A chuckle sounded. Oops, maybe she had insulted the Goddess by her address. Well, what did She expect? She had never deigned to talk to Keara before.

Keara, walk toward the closest light. Are you there? Good, now touch it. Allow the light to surround you. Listen to my voice and let the light surround you.

Whew, she hadn't insulted the Goddess after all. Keara placed her hand on the ball of light. Peace washed over her as the yellow glow surrounded her, drawing her into the globe. But being thrust through a narrow opening into a light brighter than the sun did not bode well for remaining pain free.

Her scream echoed in her ears as her body jerked against the bed.

A bed? Why was she on a bed instead of in the woods with Thoren? Shudders ran through her limbs, cramping the muscles and she forgot the question.

"Keara, open your eyes."

The voice of the Goddess again! The light must be a transport to the Afterlife. Why then did she feel so much pain? Wasn't the Afterlife pain-free? Maybe it wasn't the Goddess. Maybe it was some other woman who had found her. Found them.

Where was Thoren?

Nothing to do but obey the voice.

Her lids felt like coins lay upon them, heavy and weighted. With effort, she pried them half-open, took a quick peek and let them fall shut. Much less effort that way.

"Keara?" Hands patted hers.

Wonder if her arms were still red. *Open eyes, open.*

This time her lids didn't feel as heavy and she managed to open them. Two dark-haired women sat on either side of her, holding her hands. Relief flashed through their eyes as their lips curled into a set of matching smiles.

"There you go, girl. Nice to see you," the one with long straight hair said.

"Hello, Keara." This voice belonged to the curly-haired woman, the one that looked older, if only by the age shining through her eyes. Something about her looked familiar, but Keara couldn't figure it out. Her eyes maybe? Keara gave a mental shrug. Other things were more important than why the woman looked familiar.

"Where am I?"

"You're in the Temple of the Goddess in the land of Draconia. As the High Priestess of the Temple, I bid you welcome," Straight Hair said.

"Um. Thank you." *Where was Thoren?*

"Thoren's down the hall."

"Did I say that?"

"You mind-spoke." Curly Hair.

"I can do that?"

Both women chuckled. Nice to know she made the priestesses happy. What a change from the priests back home.

"Of course, you are Draconi. I see I will have to educate you in the ways of our race." Straight Hair.

"Your Highness?" Keara turned toward Straight Hair. She couldn't keep calling them Straight and Curly forever.

"You may call me Aryana. Everyone else does."

"And I'm Annaliese, the Temple Healer."

Did they hear her thoughts again?

Yes, chorused through her brain.

She really needed to work on this mind-speaking thing.

"That's what we're here for. To help you. Just not now, since you need your rest."

"Thoren mentioned that you were an apothecary, so I thought you might like to go on rounds with me as I attend to the sick. Once you're well, that is." Annaliese's eyes sparkled.

"I'm allowed to do that? What does Thoren think of that?"

"Why should he care?" Aryana asked.

"He's my husband. He dictates where I go."

Both women blinked, looked at each other, looked back to Keara.

"Pardon?" Aryana tilted her head as she stared at Keara.

Were things so different here? Apparently. "According to my customs we're married—"

135

"Does Thoren know this?"

"I told him that's what it meant, but he said he wasn't."

Aryana patted her hand, little strokes meant to soothe. "Keara, love, Thoren cannot be your husband. Even if it was by your laws, it is not by our customs. We have exact rituals for mating and a Draconi has only one mate. He could not have married you because he knows he needs to find his mate.

"Now, now, don't fret." The hand patting quickened. "You are welcome here for as long as you want to stay. You may look for a mate too, if you so desire, but you must remove from your mind that Thoren is your husband."

Keara blinked, hoping to catch the tears before they fell. If she didn't have Thoren as her husband, what would happen to her? Did these people really want her or would they hate her because of her red hair? What if she didn't fit in? Where would she go?

A cup pressed against her lips, the smell of lemon balm and valerian filling her nose. "Drink. Be calm." Annaliese demanded it and Keara had no choice but to comply.

The tea tasted bitter despite the lemon balm, its heat spreading outward, relaxing her. Annaliese placed a hand on her forehead and all went dark.

When Keara woke, she blinked against the brightness of the room. Light streamed from a window, splashing across Aryana as she slept in a chair next to where Keara lay. Shame to wake her, but Keara really needed to find the relief room. She threw the covers off and tried to roll out of the bed. Next thing she knew Aryana stood in front of her, impeding her progress.

"Not so fast, Keara. You shouldn't be up and around."

"I need the relief room."

"Oh. In that case, it's right in here." Aryana opened a door, then returned to the bed and helped Keara stand.

Good thing too, as her knees wobbled enough for her to collapse against the High Priestess. Holding on to the doorjamb, Keara waved at Aryana.

"I can get it from here." She slipped into the relief room and shut the door.

Aryana stood by the door when Keara opened it and wrapped an arm around her waist, helping her to the bed. How long had she been lying there to have problems walking?

"Three days."

"Three days? Truthfully?" Keara sunk into the mattress, leaning back against the headboard.

Ari sat next to her. "Yes. Three days before you woke and then Annaliese spelled you into rest yesterday evening. We've taken turns watching you."

"And Thoren?" Keara's voice hitched.

"He has been around, checking on you. He's out right now, but I will let him come to see you if you'd like."

"I'd like."

"Remember what I told you yesterday?"

Did she ever. Thoren wasn't her husband. Thoren had to find his own mate. Thoren neglected to tell her a good many things. Very well. If he didn't want her for a wife, then she would stay at the Temple.

Annaliese told her she could learn the Draconi way of healing and that sounded like a good start. Already these people liked her better than the folks had in her hometown and if she remained on the Temple grounds then she wouldn't have to deal with anyone who might find her offensive.

But she really wanted Thoren by her side.

If wishes were gold, she'd be rich.

"I remember. I would like to take Annaliese up

on her offer, if that does not offend?"

"Why would it offend?"

As if she was going to offer the why. If the priestesses weren't offended by her, then she was not going to give them ample fodder. They actually seemed to want her and wasn't that a complete change? She could get used to people smiling at her instead of warding off evil behind her back.

Keara shrugged. "Just checking."

"It would be fine for you to work with Annaliese."

What a change.

She could barely believe her luck. People liked her. People who were like her, who didn't mind smoking ears and energy bursts strong enough to topple trees.

Uh-oh. Just thinking of the magic Thoren unlocked caused her limbs to shake and not in a good way. With an ear-piercing boom, the nightstand exploded, raining wooden splinters over the room. Keara clutched her head and ducked.

Well, they had liked her and wanted her to stay. After the exploding nightstand, she doubted they were still of that mindset.

Keara peeked out from under her arms. Dust motes streamed through the air, catching on the sunlight. She coughed.

"My, that was a good one. Most don't manage to blow up a nightstand. I'm impressed." Aryana waved her hand and wood particles throughout the room coalesced into a nightstand. Keara's hand slapped over her mouth, her eyes darted from the reassembled nightstand to Aryana.

"How?"

"A Draconi can reassemble objects that have already been built. A craftsman designed the nightstand. You and a hundred others can blow it to smithereens and I can still reform it. But Draconi cannot create things from nothing. Our magic is limited in that regard."

"Can you show me how to do that?"

"Of course. It will be part of your training. You have much to learn. We usually rescue Halflings at an earlier age, which exposes them to magic sooner. But your powers are strong, so I'm sure you'll do fine."

Great. She went from cursed in her hometown to deficient here. Which was worse?

At least here, they didn't mind a deficiency.

"Now, what we really wanted to know was how you managed to absorb Thoren's energy without dying. We have vessels specially created to channel the energy from a male's Change into the ground where it disperses harmlessly. How did you do the same?"

"I'm not sure. I was surrounded by a red fog and I found that if I swallowed it, it disappeared. Then there were these lights and I blew one up and as soon as it shattered, a voice told me to go into the light. So I did and there you two were."

"Interesting. We set the lights up and hoped you'd find them to leave the darkness. But we didn't think you'd live. We could only hope and pray you'd heal."

Keara felt like she'd fallen and landed flat on her back. She'd almost died.

Maybe her grandmother was right, maybe magic was evil.

Or maybe magic was like certain herbs, too much could kill, just enough could heal.

"I'm glad I'm here."

"So am I, Keara, so am I. Now, I have some duties to attend to, so I'm going to leave you in your room. If you feel like it, we can teach you things later today or tomorrow."

"I'd like that, thank you."

Ari patted Keara's hand and stood. "I'll be back soon."

The door clicked behind her, leaving Keara alone with her thoughts.

Chapter 13

Thoren sat by the reflection pool behind the Temple, staring into the shallow waters and wishing Keara would wake. He'd heard no word of how she fared. As of last evening she was still in a coma.

So here he sat—waiting.

It would be more productive to go see his mother and assure her he lived. Alleviating her worry was normally his top priority. But she came as a double package deal and seeing his father right now was not on his agenda. Listening to how Thoren needed to find a mate, how he needed to get busy searching while Keara lay in a coma would just upset him. Thoren loved his father, but having to hear the older male pester him about finding a mate was enough to make a dragon breathe fire.

He'd contact his mother once Enar arrived and they made their report to the Council. As far as he knew, the Council didn't realize he'd returned.

Birds chirped in the tree branches, calling happily to each other as he watched their reflections in the pool. Ari needed to let him see Keara instead of keeping him away from her. He was done with this sitting around waiting business.

Once on his feet he turned, running into Ari.

Too much thinking made him deaf. "How is she?"

"She woke last night—"

"You didn't call me?"

One fine eyebrow shot upward. "She became...distressed. She's awake now. You may see

141

her. How did you become her husband? You failed to mention that."

Thoren set off at a brisk pace toward the Temple, Aryana matching his strides. "I showed you. Simon wanted to make her his so I rescued her."

"I thought she said you married her."

"That was the custom. Take the woman to the square and pronounce her yours. Take her home. There you go." He yanked open the door to the Temple and walked into the stone structure.

"How barbaric!"

"Uh-huh. You should've seen the place. Is she still in the same room?"

"Yes. And Thoren, she is going to stay with us and learn healing from Annaliese."

Thoren stopped so fast he almost fell. "What?"

"What did you expect her to do? She has no mate. We don't know who her family is, although if he is inclined, Alviss can discover it. But she needs something to do until then and she has powerful magic. Why shouldn't she serve us here?"

Because she's my mate and she belongs with me!

But if she didn't want him, then he couldn't have her. At least not now. He needed to persuade her that she belonged to him, that she was his.

And then he needed to find something else to do besides his job, his life.

Maybe Keara staying at the Temple would work out for the best. He could work until he grew tired of it and she would be protected. An ache pounded in his chest.

Ari stared at him like she was waiting on his response. Had she asked a question? She had. He really needed to stop all this thinking as it made him deaf and absentminded.

"Thoren, are you all right?" Her green stare pierced him, seeing through to his soul.

He ran a hand through his hair. "Yes, sorry.

Have something on my mind. Are you going in with me or will you leave us alone?"

Aryana's head tilted, eyes narrowing. After several seconds, she motioned to the door. "I'll be back later."

Taking a deep breath, Thoren pushed open the door to Keara's room. Empty. She wasn't in the bed. His heart thudded to a stop and then quick-timed it. Where was she?

"Hello?" Her voice shouldn't sound that weak.

Thoren shoved the door wide open and turned to Keara's voice. She stood by the window, pale and fragile, her white robe clinging to curves begging for his touch. If she hadn't been in a coma the last three days, he'd back her against the wall...

"Thoren?"

"Hey. How're you feeling? Ari said you woke."

"Yes, I did. I got tired of lying around in bed so I thought I'd take a tour of the room."

Her legs wobbled. Two strides and he wrapped an arm around her waist. "Why don't I help you back to the bed?"

"Thanks."

She sagged against him, obviously relying on his strength to walk her five steps to the bed. He wished the distance was greater so he could feel her curves against him for longer. Wished she relied on him for more than just help to the bed.

He was a lovesick fool.

She swung her legs over the edge of the bed and Thoren tucked them under the covers. Was that a chill that shook her limbs? He pulled the sheet to her waist. Maybe he should try to put it around her shoulders.

"I'm fine, Thoren." She pushed the sheet down to her waist.

"All right." If she insisted, but he'd feel better with her covered and warm.

Keara scooted her legs over and gestured for him to sit. He sat.

"Thank you for bringing me to Draconia."

Leaving you in Cautasia was not an option. "You needed the priestesses. I'm glad you're better."

She smiled and took his hand. Amazing how such a small touch affected the beat of his heart. Such delicate fingers graced his own. Delicate fingers whose touch burned lines of pleasure wherever they stroked. He remembered their feel on his skin.

And he wanted her again.

A wanting that wasn't going to be fulfilled right now.

Keara glanced out the window. "It's so different here." Her gaze returned to his. "I'm not sure if they'll accept me."

"Ari said you have powerful magic and you will be a great asset to them."

"She did? I mean, they asked me to work with Annaliese to learn healing, but I wasn't sure if they were just being nice. Things are different here."

"Different isn't always bad." Unless it referred to where she was from. No wonder she worried about acceptance among the Draconi. But she shouldn't have worried. All magical beings, no matter how little magic they possessed, were accepted.

"I guess. What will they expect of me?"

"Just what they said. Aryana is straightforward. If she didn't want you to stay, she wouldn't have asked."

Keara nodded, looking at their hands, her lips pressed together. She took a deep breath, shoulders rising and falling. "Will it bother you if I stay at the Temple?"

As opposed to with him where he could watch her, protect her, mate with her? Yes. But what could he do about it? He needed his work for his own peace of mind. There was plenty of time to mate. "No. Should it?"

Her eyes widened. Another big breath. "I thought...no, it shouldn't matter." A smile again, this one not heading to her eyes.

What was wrong? Did she want him to say it bothered him? Was there a chance she actually wanted him or did she feel obligated since she thought he'd married her? What had Ari said? He should have paid more attention to his aunt instead of losing himself in thought.

"So," Keara started, dropping her gaze to the bed. He waited. Two breaths later, the rest of the sentence came tumbling out like a steep waterfall. "Our marriage is over?"

He cursed. "Keara." Thoren placed his other hand on top of hers. "We were never married according to my customs. I saved you from Simon. I brought you to your proper home. That is all." *Oh, and by the way, you're my mate, but I can't join with you now since I'd have no work if I did.* She was nervous enough without that happy bit of news.

Her shoulders drew up and dropped. "All right." Another fake smile. "They have plenty of new things for me to learn. Are you sure they won't mind my coloring?"

"They won't."

She nodded. Looked to the window and back at him. He loved her eyes, how the lashes faded from black to red, how her green gaze locked on his, drawing him under her spell.

"Will you come to visit me?"

He smiled. "I'd love to. Once Enar returns, we will need to speak to the Council about you and Jamie. You'll probably need to make an appearance."

Keara sat straight, her grip on his hand tightening. "What do they want?"

"They will want to meet you."

"Who are they?"

"The Council is composed of thirteen males that ensure the welfare of the race. I and many others work for them, traveling to different lands and making sure that no one is trying to attack us."

"People would attack dragons?" Her mouth gaped.

"You'd be surprised. Anyway, the Council wants a report of what Enar and I found since we were supposed to find a Halfling boy—Jamie—but in addition we found you. So of course they'll want to meet you."

Her face turned the color of her robe. "Of course."

"Don't worry. They mean you no harm." At least he knew the Draconi meant her no harm. He still wasn't convinced about the Watchers. Enar was the only Watcher Thoren trusted; the rest hid eyes of hatred behind blank faces. "You need your rest now."

"I think I'm all right. I would like to take a tour of the place."

"You look tired."

Her eyes flashed. "Thanks. But with you here to support me, I can walk around and see what my new life is going to be like."

"You should lie down."

"I've been lying down. For three days. I. Am. Tired. Of lying down!" She threw the covers back. "Now, are you going to help me, or not?"

Thoren looked into her sparkling green eyes and smiled. His female possessed a temper. Not that he needed to be thinking of her as his, not yet.

Too late. His body leaned halfway toward her before he realized what it was doing. Her wide eyes stopped him. Halfway to kissing her, to touching her, to proving to her she belonged to him, he reigned in his desire. Hadn't he finished telling her he only rescued her, that he wasn't her husband?

146

His body needed to get in step with his mind's decree.

He pulled back and stood, holding his hand out for her. "As you wish." Her smile about did him in. Keara placed her hand in his and let him pull her up. He wrapped an arm around her waist, hugging her curves against him. She wanted him to walk her around.

He was the male.

"If you get tired we'll come back."

"As you wish. Lead on, my dragon."

****

Keara leaned against the headboard of the bed and watched the door. Any minute now, Thoren would walk through it and maybe today they'd make it outside. Yesterday they walked to the infirmary where Annaliese used her healing skills on some poor child that had sliced open his arm.

Annaliese was talented, no doubt of that, but Keara saw no evidence the priestess possessed the same unusual skill Keara did. No evidence at all. If the primary healer had to resort to herbs and spells instead of passing her hand over the cut to heal it, then Keara needed to keep her mouth shut regarding her own ability.

Passing her hand over a cut and healing it without a scar was the least of it. Her hidden ability would scare the Draconi and then where would she be? On her own, banished from her people.

They were her people. Despite her unease over their promises that they really meant her to stay— she had yet to see another Halfling—they treated her better than anyone else had over the years.

Anyone else but Thoren.

And he no longer wanted her. The one person she convinced herself she could count on in this new life and he agreed with the priestesses that she would enjoy Temple life. Good thing she wanted to learn new healing skills. Otherwise, she might cry.

A tear rolled down her cheek, dropping onto the sheet. Oh, no. She would not cry. He didn't want her. Another tear rolled.

"Keara?" Thoren knocked on the door.

She cursed. Of all the luck.

He stuck his head in the door. "Are you all right?"

Oh, great. Now he saw her tears. How embarrassing. She swiped under her eyes.

"I'm fine. I just got something in my eyes and they're watering."

"Want me to look in them?"

Yes, but not in the way you mean. "No, that's all right. Are you ready to walk outside?"

"Sure, but I want Annaliese to clear the walk first."

So protective. Anyone else and the whole I-know-best thing would be annoying. On Thoren, it was endearing. Yet another thing she'd miss when he left her. She started blinking.

"Maybe Annaliese can look at your eyes too."

Not if she could help it. "All right. You ready?"

Thoren wrapped his arm around her waist, supporting her as she stood. Not that she needed supporting. After he left last night, she walked all over the room and up and down the hall, but she liked the feel of his arm around her. Her grandmother didn't raise a fool.

Leaning against him made her blood hum, made her almost beg to have him stay with her.

So far, she wasn't that desperate.

Maybe tomorrow.

For now, she'd take what she could and deal with the wanting on the morrow.

"I'm glad you're feeling better. Hopefully today won't bother you too much."

"I'll be fine. I really don't need to see Annaliese."

"I'd feel better if you did."

Wasn't that sweet? It felt good to have a man care about her. If only he thought enough of her to want her for his wife.

Did they even have the term "wife" in Draconia? Come to think of it, Aryana used the word "mate" to refer to the woman Thoren would marry. And did the priestess even use the term "marry"? No, she hadn't. The Draconi even called the sexes male and female instead of man and woman. Guess that figured since they were part dragon.

"Zeke?"

Startled from her thoughts, Keara focused on the man—or she should say male—sitting in the hall outside the infirmary. His head pressed against crossed arms resting on knees pulled to his chest. Shoulder length black hair fell over his arms, his shoulders hunching forward. At the sound of Thoren's voice, he raised his head, his face pale. Keara's breath caught. The hair length differed, but other than that, Zeke looked like Thoren's twin.

"Zeke, what's wrong?" Thoren tightened his grip around Keara as he hurried to the other male's side.

Dropping his arm, Thoren knelt and Keara squatted beside him. Grief slammed through her like a palpable wave and she doubled over, surprised Thoren didn't seem bothered by the emotion. Could he not feel the smothering blanket of sadness?

"She's dead, Thoren. I got there too late. I didn't know about the sickness! And now he's not expected to...to..." Zeke buried his face in his hands, shoulders shaking.

Her hand trembling, Keara reached out and touched Zeke's forearm at the same time Thoren touched his shoulder. Her vision narrowed, swirling around, then popped into focus as in her mind's eye she flew through fluffy, white clouds.

A village stood ahead, buildings pointing to the

sky. She landed, but no one came to greet her. Where were they? In rapid succession the visions flickered, a woman—dead, a village with no movement but the wind, a boy—a red-haired Halfling—barely alive. Grief battered her as a high-pitched wail shook the silence. Her voice, and yet nothing like her voice. Deeper. Like a dragon.

With a snap, the visions vanished and Keara rocked backward, losing touch of Zeke's arm, falling on her butt. Her breath came in ragged puffs and she felt dampness on her cheeks.

The emotions evoked from Zeke's memories clamored through her system, grief fluttering her heart. How had she seen his private thoughts?

Two sets of green eyes stared at her, one with grief, the other with concern.

"Forgive her. I just found her and she doesn't know what she's capable of." Thoren patted Zeke's shoulder.

"What was that?" Did she really see Zeke's memories? How was that possible?

Zeke grunted and leaned his head against the wall. "Doesn't matter what she saw."

"Who is in the infirmary, brother?"

Zeke squeezed his eyes closed, his voice a gravely whisper. "My son."

Thoren blinked. "Your son?"

Zeke shot Thoren a glare that turned Keara's bones to ice and she wasn't even in its path. "Did you never wonder why I Changed and took no mate?"

"I figured the Seer—"

"I didn't care about the cursed Seer! I met Shalorna years ago. On a mission. We fell in love. Who cares what the Seer said?"

"What did the Seer say?" Thoren asked.

"What's a Seer?" Keara said simultaneously. Of course, no one paid her any attention.

Zeke slammed his fist against the ground.

"Forget it. He's in there and she won't let me in."

Thoren's jaw worked like he had something to say and couldn't get his lips to open. But she didn't have to hear his words, or mind-speak with him to know he was not pleased about his brother's revelation. Why? Maybe he didn't like Halflings, which would explain why he refused to admit she was his wife.

She needed to change his mind about that belief. Not now though. Now they needed her help.

Drawing her feet under her, she rose.

"Where do you think you're going?" Thoren grabbed her hand.

"To help." She gave Thoren's hand a squeeze and headed toward the door Zeke had indicated his son lay behind. So what if she didn't take her grand tour of the outdoors? She hated to see children hurt or sick. Healing the sick and caring for the ill were the parts of being an apothecary that she loved.

"Wait! You can't go in there." Zeke's eyes seemed to fill his face.

"I'm an apothecary by training and Annaliese has asked me to assist her in the infirmary. I might be able to help." With that, Keara twisted the dragon-shaped knob and pushed.

The door stuck, but she shoved it with her shoulder and it opened enough for her to squeeze through.

"Hey! Wait!" Thoren appeared in front the door quicker than she could blink, but lucky for her, shutting the door was easier than opening it.

The resulting bang and ear-popping change in pressure was loud enough to hear through the stone walls. Keara rubbed at her ears, opening and closing her mouth.

Annaliese looked up from where she bent over a bed. A fuzzy haze covered the bed, obscuring the person lying there from sight.

"How did you get in?" Annaliese rose to her full height, her normally placid face a rush of emotion.

Maybe this wasn't such a good idea after all. "I opened the door." Annaliese continued staring. What else did she want? "It was rather hard to open."

"That could be because I have a containment spell on it. Which is why your overprotective dragon is roaring in the hall."

"He is?"

Annaliese waved her hand back and forth, as she walked toward Keara. "Never mind him. It's you that interests me. No one, with the exception of the High Priestess and me can get through that door when there is a containment spell on the room. Not even a male with full powers."

"Why a containment spell?"

"I do not know what sickens the boy, but it felled his entire village. The only reason he still lives is because Draconi do not often get ill. We tend to repel illnesses. But this illness has brought the child to the edge of death. I put two containment fields in place. One on the room and the other over his bed."

"That's what the fuzzy haze is?"

The priestess nodded. "Why did you come in?"

"Because I thought I could help."

"You felt drawn to him, did you not? Like you had to help no matter what?"

How did she know that?

"Because I feel it too."

Great. Learning to mind-speak, or more correctly, how not to project thoughts, was now in top place on her to-do list. Forget the great outdoors, once she made it out of this room, Thoren was teaching her all about mind-speaking.

"To feel the draw to heal another is part of what being a healer is about. Some like the thought of helping others, but have no affinity for it. But others, like you and me, can't stop the ability no matter what we do. It's in our blood. It's part of who we are, what makes us us."

"True." Keara smiled. Annaliese understood her. Words couldn't describe how much that meant. "So what's wrong with the child?"

"High fever, wet cough with blood. Zeke said the village residents bled from their eyes, nose and mouth."

Keara felt her forehead wrinkle. "I've never seen an illness like that." But she had no doubt if she touched him, she could draw it into herself and heal the boy. "May I look at him?"

"Yes. You may touch him. The containment field will purify your hands."

Keara walked to the bed. Up close, the haze dissipated, allowing her a clear look at the child. Red hair stood straight up from his head, drenched in sweat. A light sheet covered him, leaving his arms exposed. Pale white skin, peeling around blackened nails, gleamed through a map of red mottling. A sickly sweet smell hovered around the boy and she swallowed.

Don't gag, don't gag, don't gag.

Keara looked across the bed at the priestess. "Are you sure it won't hurt me to touch him?"

"You walked through a containment field. I don't think much of anything will hurt you."

Maybe not physically, but when Thoren left it would break her heart.

Enough moping. She had a healing to attend.

Tentatively Keara reached her hand through the containment field surrounding the boy, garnering a raised eyebrow and a half-smile from Annaliese. Cold seeped through her skin wherever she touched the field. A shudder shook her spine. Her fingers brushed the boy's skin, softly so as not to cause more bruising. Heat rushed into her fingers from his skin, darting through her veins, burning at the cold of the field.

She wanted to pull away from the heat, instead she concentrated on drawing the illness up from her fingers into her body. Heat raced up her arm as far as the containment field and then stopped, only small tendrils snaked past the field. How was she supposed to heal, if the illness went no higher than her elbow?

Gritting her teeth, Keara concentrated on drawing the sickness past the containment field but couldn't. Heat built in her forearm and hand, pulsing in time with her heart. What did she do now? Ask for the containment field to be dropped? Disperse the illness?

Wait. What had Aryana said to her about dispersing the magic from a male's Change? Didn't she say that the priestesses threw the magic away? That there were special urns for that purpose?

Keara's gaze darted around the room. Maybe one of those urns rested in here. There. By the brazier. A bronze urn.

Pulling her hand out of the containment field, she aimed it at the urn and released the energy. Zap, bang! The urn flew a foot in the air and landed with a clatter, firing sparks of energy into the ceiling.

Good thing the containment field over the room held in magical outbursts.

Annaliese raised an eyebrow. "Try not to destroy the room."

"Sorry."

Keara stuck both hands through the field, resting her fingertips lightly on the boy's arm. Closing her eyes, she imagined the illness drawing toward her fingertips, running out of the boy's veins. Her hands pulsed with heat, her forearms turning red with mottling. Yanking her hands free, she aimed them at the urn and zapped it again. This time it shattered, pieces flying toward her.

She ducked, throwing her arms over her head, but she didn't feel the pieces hit. Raising her head in small movements, she stared at the bronze pieces hovering in mid-air.

"You're lucky I have practice stopping shattered items."

Wasn't that the truth? Without Annaliese, the urn particles would have sliced through her skin. Keara shivered. Annaliese flicked her hand and the pieces joined to reform the urn.

"What do you normally do when you heal?"

"I normally draw it into my body and change it, but I can't draw the illness past the containment field."

"Then I will place you and him in the field and see what happens."

Narrowing her eyes, Annaliese stared intently at the field until it started to expand. With another ear-popping snap, the field swallowed Keara, hovering around her. This close the smell of death assailed her nostrils and she clamped a hand over her mouth. Would the boy even live?

Ah, the red mottling seemed like it lessened where she had touched. Yes! She was helping.

This time when she touched the boy, the heat poured through her, circling in her veins, pounding against her skull. She let go and shook her hands. Her red mottled hands. Her breath caught, and for a split second, she felt fear ice her veins.

But why should she fear? She'd done something like this a million times.

Just never with an illness this serious, but it was the same concept. Wasn't it?

At least the boy's mottling looked better. Not as angry. Like a mild sunburn. Much better.

His skin felt cooler too, the heat slackening. Lids scrunched, Keara concentrated on drawing more of the illness into her, on transforming the boy's illness inside her into something innocuous. But no matter how hard she tried, nothing changed, except the red mottling in her skin disappeared. The boy's skin remained the same.

She tried again, this time touching his other arm. Still nothing. Since when could she not draw an illness into herself? The tightly curled ball of magic deep inside her creaked, a tendril slipping out. Her hand smoked.

And she'd been doing so well holding it together.

The containment field felt cold to her heated skin as she pushed through it, stepping beside Annaliese.

"I couldn't fix him." A bolt of magic shot out of her hand, bouncing off the wall.

Keara and Annaliese ducked and the energy bolt slammed into the urn, clanging it into the wall. Annaliese glanced at the urn.

"Well, it held together. You need to work on—"

"I know, I know. Keep my magic inside. But I couldn't heal him." Tears pressed against the back of her eyes and she dashed her fingers under them. Apparently, the lack of magical control brought on a crying fit. Lovely. And the poor boy remained ill.

Annaliese walked to the child's bed, peering through the containment field. "He looks better." She reached a hand through, resting it against the boy's forehead. "He feels cooler too."

The boy coughed, a deep hacking noise, and blood seeped out the side of his mouth. Annaliese wiped at the blood with a cloth lying on the bed.

"Well, that cough hasn't changed, but I'd say overall he's improving. How do you draw the illness into yourself?"

Keara leaned against the wall and sank to the floor, resting her arms on her knees. For some reason, this healing didn't make her as tired as they usually did. Maybe because she didn't really heal the boy. Or maybe it had to do with her powers being unlocked. Despite the lack of normal post-healing tiredness, her recent experiences left her weak. Sitting sounded like a good idea.

"I don't know. But it works the same with cuts and bruises too."

"Do you become ill?"

"Never have before, but in there," Keara pointed at the bed, "my forearms turned red and mottled like his. But I imagined the redness disappearing so they're back to normal."

Annaliese tilted her head and pierced Keara with an eyes-narrowed stare. As if Keara was prey and the priestess the hunter.

"Where did you say you were from?"

What did that have to do with anything? "River's Run in Cautasia."

Annaliese grunted and pressed her lips together. "My mother had that ability. It's very rare."

Keara shrugged. So she was an aberration in Draconia too. Nothing new. But if taking an illness into herself and changing it was rare, she could only imagine how her other ability would be perceived.

"Momma?" the boy croaked.

Annaliese whirled, her dress flaring around her legs. Keara tried to rise and sank back to the ground. Wobbly legs did not make for good standing.

Keara watched Annaliese touch the boy as she spoke in soft tones. Why had she not been able to heal him? What caused her powers to stop working? If she couldn't heal and contribute to the infirmary, the priestesses would have no choice but to let her go.

And Thoren didn't want her.

Her day was shaping up nicely.

Keara sighed and pressed her head against her arms. Wetness seeped down her cheek and she swiped it away. Overactive tear ducts. Something about this place set them off.

Crying had never been her thing. Getting done what needed to be done was her motto. No use crying over things she couldn't change. But with Thoren not wanting her, her inability to hold her magic in place, and her complete failure at this healing, the tears spilled like a slow leak.

She dashed her fingers under her eyes and tilted her head back with a thud against the wall. Annaliese glanced over at the sound. Maybe she should stare at the ceiling instead of thud her head against stone.

Keara blinked as she looked upward. Fluffy white clouds danced across the ceiling, hiding dragons that weaved in and out. Amazingly beautiful. The artist had some skill to paint on the ceiling. Did he or she have to hang upside down to finish the picture?

Keara? Can you hear me?

Keara jumped at the voice in her head. So much for the pity party. How did she answer?

Thoren?

Are you all right? What in the name of the Goddess did you think you were doing walking in there?

I'm fine. Calm down.

Calm down? You walked through a containment field. No one walks through a containment field and Zeke's son is dying of an illness you could catch. Have you lost it?

His protectiveness should bother her. Instead, it made her feel loved. No one else in her life had ever cared like this, not even her grandmother. But Thoren was protective of her. What a shame he didn't want her for a wife.

She would change his mind about that.

Thoren, I'm a healer. Healers heal. It's a calling. I can't resist it.

She saw a mental image of Thoren pacing the hall outside the room, hands shoving through his hair like he was digging for treasure. The mantle of failure smothering her lightened at his concern.

Are you even allowed out of that room?

Good question. Why hadn't she thought about being quarantined before she darted through the door? *I don't know. I couldn't heal him.*

Is he...?

No, he just woke and asked for his mother. Annaliese is tending him. I tried, but I just couldn't heal him.

But that's good that he woke. I'm sure you helped.

Annaliese thinks I did, but I've never been unable to heal someone before.

Think Zeke can come in?

"Annaliese?"

"Hmm?" The priestess patted the boy's head and turned to Keara.

"Can Zeke come in?"

"I suppose he can now." She started toward the door. "I meditated and saw no illness inside me. I've checked on Zeke several times since he brought his son and he has not fallen ill. It is doubtful that full-blooded Draconi can catch this illness. The precautions were mostly set for Halflings. They apparently can catch the illness."

"Wait. Am I allowed out? Or am I under quarantine?"

Annaliese tucked a strand of hair behind her ear. "The containment field keeps everyone in this room and alerts me if whoever tries to leave has the illness. If you don't have the illness, you should be able to walk out of the room. But since you walked in when you weren't supposed to, I'm not sure if it will work on you. I can cast another spell for you, but I'm not convinced it would work either."

"So I should stay here?"

"Probably overnight. Since this illness doesn't seem to affect full-bloods, Thoren can come in if you'd like. He's not very happy out in the hall."

Keara smiled. Her dragon was protective. She needed to stop thinking of him as hers. He wasn't.

Not yet anyway.

"Are you sure I shouldn't stay longer?"

"The child has been here since yesterday evening. Zeke was at the village the day before that and all was fine. He went back yesterday and all but his son were dead. We should know tomorrow if you are ill."

Keara shivered. What if she caught the illness? No use dwelling on the what ifs. "So Thoren can come in?"

Annaliese smiled and turned toward the door. Raising her hand, she spoke words in a language Keara had never heard and the door swung inward. Thoren stumbled inside, righting himself before he tripped into Annaliese. Zeke pushed past Thoren and ran to the bed.

"May I touch Keara?" Thoren asked Annaliese.

"Of course." She headed to the bed, talking to Zeke, but Keara didn't hear the words.

All she cared about was Thoren as he walked toward her. Dropping to his knees, he ran his hand up her arm, down her hair. His hand caught her neck in a tight grip, and yanked her to his chest, his arms banding about her torso.

Breathing became somewhat difficult. Not that she was complaining. Oh, no. One didn't complain when one's lover crushed you against his chest.

Provided he was still her lover.

Her arms hugged him back as she rose onto her knees. He would be again. No matter what else happened.

****

Thoren clasped Keara against him, running his hands over her back and hair, assuring himself that she was unharmed. Watching her walk into the infirmary like nothing was wrong had frozen his heart and lungs. They'd kicked back in with a wheeze and a thud, knocking him halfway to his knees. Unlike Keara, he had been unable to get through the door and no amount of pounding, yelling or throwing magical spells opened it.

But he was with her now and he'd make sure things stayed that way.

At least until his next assignment.

His hand slid through her hair to the base of her skull. Fisting his hand into her braid, he pulled until her widened eyes stared into his. He needed her, needed to assure that she lived, needed to sink inside her warm folds and lose himself in her softness.

Were all dragons this way around their mates?

He refused to throw her down on the floor in front of the Temple healer, his brother and his nephew. The dragon could take a hike.

But a kiss. Now that he could do.

He looked into her eyes, their pupils dilated. Saw the vein beat in her neck. The vein he would bite to join their life-forces when they bonded. Which wasn't going to happen any time soon.

Her lips parted and he took the invite. Crushing his lips against hers, he tightened his hold on her waist, pleased when her arms wrapped around his neck, fingers running through his hair. His tongue played at the seam of her lips and she opened for him, drawing him in, brushing her tongue against his.

Goddess, but he wanted her. Here. Now.

Running his hand down her back, he grasped the firm globes of her arse and pulled her against him. Aaah. She felt good.

"Ahem. There are other people in here," Annaliese said.

Hadn't he just finished telling himself it was only a kiss? Obviously obeying self-talk was not high on his to-do list. Releasing Keara, Thoren rose to his feet. Maybe distance would help the almost overwhelming desire to take her despite the onlookers.

"Sorry." Thoren gave Keara's hand a squeeze and walked to the bed to look at his nephew.

Nephew. Now that was a word he hadn't expected to be using for some time. He wiggled his jaw, trying to get the tick to stop. The last thing Zeke needed was for him to yell. But when he thought of Zeke lying with a non-Draconi female...he shuddered. Bad image. Think of something else, like Keara's full lips.

Or not. Thoren clasped his hands in front of his body and stood by the bed, staring down at his nephew. His older brother contributed to the mess otherwise known as Thoren's occupation.

Thoren should be happy there were those like Zeke who didn't mind where their scales rested. On the other hand, bedding a non-Draconi just plain gave him the shivers.

Zeke's hair fell across his cheek, obscuring his face from view as he bent his head to his son. Five years Thoren's senior, but with almost identical features, his brother had been his idol. But in recent years, the closeness they'd shared as hatchlings unraveled, separating like the hem of a well-worn cloak.

For years, Thoren wondered why Zeke turned distant.

The reason lay in front of him, sickly and smelling like death.

A hand touched his back and he wrapped an arm around Keara's shoulders. As everyone was busy watching the child struggle for breath, he supposed no one would notice what was going on in his leathers.

Thoren dropped the hand hiding his embarrassing bulge and placed it on the containment field surrounding the boy. Or tried to place it on the field. His hand slipped through the shimmering haze and landed on the boy's leg. Lids fluttered open and green eyes stared out of a face that mirrored his own.

All the anger he felt toward Zeke and his unnatural bedding practices vanished with that one gaze. This was his nephew. His blood.

"How're you doing, hatchling?"

One side of the boy's lip turned upward and his eyes closed, his breathing rapid.

"His name's Conr. His mother named him." If Zeke pulled his chair any closer to the bed, his knees would fuse to the mattress.

"Was he...hatched?" Thoren took his hand off Conr's leg as he looked at his brother's bowed head.

"No. He was born."

"Hatched?" Keara tilted her head to him, one eyebrow reaching to her hairline.

"Male Draconi hatch. Females are born," Annaliese explained. Judging by the look on Keara's face, that news didn't go over well.

"Hatch?" Keara's voice hung around the ceiling.

"If a female is expecting a male, she will give birth to an egg, which is then incubated for a couple of months before it hatches. A female child is carried to term and is delivered with much pain."

Keara blinked her lashes like a butterfly's wing. "I feel a bit weak." She gestured toward the wall. "I think I'm going to go sit back down."

She needed a better idea if she thought she was going anywhere without him. Even the short distance to the wall. Where she went, he went. As long as he didn't touch her or think of her soft body pressing against his, how she looked moving on top of him, the feminine whimper of pleasure when he took her. As long as none of these thoughts dropped by for a visit, he'd be fine.

But seeing they'd moved into his room of wishful remembering, he was screwed. No, that's what he wanted to be.

Show control, Thoren.

"Please teach me to mind-speak," Keara placed her hand on his arm. His emotional grip slid toward the cliff of no-control as her fingers touched him.

"All right." Teaching such a basic concept should be a snap, along with the added benefit of giving him something else to think about besides what he'd rather be doing with her.

She learned faster than a dragon flew. In no time at all, she understood the basic concept of how to block her thoughts from leaking into other's minds. So he moved on to other things, like how one used magic.

Dinner came and went, an aroma of pleasant scents drowning out the ever-present smell of sickness. Zeke remained by the bed, only leaving it to visit the relief room, his hand resting on his son's arm. Annaliese hovered between the bed and a table where she prepared droughts, the soft slide of her shoes whispering against the stone floor as she moved.

Keara rested her hand on Thoren's forearm, her head against his shoulder. He continued to check her for Conr's illness, for the red spots and high fever, but the only symptom she exhibited was tiredness.

Not that he minded.

She could rest her head on his shoulder for as long as she wanted. He rested his head on top of hers, shutting his eyes for a minute. Only a minute...

Thoren woke to Keara moving against him.

Weak light shone through the high window, coating the room with a pale glow. Had he fallen asleep? Considering he lay flat on his back, muscles aching from sleeping on a stone floor, he supposed the answer was a yes. Keara lay on top of him, using his body as a pillow.

She moved and he groaned as she rubbed against him. It was about time he put his morning erection to good use. Tightening his arms around her, he rolled them over.

"Good morning! Nice to see you awake." Annaliese's voice cut through the strands of light like shards of glass.

Thoren looked down into wide green eyes. Keara's mouth opened in an "oh" and not the kind of surprise he wanted to see on her face. He rolled to his feet, squatting next to Keara.

"Good morning, Annaliese." Thoren looked to Zeke who lay on his side on a pallet. A soft, comfortable pallet. He squelched the stab of jealousy. He shouldn't complain. His brother's son might die.

Keara scrambled to sit, straightening the bodice of her dress. Annaliese knelt beside her.

"Let me have a look at you. How do you feel?"

"Great. Actually, this is the best I've felt since I was brought to the Temple."

"Good, good."

Thoren watched as Annaliese examined Keara's skin, looked in her mouth, pulled down her bottom eyelids and pronounced her able to leave the room.

Praise the Goddess!

Grabbing Keara's hand, he helped her to her feet.

"How's Conr?"

"The same as yesterday evening, but I think he's on the downhill slope of improvement. Zeke can stay with him. Now you two take a walk around the

Courtyard. Get some fresh air. Keara's been cooped up inside too long."

Keara patted her hair, trying to smooth the rowdy tendrils into her braid. It was like putting cats in a carrying container. She apparently realized this, since she quit touching her hair and grabbed hold of Annaliese's hand. They exchanged a silent gaze and then Annaliese nodded.

Thoren stood a little taller. He'd taught her how to mind-speak.

Which was rather annoying, come to think of it, since he couldn't tell what they were talking about.

With one last glance toward Conr, Keara opened the door and walked out. Thoren ran smack into the containment field. Ouch.

"Sorry," Annaliese said, waving her hand.

This time when he walked through the door, nothing stopped him.

When she arrived at the door to her room, Keara looked at him from under her lashes, then at the ground, then back at him. His breath caught.

"I need to change before we go out."

Maybe she'd let him come in and watch.

"So do I."

But if he came in and watched her undress, he'd want her. Want to lay her on the bed, lick up the insides of her legs, take her core between his lips.

"See you in a bit."

She closed the door. In his face. Smoke steamed from his ears as his dragon strained to reach her. She belonged to him. And he wanted her. Why in the name of the Goddess was he leaking smoke? Who was in charge here? Him or the dragon? Clearly the dragon, since his hand hovered halfway to the door, ready to knock it down.

Thoren took a step back and stalked down the hall to his room. A twist of the handle and a slap against the wood sprung the lock. The ensuing kick shut the door with a satisfying snap.

What had made him think putting off mating with Keara was a good idea? It seemed plausible at the time. It must have, or he wouldn't have thought it. Now? If putting his job over his mate was the best he could come up with, he was dumber than a catch of glittering stones.

His dragon understood. It was about time his higher reasoning caught up with what he instinctively knew—Keara was his mate. Unable to live apart from their mates, male dragons craved their females, protecting them at all costs. He'd heard the stories, but thought he was above basic biology. He enjoyed his work, loved it, couldn't imagine life without it, but despite that reasoning, his body needed Keara like it needed air to breathe. Without her, he was nothing. Plain and simple.

Yanking his tunic over his head, he threw it on the mattress and started to pull off his leathers. He needed a bath if he wanted to convince Keara to bond with him. Biology only went so far. A clean prospect meant a lot.

Once finished, he waited outside her door. Had he really considered knocking it down to get to her? Good thing he put the dragon on a leash, no telling what the beast might do.

"Oh, hey. Sorry to keep you waiting."

Keara appeared in the open doorway, another white dress on, this one trimmed in green. Her hair was pulled into a sloppy bun with curling tendrils escaping. His heart kicked like he'd been hit in the chest. Goddess's teeth, but she was the prettiest thing he'd ever seen.

"Does it look all right? I'm not used to dresses, but that's all the priestesses seem to have." Her hands fluttered down the front of the skirt.

"It looks good."

Her face broke into a smile. "Thanks! Are you

ready to give me a tour?"

Definitely yes. A tour of his body and then he'd take a tour of hers, or maybe he'd go first.

Get it together, Thoren. You have to prove to her she needs you.

He stuck out his elbow and she slipped her hand in the crook of his arm. Together they walked to the Courtyard.

Chapter 14

Ah, the warm feel of sunshine on her skin, the merry chirping of birds filling the air, her hand on Thoren's arm. This day was shaping up nicely. Much better than yesterday. Thinking about how she failed to heal Conr made steam start rising in the back of her throat and her mostly-controlled powers fluctuate.

The birds continued their songs, Thoren's arm felt warm beneath the fabric of his tunic and the sun warmed her, but the cold anger she felt for herself simmered below the surface. What happened to her ability to take an illness into her body and change it into something innocuous? Was Conr's illness too great, or had unlocking her magic shriveled her healing ability?

"I can't believe I couldn't heal Conr."

Thoren's lips pressed together, like he had something to say and couldn't decide how to say it. "What?"

"I said, I'm mad that I couldn't help Conr."

The next thing she knew, rough bark rasped against her butt through the fabric of her dress as she teetered on a branch high above the ground. Grabbing the nearest limb, she held on with a grip of a dying person—which she just might be if she didn't figure out how to get down before she fell. The leaves rattled as her arms shook. It took her a couple of tries to get the words past the thickness of her tongue and lips.

"Thoren!" Even to her ears, the cry sounded

weak. He might not hear her shout.

Keara?

Mind-speaking! In her panic, she forgot her newly acquired skill.

Thoren, I'm up in the tree, get me down!

What are you doing up there?

How am I supposed to know? Just get me down!

She looked down and wished she had not. Red and gold leaves and brown limbs formed a map running down a trunk that seemed to go on forever. Closing her eyes, she counted to three and then opened them again. Still in the tree.

Perhaps now is a good time for another lesson.

What? She sat stuck in a tree and he wanted to teach her something? Were all males this crazy?

Thoren. I. Am. Stuck. In a tree. Why are you talking about lessons?

If you knew how Draconi traveled, then you could get down from your perch without asking me for help.

Fine. Get me down and you can teach me whatever you want.

Dizziness, accompanied by an out-of-body experience, assaulted her as she disintegrated piece by piece, reappearing in Thoren's arms. Hopefully she'd adjust to that mode of travel as she had a sneaking suspicion it was her newest lesson.

Thoren's grasp tightened until her ribs cracked. Keara refused to complain, at least her feet stood on the ground.

"What happened?" Relief distorted his words.

"I don't know. I was upset and started to lose the grip on my magic and then I was in a tree. At least I didn't blow anything up."

"You're getting better at controlling your powers. It's starting to come as a second nature to you now. But anger has a way of interfering with magic, making it harder to control."

"Anger interferes with a lot of things. How did you get me down?"

"Draconi can move around simply by thinking about it. See, I'm here now." One blink later and he stood a stone's throw away, "Now, I'm here," Thoren reappeared in front of her, "And now I'm back to you. But until a Draconi male goes through the Change, he can't move other people, so you're lucky I've Changed. Ready to learn how to move around?"

She closed her eyes, waiting for it all to disappear and her to wake in her shop in River's Run. But Thoren remained standing in front of her in the Temple Courtyard. No dream. If she hadn't seen him disappear and reappear, she never would have believed people, even Draconi, had the ability to transport themselves in that way.

But she lived in Draconia now and magic abounded so she might as well embrace her new life. What a relief to know her Grandmother and everyone else in River's Run were wrong about magic. Instead of being evil, it was fascinating.

"Sure. How far can you travel by transporting?"

"You have to be able to see the place, or to know where it is. So I can transport back into my room in the Temple without seeing it because I know where it is. But there are wards surrounding Draconia that prohibit you from transporting in or out of the land. The only exception is if your mate is in jeopardy. Then you can transport to wherever he or she is, even if you haven't been to the place where they are."

"How's that?"

He shrugged. "Don't know. It's part of being mates and it's a test of sorts in case you don't know if a person is your mate or not. Now are you ready to try?"

By the time the sun rose to its full height, and her stomach growled, she had learned how to

171

disappear and reappear around the Temple grounds, Thoren giving chase. It was the most fun she'd ever had. What an enjoyable morning.

Thoren's presence made her happy. Being around him, learning new things, his patience with her, all made her realize how much she cared for him. Dare she use the "L" word?

Keara glanced at Thoren, smiling as his eyes twinkled. How did she go about convincing him to marry her? To love her? He seemed to enjoy her company, which was a plus in her favor. And yet, sometimes she saw a distance in him too. As if he'd rather be doing something, anything, besides being with her.

At least that distance was gone today. Today, he acted like she was the best thing in his world. Why had she not paid more attention to relationships and less to herbs? Maybe then, she'd know how to keep alive his attitude toward her.

Picturing herself sifting through space, she reappeared in front of Thoren. He grabbed her about the waist and swung her around. She squealed.

"Great job! Let's go eat lunch. I can hear your stomach growling."

****

Thoren had no sooner crammed his mouth full of food when he heard dragon-song billowing through the windows of the dining room. His fork froze halfway on the down stroke to his plate. Why was an adult male flying around the Temple? The males who remained in dragon form stayed on lands some distance from the Temple and they only flew in on holy days. Since today was not a holy day, why was the dragon here?

Judging by the looks on the priestesses' faces, he wasn't the only one with that thought. Keara continued to munch her food, but even she realized something unusual happened since the entire room stopped eating and turned to the windows.

Aryana hurried to the panes of glass overlooking the Courtyard, Thoren behind her. As if given permission to move, the priestesses and acolytes trailed behind, crowding around the open windows.

A dragon landed in the Courtyard, blood-red scales gleaming in the sunlight, his wings flapping before settling against his back. The beast's thoughts drifted through the minds of the curious faces watching him.

I need to speak to the High Priestess, please.

Fafnir? Thoren squinted. It definitely looked like the dragon he'd left to Enar's care. So where was Enar?

"Is that Fafnir?" Keara asked, pushing aside a priestess to stand beside him.

"I better get down there." Which was the last thing he wanted to do. He'd rather ask Keara to be his mate, but getting the words to come out proved harder than imagined, and he might as well do something useful. Starting with finding out where his Watcher was.

Ari disappeared, followed by half the priestesses. Giving Keara's hand a squeeze, Thoren transported himself to the Courtyard, reappearing next to Fafnir.

The dragon stood, wings folded, the expression on his face suggesting he'd rather have his scales bent backward. Thoren felt a stab of pity, knowing he would hate to be in Fafnir's scales, so to speak. After spending years away from Draconia—and those years in a cell—Fafnir had to be feeling shame mixed in with a heady dose of freedom.

Or at least that's what Thoren would feel. How embarrassing to admit that non-magical beings managed to confine you in a cell for over twenty years. It gave him the chills to think about it.

Where was Enar? And Jamie? And Keara's

friend, Lily? Why did Fafnir arrive without them? Had something happened?

Fafnir raised an eye-ridge at Thoren's appearance. Thoren looked over his shoulder, expecting his aunt to be behind him, but instead he faced a whole lot of landscaping.

Things have changed if the High Priestess is requested and I get you instead.

Thanks. Thoren crossed his arms. *Where's my Watcher?*

A few hours behind me. Where's the Halfling female?

Safe.

She lives?

Yes. She's watching.

Fafnir's head swung toward the windows of the dining area. Thoren turned in time to see Aryana walk through the Temple doors in all her splendor followed by an array of priestesses. No wonder he arrived to greet Fafnir before she did. He forgot the requirement that the High Priestess greet first time male guests in the robes designating her station.

The dragon's eyes widened as he watched Aryana approach. Fafnir's nostrils flared and Thoren clenched his fists. The dragon should know better than to make eyes at his aunt, the High Priestess. Head held high, Aryana seemed oblivious to the male appreciation turned her way.

She stepped next to Thoren, wearing the green velvet dress that signified she was the High Priestess. Gold embroidered dragons danced down the front of the dress, gold roses circled the hems of the sleeves. Upon her head sat a gold tiara in the shape of a dragon, his thin body elongated into a circlet that highlighted her black hair.

As she approached, Fafnir remembered the politeness protocol and dropped his gaze, bowing his head, male appreciation banked.

"I am the High Priestess Aryana. How may I help you?"

Thoren listened as Fafnir explained his predicament, ending by asking if anything could be done to reverse his dragon form.

Ari placed a hand on Fafnir's flank, a strange look dancing across her face before disappearing. "I'm sorry, but I am unable to help you. However, I will research the matter. There might be a way, but I cannot promise you anything."

Fafnir sighed, his breath blowing beads of dirt across the grass, ruffling the hem of Aryana's dress. *I had to ask.*

His head popped up, twisting away from Ari, his gaze sharpening on a point behind Thoren. Thoren didn't need to turn to know Keara stood behind him. Fafnir's interest in Aryana was one thing—she was an attractive female who garnered a lot of male staring. But the fact that Fafnir focused so intently on Keara's presence made steam rise in the back of Thoren's throat.

She belonged to him.

Thoren pressed his lips together in an attempt to keep a snarl off his face. Wasn't this wonderful. The dragon inside wanted a fight with the dragon standing in front of him.

Focus, Thoren, focus. No fighting on the Temple grounds.

Keara stood beside him, one hand raised in greeting. "Hey, Fafnir. Nice to see you again. Where're Lily and Jamie?"

Fafnir's lip curled, exposing a row of pearly whites in a dragon grin. *They are coming. How are you? Is this male treating you well?*

Keara wrapped an arm around Thoren's waist. "Very well, thank you."

Fafnir nodded and glared at Thoren. *He better.*

Why did the dragon act protective of Keara?

Probably since she came from the same dilapidated town he was found in. All Draconi males tended to be protective of females, whether or not those females belonged to them.

But still. Keara belonged to him. Did Fafnir imply Thoren couldn't keep care of his own female?

Aryana narrowed her eyes at Thoren and turned that look on Fafnir. Her lip caught between her teeth as her eyes darted between the three of them. Thoren recognized her look, that brain-whirling look of concentration. Problem was, he didn't care. Something about Fafnir's focus on Keara brought his dragon halfway out and it was all he could do to keep the other half in place.

"Fafnir, you must want purification. If you would follow me, I'll lead you to the ritual baths." Ari gestured with her hand and with one last glare at Thoren, Fafnir turned and walked with her around the corner of the Temple, the priestesses following, their murmurs like a flock of gnats' wings.

Closing his eyes, Thoren breathed deeply. A couple of breaths and a cleared Courtyard later, he managed to bury the possessive, jealous dragon deep inside. When he opened his eyes, Keara stood in front of him, arms crossed.

"What was that about?"

"Fafnir asked if Ari could change him back into human form. She can't."

"I caught that. I mean that stare and glare between the two of you."

She caught him in the act. He shrugged. "Fafnir doesn't seem to like me."

"You think? Why?"

"We're both...protective of you. This creates problems."

Her brows dug a trench through her forehead. "Why? I think it's nice that you both want to protect me."

She didn't understand. Now was the perfect time to inform her. To let her know she had a mate who would bond with her for life. But did she want him?

What difference did that make? It was biology, plain and simple. Plus he was giving up a promising career to be her male, didn't that stand for something?

Yes, yes it did. And yet, Thoren wanted her to need him. It meant more to know that the female he bonded with chose him too. Would Keara find the news she belonged to him no matter what a good thing or a bad one?

He needed to ensure she found him a good thing.

"I'm glad you think so. Because I'm very protective of you. I don't like other males focusing on you the way he did."

"He was just being nice. Speaking of other males, why aren't there more here?"

"Because the Temple is run by females. Females have the direct link to the Goddess. Males only visit here. Would you like to return to lunch? I'm hungry."

Smiling, she disappeared. Once Enar arrived and they met with the Council, he'd talk to Keara about bonding. With any luck she would be receptive.

A Draconi male was nothing without his mate.

Chapter 15

How did the Draconi choose their mates? Maybe Aryana told her and she didn't listen. Was it common for a female to ask a male to join with her, or was that taboo? Was sex casual or only offered during rituals? What did she really know about Draconi customs?

That question Keara knew the answer to: little to nothing.

Aryana returned to the dining room as Thoren and Keara rose to leave. The High Priestess would know the answers to all her questions. Provided she would talk to her.

"Thoren, I need to speak to Aryana."

"What? Why?"

Wild dragons couldn't make her tell. "I need to speak to her about what expectations she has for me. Now that I've returned to the land of the normal I need to know."

"She's busy. She'll need to return to Fafnir to complete the purification ritual. You can speak with her later. We need to return to your lessons."

"Maybe, but I think I'm going to ask her anyway."

Using her newly learned magic, she appeared in front of Aryana. The High Priestess blinked, her fork hovering in midair.

"I need to speak to you."

"About?" Aryana stuck a piece of food in her mouth.

"I need to know some things."

A chew and a swallow. "Can it wait until tomorrow?"

"Um," Keara looked over her shoulder at Thoren, who stood where she left him, arms crossed, a glower like an impending storm on his face.

"I see. Have a seat while I finish eating."

Keara sat across from Aryana, looking at her clasped hands.

"Might as well loosen those lips. I have things to do."

"Sorry. Thank you for listening. I...I need, I mean want... I want to know mating customs."

Aryana took a sip of water. "What about them?"

"Everything. I mean, how does one go about convincing a male that you want to join with him?"

"Keara, love, a male only has one mate. There is only one female who complements him. When he finds her, he becomes possessive to the point of idiocy. There is a test for mating compatibility. If you are not compatible, then you are not mates. Even if you want Thoren, if you are not compatible, you are not his mate. Do you understand this?"

A hollow cavity formed in Keara's chest. What if he wasn't hers? What if he belonged to another? "Can you do the testing?"

"Of course. Would you like to be tested?"

Might as well. Finding out now would save her heartbreak later. "Yes. Can you do it now?"

"Not now, but later." A pause. "You're not going to ask what the test involves?"

Not that it mattered. "I guess I should. What does it involve?"

Aryana took a sip of water. "We put one of you in danger in a place where the other has never been and see if you can transport to the one in danger. Now, don't worry, you won't be hurt. Your instinct takes over when your mate is in danger, be it real or imaginary, so you'll react as if they are about to be harmed."

Keara gulped. What kind of danger? Would the dragon's instinct really overtake her higher reasoning and convince her Thoren was to be harmed when she knew he really wasn't? What a strange test.

"Was there anything else you wanted to know, Keara?"

She might as well ask all her questions while she had a semi-willing audience. "What will happen to Fafnir?"

"He will go live with the other males in dragon form. Why?"

"Maybe I could help him. I can take illnesses into myself and turn them into something no longer harmful. Perhaps I can absorb the energy it takes to remain in dragon form and allow him to turn back into a man."

Aryana's mouth gaped like an opened present.

"I didn't think of that. If I remember correctly, there is an ancient ritual, but it would involve using the male's offspring. Fafnir says he never mated, so it probably wouldn't work, but perhaps using a priestess or other female relative would. Strange, I don't recall anyone named Fafnir going missing years ago, but there are many Draconi."

"I wouldn't expect you to know them all. The priests in my town didn't know everyone. If you need help, I'd be happy to assist anyway I can. I like Fafnir."

"I'll ask if the time comes. Thoren is waiting for you and I need to run. Stop by my room tomorrow if you have any other questions." Aryana stood and rested her hand on Keara's shoulder. "We're glad to have you here."

"Thank you. I appreciate you taking time to talk."

"No problem."

As Aryana walked away, Keara wanted to cry. Thoren might not be her mate. Although Aryana welcomed her, Keara couldn't imagine a life without Thoren in it. And watching him take another mate? She swatted at the tears. Silly things. She'd cried more since she came to Draconia than she had in her entire life.

"What's the matter? Did she upset you? Do I need to have a talk with Ari?" Thoren's fists slammed into the table as he leaned against it.

"I'm fine. There's just something about the air in Draconia that makes my eyes tear up."

Thoren's face held doubt as he pierced her with a stare. "So, you want me to give you another magic lesson?"

Just what she needed. More reason to fall in love with him. Oh, Goddess, did she use the "L" word? Yes she did. She pulled out the big, scary word. Only love explained the thrill of her heart when Thoren came near, the happiness felt when he spoke to her, the pride when his protective side roared in defense of her. And if he wasn't her mate? If Aryana tested them and found them incompatible, then what?

Her eyes would be stuck on permanent water mode, her heart aching from ribbon-like slashes.

"I'd like that."

"Great! We can practice my favorite move, throwing an energy ball."

****

She was not meant to throw energy balls. Keara rubbed her upper arm while watching Thoren demonstrate an underhanded throw. Overhand, underhand, it didn't matter, her arm muscles apparently weren't designed to lob an energy ball.

"Now watch. To get maximum velocity on this..."

If she threw one more energy ball..."Thoren?"

He stopped moving mid-motion. "Yes?"

"I need to go check on Conr."

His gaze darted from her arm-rubbing to her face. One hand ran through his hair. "I'm sorry for not noticing sooner that your arm hurts. Want to take a break? There's a really nice reflection pool behind those bushes. I'm sure Annaliese has Conr under control."

As much as she wanted to check on little Conr, Thoren was right. Annaliese knew how to take care of him. And if the child took a turn for the worse, they would know about it. Zeke would want Thoren there with him.

"You haven't shown me the reflection pool. I'd like to see it."

Thoren grabbed her hand, his green eyes twinkling, loose strands of his hair blowing across his face. Priestesses milled around the Courtyard, the noise from their conversations drifting around her like the wind, but when she looked at Thoren, the noises faded.

What would she do if he wasn't her mate? If the testing showed them incompatible?

She refused to think that way. He belonged to her and that was that.

The warmth of his hand caressed the skin of her palm as they strolled along stone paths. Keara held out her free hand, touching the bushes blooming with autumn flowers. The pleasing scent of nectar wafted on the air, carried by the breeze. How peaceful and relaxing the Courtyard was, with its red and gold trees, flowers, and bush-lined pathways.

Thoren led her to the reflection pool, a rectangular shallow pool surrounded by thick bushes, giving it a secluded feel.

"It's beautiful!"

"Not as beautiful as you."

Keara's heart flip-flopped. He liked her. Or at

least he thought her beautiful, which was a start. A really good start.

She felt her cheeks warm and glanced at the ground, looking up at him from under her lashes. "You're pretty good-looking yourself, you know."

Thoren's hand lifted her chin, his lips brushing against hers. And as quick as a snap of her fingers, she became lost in his kiss, in the strokes of his tongue against hers, the feel of his hands on her back. Their bodies pressed together and she felt the hard length of him against her stomach, her core flooding with wetness. His hand stroked to her hip, his fingers gathering her skirt. At this moment, he belonged to her.

And then he stopped.

Keara tightened her grip around his neck, trying to draw his lips down to hers, but he grabbed her wrists.

"There's a commotion in the Courtyard."

And that mattered, why?

Footsteps slapped in a dash against the stones, bushes rattled and an out-of-breath priestess darted into the clearing.

"Thoren!" she gasped. "The High Priestess sent me to find you. Your Watcher, Enar, has arrived."

Lily! Keara stepped from Thoren's arms, sexual heat forgotten as she hurried to the main area of the Courtyard, Thoren and the priestess behind her. Was Lily all right? Had Enar hurt her? And Jamie. How was her apprentice? She hiked her skirt above her knees as her feet flew across the stones and grass.

Enar stood in a circle of priestesses, his blond hair easy to spot in a crowd of black-haired beauties. Keara scanned the area, looking for Lily or Jamie. Where were they? They had to be here. Enar wouldn't have left them behind, would he?

As if hearing something she didn't, the gawking

crowd turned as one toward the Temple, watching as the High Priestess made her appearance. Aryana strode across the paved stones, still wearing her finery from meeting with Fafnir. As she walked toward Enar, the crowd of white-clad priestesses parted, allowing Keara a glimpse of her friend.

Lily stood nestled against Enar's side, his arm clamped around her shoulders. Her wide blue eyes stared at the crowd surrounding them, her face paler than usual against the black of her tunic. Keara didn't see Jamie.

"Lily!" Keara pushed past a gaping priestess and sprinted to her friend, grabbing Lily in a hug.

A little thinner, but other than that Lily felt the same. Red tinged the pale skin of her face from where her cloak failed to cast shadows, and dirt stained her clothes, but overall she looked fine.

Keara released the breath previously frozen in her chest. Her friend was unharmed.

"Enar, my friend. How are you?" Thoren stepped around Keara and clasped hands with Enar while simultaneously smacking him on the shoulder. Enar returned the whack-on-the-back. All fine and dandy for them, where was her apprentice?

"Keara!"

Keara snapped her head toward the sound of Jamie's voice as a brown head poked up from behind Enar's back. The little imp had turned the Watcher into a packhorse. How had Jamie managed that?

Keara reached for Jamie, stopping when she saw the crudely fashioned sling he was wrapped in. Why was he in a sling?

"Jamie?"

Pain-filled eyes focused on her. Oh, Goddess, he was hurt. Steam roiled in the back of her throat, her hands cranking into fists.

"What did you do to him?" She hissed at Enar, steam escaping through her teeth.

Thoren placed a hand on her shoulder. "He didn't—"

"I carried him for the past four hours. It wasn't easy. The lad's more trouble than he's worth." Enar shook his head, ignoring the steam wafting across his vision. Removing the sling, he lowered Jamie to the ground.

Keara knelt by Jamie's side, noting the pain lines etched in his pale face and the odd bend of his limbs. *Tell me no.*

"What did you do?"

"He fell out of a tree." Lily knelt beside her. "Broke his arm, sprained an ankle and broke his leg. We didn't know how to set it."

"Can you heal him?" Thoren asked.

Keara swallowed. It was worse than she thought. The longer a broken arm and leg remained unset, the more difficult it was to reset them. Once she moved the broken ends into alignment, she could run her hands over the break and join the ends together. It took several tries, though. And that was only if she could pull the swollen limbs into place.

The sooner she started the better chance of success.

From her peripheral vision, she saw Aryana step closer, and the priestesses move out of her way.

"Greetings, Enar," Aryana said, peering over Keara's shoulder. "Is this the male Halfling?"

"Male trouble-maker is more like it," Enar said. "Your Highness."

Keara glanced up in time to see Aryana place a hand on Enar's arm, a look of sadness on her face. By the time Keara finished blinking, the moment had passed. Not that it was any of her business, but it sure seemed like Aryana had a liking for Enar.

Definitely none of her business. She had more important things to think of.

"His arm and leg are broken. I need to get him

to the infirmary."

Aryana knelt at Jamie's feet. "My apologies for not noticing earlier, young one. Hang on and I'll send you to the infirmary where Keara and our priestesses will help you."

Jamie's eyes bugged at the High Priestess, but the speechless performance didn't last.

"You're the High Priestess? You don't look old enough. My Daddy said you were old."

"Who has my herb bag?" Keara looked at the sacks hanging from Enar's belt, spying her own, hoping Jamie hushed.

"I'm older than I look. When you feel better you'll have to tell me all about your father." Aryana touched Jamie's shoulder.

The air around Jamie warped, shimmering like the reflection off water on a hot day. He started to disappear right when Enar spoke.

"Catch." Enar pulled her herb bag from around his waist, tossing it to Keara. Her hand grasped it a second before she felt every small particle in her body rip apart. Shimmering waves of air flooded her vision as she reappeared in the infirmary. Jamie lay on the bed, a smile evening out the pain lines etched on his face. Aryana had strong magic to transport Jamie into the healing room and land him on the bed.

Good thing her eyes were already green.

Before the jealousy grew roots, an ear-piercing shriek filled the room followed by Lily appearing in front of her. Keara clamped her hands over her ears as she hurried to her friend.

"Lily! Stop that! You'll wake the dead!" Keara elbowed Lily until she stopped screaming. Who knew her friend had a set of lungs like that?

Jamie turned his head toward Keara. "That was fun! Can we do that again?"

"Sweet Goddess, I hope not. What happened?"

Lily's hand fluttered at her chest.

"It's how the Draconi move about. Takes awhile to get used to it. But once you do it's amazing." Keara rummaged through her herb bag. Where was that datura? She needed it to put Jamie into a deep enough sleep to reset his limbs. "It's fun to be able to pop around the Courtyard. Where is that packet?"

Calm down, take a breath. Once she relaxed a bit, her fingers found the packet by touch. Unlike her grandmother, who had tied each packet in a different knot to differentiate between the herbs, Keara always knew what each packet held by touch alone. Yet another reason for her grandmother to fear her.

She shook the memory from her head, focusing instead on Jamie's injuries.

His right arm had been broken above the elbow, the fractured lower half of the bone riding over the upper half, giving the arm a bulging appearance.

"Did you dose yourself?" Keara glanced at his face as she set the packet of datura on the bedside table.

He shook his head, grimacing. "I could only remember the willow bark. You never showed me the stronger herbs."

"Well, Jamie. I hope you've learned your lesson about climbing trees." As if that was possible. Boys attracted trouble like bees to nectar. She ran her fingers over his lower leg feeling the break in the bones.

"That part stuck straight out when I landed. Pale as Lily. Enar pulled on my leg until it went back in, but it don't feel right. It's hot to the touch too. All red-like. That's not good, is it?"

Keara didn't answer, losing herself in her work. The ends of the bones in his leg didn't line up correctly and would have to be reset. Lily would need to help her realign the bone once she relaxed the lad.

Using her knife, Keara cut Jamie's pants leg off. Blood oozed from the skin where the bone had broken through, the surrounding area fiery red.

She needed to relax the muscles to reset the bone, then clean the wound, and hope infection didn't set in.

"Lily? Would you mind setting the pot of water to boil?"

"Of course not. Where's the pot?"

Keara gestured to the stack of pots against the wall and left Lily to draw the water from a pump in the corner of the room.

Her poor apprentice. Who wasn't an apprentice in Draconia, was he? She was the apprentice to Annaliese. Jamie...would he be allowed to live here at the Temple with her? Her heart kicked a solid thump against her chest at the thought of not having him around. Where did orphans live in Draconia?

All questions for another time. She needed to focus on the work at hand and pray she managed to set the bones correctly.

Jamie touched her hand. "Are you all right? He didn't hurt you, did he?"

"Who? Thoren?" Keara brushed the hair off his forehead.

"If he hurt you, I'll get him back."

Keara tried to wipe the smile off her face and failed. It was nice to be looked after. Even if it was by a ten-year-old boy. "He didn't hurt me. Not at all. He helped me a lot by bringing me here. Everything is good." *Except I don't know if Thoren is my mate or what I'll do if he's not.* That unhappy fact would not be mentioned to Jamie. "It's you I'm worried about."

His face fell, gray eyes sorrowful. "That bad, eh?"

"I doubt you'll die from it. But it will hurt when

I reset the bones. What were you thinking to fall out of a tree?"

"I didn't mean to fall. I wanted to see the bird's nest. It was this giant bird, I mean ginormous. Fafnir said I should be able to fly one day so he'd let me climb and then I'd jump and he'd catch me. He'd just appear out of nowhere. So I thought I could jump and he'd catch me and how was I supposed to know he had already left camp?"

"You're lucky you only broke an arm and leg and not your head. And what was Fafnir doing encouraging you to jump out of trees? Doesn't he know that's dangerous?"

"But it's fun!"

"Sure it is. See all the fun you're having?"

"But I did get to be transported here."

Boys. She couldn't stay angry at him, though.

Lily sat on the edge of Jamie's bed, patting his good leg.

Might as well continue the lessons. Teaching took her mind off the twisting hops her heart passed as beats when she thought about Jamie's suffering. "Once the water boils, I'll make a tea with datura. Do you remember what that does?"

Lily and Jamie both shook their heads.

"It will relax your muscles, allowing me to reset the bone. The potion has to be made just right or else it could put you into a sleep you won't wake from. A potion made from the root would allow you to see into the future, but at a cost. Too much can be dangerous."

"Try not to kill me."

Lily patted his good arm. "Don't worry. I'm sure Keara knows what she's doing. She's done this before, you know," Lily assured him.

Keara let Lily comfort Jamie while she devoted herself to preparing the datura potion. Dangerous stuff. Too much and she could kill him. Only a practiced apothecary knew how to use datura. Good thing she was accomplished.

Once made, she held the bitter brew to Jamie's lips. "Bottom's up."

He made a face, but drank the cup dry. Soon his eyes closed and he drifted to sleep.

"What do you need me to do?" Lily sat on the opposite side of the narrow bed from Keara, face pale under the sunburn.

"Stabilize his arm. I'll pull and adjust the bones, but I need you to hold it like so," she demonstrated for Lily, "and not let go. Can you do that?"

Lily nodded as she stood. Keara grabbed Jamie's arm, one hand at the wrist, the other at his elbow and tugged, applying steady pressure. Lily held on until the bones slipped into place, the bulge in Jamie's arm straightening out, then her eyes rolled into the back of her head and she crumpled to the ground.

Oh no. "Lily!"

Her friend didn't move. Not good at all. Nothing to do about Lily, Jamie's injuries took priority. Keara sandwiched Jamie's arm between two flat pieces of wood, wrapping the pieces tightly with strips of cloth. Thank the Goddess the room was well stocked with bandages and wood for splints.

Once Jamie's arm was bound, Keara knelt beside Lily, feeling the rapid pulse in her neck. Her friend moaned at Keara's touch. At least she hadn't hit her head when she crumpled neatly to the floor.

But her fainting spell left Keara without a helper and she needed one and soon, before the drug she gave Jamie wore off. Maybe one of the priestesses would help.

Keara poked her head out the door, looking up and down the empty hall. Obviously, they had decided staring at Enar made a better pastime. She sighed, closing the door.

Keara stood still, opening her mind to the thoughts of others. Other's thoughts, like butterflies' wings beating against her mind, whispered to her as she filtered through them until she found the pattern distinct to Thoren. Then she called for him.

Chapter 16

Thoren stared at the spot where Keara knelt moments earlier. "Where are they?"

"In one of the healing rooms," Aryana said. "If Keara needs help Annaliese is nearby."

"With Zeke and Conr?"

"Zeke's sick?" A wrinkle folded between Enar's brows.

"His son."

Enar blinked. "Son? He's mated?"

"His son, Conr, is a Halfling," Ari said.

Wait for it. Enar reacted as expected, brows slamming down over his eyes. Thoren slapped his friend on the back, warding off whatever Enar might have said.

"So, how was your journey?"

"Besides you leaving me with a hellion?"

"You shouldn't speak of Fafnir that way."

Enar shook his head. "It wasn't too bad. We made it here in mostly one piece."

"Would you like food or drink?" Aryana waved a hand toward the Temple.

Wasn't it time for his aunt to make a disappearing act? Why was she so interested in hanging around Enar? Only acolytes and young females fantasized about Watchers. And yet...it didn't bear thinking on.

"I thought you'd never ask." Enar picked up a bag and strode with the urgency of a starving male to the Temple door.

Thoren followed, catching up with his friend.

"We need to talk."

"How about you talk and I'll fill my stomach?"

"Are you even allowed in the Temple?"

Enar raised an eyebrow. "It hasn't fallen down, has it?" He strode through the door like he owned the place, heading for the dining room.

How did he know the location of the dining room? Thoren glanced behind them at Aryana hurrying to keep up. Surely not. Priestesses did not have fantasies or liaisons with Watchers. Adult Draconi knew how dangerous Watchers were and shied away from them.

Unless they were females around Enar. But still. His aunt?

"Enar, please help yourself to the food. I am needed at Fafnir's purification ritual. It's nice to see you again." Aryana flashed an upward turn of her lips before disappearing.

"So how bad was it?" Thoren dropped into the chair next to Enar's, holding back a headshake as the serving acolytes nearly tripped over their hems trying to wait on Enar. What was it with his friend and females? Was it the forbidden aspect that made him so appealing?

Enar swallowed a mouthful of apple. "Jamie is more trouble than he's worth. Climbing trees, disappearing, reappearing in places he's not supposed to be, falling out of trees." He took another bite of the apple. "Surely we weren't that much trouble as boys."

A vivid image of his mother scolding them after they disappeared to go exploring flashed across his mind. He grinned. "Of course not. We never got in trouble."

"That's what I thought. But I did learn how he came to be in River's Run."

"You did? How?"

"Well, it was really Lily that learned it from

Fafnir, who Jamie confided in..."

"Listening to gossip, now?"

Enar snorted. "As I was saying, his parents were killed in front of him."

"That's horrible!"

"It was a surprise attack. Soldiers came, killed his mother first when she went outside for water. His father helped him escape and told him to hide in the woods, but he still witnessed their deaths. He said it seemed like his father had no magic, that he'd try to fight but nothing would happen."

"What? How could that be?"

Enar looked at him. *Titanium.*

Unbidden, he saw Fafnir in a titanium cell. Titanium, the bane of Draconi. How did humans discover their poison?

"I don't know, but it seems odd that Fafnir was in a titanium cell. Especially when combined with Jamie's father being killed by titanium-wielding soldiers."

"Why did the soldiers come to his house?"

"He heard them say something about 'the boy', who he assumed to be himself. It seems like the soldiers were after Jamie. If the rogue Draconi was working with the lord in River's Run, then maybe they tried to get Jamie first and settled on Keara when Jamie escaped."

"We need to report this to the Council."

Pain slammed through his head as he heard Keara silently yelling for him. He obviously needed to repeat his lesson on yelling while mind-speaking. So much for reporting on a security threat.

He rubbed his ear—hoping that would stop her screaming. *What's wrong?*

Lily passed out and I need help setting Jamie's leg.

Where's Annaliese?

I thought maybe you could help me?

The Council report could wait. If Keara wanted him, he wasn't going to complain.

"I need to go. Keara needs me. I'll come back and find you." He barely registered the look of surprise on Enar's face before he disappeared in a cloud of dust, arriving in the healing room.

Keara stood in the middle of the room, facing the door, her lips turning in a grin as he appeared. Jamie lay on the bed, one arm in a splint, one leg lying at a strange angle. Thoren winced. Fortunately, he wasn't squeamish.

"Thank the Goddess you're here. I didn't know what to do."

"I'm happy to help, but Annaliese would be better at it."

"I know, but she's busy and I wanted you."

"In that case, I'm all yours."

"Would you mind picking up Lily and putting her on the other bed?" Keara pointed to the floor, where Lily sprawled, moaning.

How had he missed a moaning woman lying on the floor? Talk about embarrassing.

After he placed Lily on the bed, he walked back to Keara. "You need help setting the leg?"

"Yes, thank you. You stabilize by putting your hands here," she pointed and Thoren wrapped his hands around Jamie's leg, "and hold on."

By the time the bones slid into place, a sheen of sweat covered Keara's face. Not that he looked much better. He wiped the sweat from his eyes on the back of his sleeve as Keara placed a splint on Jamie's leg.

Thoren watched her work, her deft fingers tying the splint together. His mate. He still needed to tell her that fact.

"What?" Keara mimicked his motion, swiping her face against the back of her sleeve.

No time like the present. Thoren opened his mouth, but the words dried up faster than a stream in a desert. Closed mouth. Tried again. Got nowhere.

One eyebrow cocked as she watched his mouth move. But her focus didn't last long. Her gaze fled from his lips, wandering to where Lily lay behind him.

"Ah! So you decided to join the land of the waking. How do you feel?" Keara hurried to Lily's bed.

And his perfect moment dissipated like steam in the sunlight.

"Not too good." A small grin turned the corners of Lily's lips. "Guess I'm not meant to be a healer, huh?"

"You were out for awhile. I was worried about you." Keara's hands fluttered over her friend, touching her skin, the pulse in her neck.

One minute he watched Keara with Lily and the next pain split his skull in half. Thoren clamped both hands to his ears—not that doing so would help quiet the mind-speaking—and doubled over. By the Goddess, could the Council not find a better way to call its spies? Why did they insist on calling in such a way that made Keara's earlier shout a whisper?

His pride stung as Keara darted to his side, asking him questions he couldn't hear over the roar in his head. What kind of a male acts like a pained sissy in front of his female?

The kind that gets a call from the Council.

But still. He tried to straighten and made it an inch. How long did the bloody deafening call have to continue? The thought had no sooner flashed through his mind when the Council's call vanished as quickly as it came, leaving him panting for breath.

Yet another pride stinger. Keara's frantic voice penetrated his aching brain.

"I'm fine." If one considered having his brain shattered, fine. "The Council summoned me."

"You don't look fine. What's the point of summoning like that? What if you were doing something important? You'd think—"

"I agree, but it's the way they call. I need to find out what they want before they call again." He doubted his brain could take two doses of that in a day.

"Will you come back?"

Thoren leaned in, pecking her cheek, wishing he had longer. Once he took care of Council business, he would tell her she belonged to him.

Hopefully she'd take the news well.

"Of course. See you in a few."

Disappearing, he transported to the Council's Chamber. The ceiling towered over walls carved from stone, ornamented with jeweled designs. Polished marble floors aided the hardness of the walls in rendering the atmosphere of the room cold and unyielding. Much like the eyes of the ones who sat in a half-circle facing him.

By the Goddess, he loved this chamber.

Thirteen carved, wooden chairs held thirteen males with countenances as hard as the wood cushioning their arses. A mixture of colored eyes—the bright green of Draconi and ice-cold blue of the Watchers—cut through him like knives.

They wanted to know what he discovered on his mission and he wouldn't put it past a few to try and read his mind. Rude bastards, but he didn't much blame them. When dealing with the safety of his people, every little memory counted. It was a game, in a way, to hide his thoughts from prying minds, so he slammed his mental shields in place.

Take that you bloody bastards.

A couple of faces scrunched as they met his shields. Score one for the reconnaissance specialist.

But he couldn't mask the voice that spoke in his head.

Hello, son.

Father.

Balthor sat to the left of Alviss, who sat in his normal spot smack in the middle of the semi-circle. Thoren tensed, ready for a wave of get-busy-and-find-a-mate nagging. Instead, Balthor's eyebrows shot into his hairline as he gaped at Thoren. To top the odd reaction, Balthor marched over to Thoren, hugged him, and stuck his nose in Thoren's neck.

Had his father lost his mind?

"You Changed."

One eyebrow popped up as he stared at his father.

"I did."

"Who was the female that aided you?"

Keara. A Halfling. My mate. But I'm too messed up to inform her of what she is. "Someone I met."

Now it was his father's turn for the cocking eyebrow routine. Clearly, he hadn't expected that answer.

Before his father spat a comeback, the twenty-foot tall doors swung open like they were loose on their hinges, all wobbly and light.

"We'll talk later."

Not if he had any say in the matter.

Enar strode through the open doors, a look of pure rage on his face. Unlike Thoren, who could cheerfully pull up a carved chair and plant his arse in this Chamber, Enar would rather lose his left testicle before coming here.

The only reason his friend even bothered with the Council was because Thoren liked it and Enar was assigned to guard Thoren. Until death do them part, so to speak.

Thoren suspected Enar's reticence for the Council had more to do with his father than it did with the Council itself. Enar's father won Thoren's meanest-male-ever-met award, a towering wall of anger, most of it directed at his son.

Thoren might disagree with his own father—especially over the finding a mate saga—but at least he knew his father kept his best interests at heart. Enar's old man couldn't care less about his son and didn't mind showing that attitude to the world.

With a crash that caused little bits of dust to rain down, Enar slammed the gigantic doors closed. Thoren bit back a smile.

"Instead of summoning me, why not just kill me instead? It's bound to hurt less." Enar stalked farther into the room, stopping beside Thoren.

"You still live, Aylasson?" Thoren's eyes widened at the insult of calling Enar by his mother's name as one would a female. "Thought you would be dead by now." The man to the left of Thoren's father grasped the arms of his chair, knuckles white, as he stared at Enar.

"It's nice to see you too, Father. Give my regards to the demon that set you free for today's meeting." Enar stood feet shoulder-width apart, arms crossed.

Viktor pointed a finger at Enar. "You ungrateful whelp! I—"

"Silence!" Alviss spoke, his words echoing off the high ceiling, settling like a shroud across the assembly.

Thoren shuddered as the spell slammed into him. Alviss was the most powerful Draconi that sat on the Council. And the oldest. His white hair hung in long locks over his shoulders, his face a map of lines. He walked with a cane, from all appearances a frail, withered man. But his magic ran strong, through his veins and the veins of his only surviving child, Annaliese.

"We are gathered today to hear the reports of Thoren and Enar, not to bicker with them," Alviss spoke quietly; even so, the words reverberated throughout the room. "Did you locate the Halfling we sent you to find?"

"Yes sir. Along with others." None of which the Council knew about. The High Chamber of the Council might sit in close proximity to the Temple of the Goddess, but Ari refused to discuss most of the happenings of the Temple with the Council members.

Although he had been back for several days, the Council would not have known about it until Enar's return. Both members of a spy pair were required to return in order to alert the Council.

Quizzical looks greeted his news.

"Others?" Alviss needed to loosen up that grip on the chair before he ripped off the arm.

"There was a mature Halfling female and a captured male Draconi locked in dragon form."

Two heartbeats later, the room erupted. A grin attempted a run on his lips and he quashed the emotion before it spread. It was always fun to bring back shocking news.

"A Halfling female!"

"What's the dragon's name?"

"Where is the boy Halfling now?"

Questions peppered Thoren and Enar faster than they could answer, rendering both silent as a defense. Eventually Alviss would call for order, allowing them to report. And as expected, a short time later the old male's cane thumped against the marble floors.

Thud. "Silence!" Thud, thud, thud. Voices died, drifting away to the edges of the room.

"First things first. How did you find the boy Halfling?" Alviss pointed the tip of his cane at them.

"When he wandered out of Thoren's containment spell. He's been wandering ever since." Enar voice dripped weariness. Going by the tone of Enar's voice, Jamie must have given his friend a larger dose of trouble than he had earlier admitted.

A bushy white eyebrow popped up. "You are two of our best reconnaissance specialists. How could you not ward an area to contain a Halfling?"

Thoren felt his cheeks heat. "We didn't realize what he was."

"Pardon? Are your eyes giving you trouble?"

"No sir. The boy does not have the typical Halfling coloring. He has brown hair and gray eyes."

Another round of murmuring followed by a thumping cane.

"We knew Bjorn had a Halfling boy, but we did not know about this."

Bjorn was Jamie's father? Thoren fought to keep his gaping mouth closed. Bjorn had been one of Thoren's closest friends as a child despite being several years his senior, but they grew apart in recent years. Last he'd heard, Bjorn had disappeared several months ago. And Enar confirmed he died. Thoren took a deep breath and closed his eyes, saying a quick prayer for Bjorn's soul. Grieving would come later.

"Does he use magic?"

"None that I saw. What about you?" Thoren turned to Enar.

"Not unless you consider a penchant for climbing trees and falling out of them magic."

"Maybe you didn't give him the right incentive. We'll question him ourselves."

Oh, that would go over really well with Keara. She protected Jamie like a mother dragon did her hatchlings.

"He's injured—"

"Falling out of a tree. He thought he could fly," Enar chimed in.

"He broke his leg and arm and is being tended by the Halfling female we found."

"And my Claim." Enar stood a little taller.

The Watchers' gazes landed on Enar and Viktor

snarled. Thoren's hands cranked into fists. What he wouldn't give for a fight with Viktor. Hatred was not an emotion he normally felt, but Enar's father brought it out like a burst from an exploding energy ball.

Alviss's questioning continued, rolling right over Enar's statement and Thoren's anger.

"Draconi heal fast. We'll speak with him tomorrow or the next day. Tell us about the female. How did we not hear of a mature Halfling?"

"I don't know the answer to that. But the town we found them in is full of superstitious people who convinced her magic was evil and she was, too. Don't worry, I've convinced her otherwise. Her name is Keara and she was...is...an apothecary. Annaliese has taken her on as an apprentice."

"You've been here long enough for her to meet Annaliese?"

"I returned with Keara several days ago. I went through the Change while on the mission," Balthor's face turned into a mask of horror, "and gave her a crash course on helping me, but she absorbed the magic and went into a coma."

Now all the Draconi faces matched Balthor's horrified glare and the Watchers looked puzzled. While the Watchers knew male Draconi underwent a Change, they didn't know what it involved.

"She lived despite absorbing magic?" Alviss's coloring matched his hair.

"She did. I turned and flew her back. Figured it was an extenuating circumstance."

"Of course, of course. Are you sure she absorbed your energy?"

"Both she, the High Priestess, and Annaliese said that's what she did. She's tending Jamie, the boy Halfling."

"We need to speak with her too. Now about the dragon." Alviss made a circular motion with his hand.

"We found him in a dungeon—"

"What were you doing in a dungeon?"

"Rescuing Keara. She'd been captured. Oh, speaking of which," Keara distracted him to the point where he completely forgot about important safety news. Mated males were apparently head-full-of-air fools. "One of her captors was a Draconi."

"A Draconi?" Alviss gripped his chair's arms in a white-knuckled grasp. "Who? Did you see this male?"

"I did not. Keara said she recognized him by his mark."

"She was also drugged up but good," Enar added.

"So it's possible she did not really see a Draconi?" Alviss asked.

"I suppose. But she was insistent on that fact and she remembered everything that happened to her. The drug didn't affect her memory. She said the Draconi wanted to use her for revenge."

"We will question her about that. It's very disturbing. Continue with the dragon."

"As I said, we were in a dungeon and there he was. Apparently, he'd been captured many years ago while in human form and he Changed while in the dungeon," as one, the Draconi shuddered, eyes wide, "and is now stuck in dragon form. He arrived at the Temple earlier today."

"Why did he not come back with you?"

Thoren shrugged and looked to Enar.

Enar's heavy shoulders bunched. "I don't know why, but he came with me, not Thoren."

"He'll also be questioned. How was he captured?"

Thoren shrugged. "I don't know, but the bars of the cell were made out of titanium."

"Titanium? How can a mcrc human know titanium renders a Draconi's powers useless?"

"I don't know." Mated Draconi males were forgetful fools; he almost missed telling about Bjorn's death. "Enar discovered Jamie's father is dead."

Alviss's eyes widened, his mouth tightening. "How?"

Enar related what he knew about Bjorn's death and his speculations regarding the rogue Draconi trying to capture Jamie before he tried capturing Keara.

"That is a major security threat. We cannot have humans working with Draconi to capture Halflings. We will send a team tomorrow to eradicate the problem. Do you know anything else about this dragon?"

"Sir, I discovered how the dragon was captured," Enar said.

Thoren glanced at Enar. Some inner voice told him Fafnir hadn't gotten all close and personal with Enar, so how did the Watcher know that tidbit of information? More gossip?

"Well, we're waiting." Alviss leaned forward.

"He was visiting River's Run and ran afoul of one of the nobles there who somehow knew of titanium's effect on Draconi. I'm not sure why the noble captured him, but Fafnir cast a spell on the noble before he was thrown in the cell and the man went crazy."

"Serves the human right. Do you know more than that?"

"No sir. I didn't discover more about his story."

"Very well. We'll question all involved and find out the answers ourselves. First we'll talk to the female, you said her name was Keara?" Thoren nodded. "We'll try to discover who her father was. Please bring her to us."

Thoren nodded and closed his eyes, sifting through the thoughts of Draconi surrounding him and the point where he last saw Keara. He found her thought pattern in the healing room and took a hop into her mind.

Keara?

Thoren? Where are you? What's wrong?

The Council would like to speak to you. Can you transport here or do you need me to bring you?

Where's here?

Hold on and I'll bring you.

Thoren used his newly awakened powers to transport Keara from the infirmary to the Council's Chamber. She took shape beside him, the scent of herbs wafting around her. One hand reached out and clutched his palm as she stared at the thirteen in front of her. The acrid scent of fear slapped against his nostrils, but her shoulders arched back, her spine straightening.

Courage in the face of fear attracted him.

He wrapped his fingers around hers, running his thumb over her mark. Her fear receded, rolling away like dust on a breeze. Her palm felt small, tiny even, in his hand. As if it needed protection. Just like she did. A female needed her mate's protection, his caring, his love. In the same way a male needed his female like he needed the air beneath his wings. Without her, he remained grounded, a useless vessel, living, but not alive. With her though...

Thoren gave Keara a sideways glance as she looked at him. He smiled and stood a bit straighter.

"May I present Keara, the Halfling female from River's Run. Keara, this is the High Council, the group in charge of security for Draconia."

Keara dipped her head. "Pleased to meet you."

Even with his thumb stroking her mark, her hand shook. Guess relaxation only went so far. Where she was concerned Alviss was an old dog with no teeth. He'd never hurt a female. The thought was ludicrous. But Thoren could understand Keara's fear. Where she came from, this little visit meant disaster.

Understanding didn't mean he agreed, though. *They mean you no harm.*

Her eyes flicked to him and then refocused on Alviss, her thoughts banked. Good to know his lessons on shielding her mind met with success.

"Greetings, Keara. I am Alviss, the Grand Master of the Council. We have some questions for you. Will you be so kind as to answer them for us?"

The kindness in Alviss's voice must have relaxed Keara because Thoren no longer scented fear wafting from her. Her hand still shook, though.

"If I know the answers, sir."

"Of course, of course. Now, tell me about your parents."

"My mother died when I was a young child and I never knew my father."

"No one knew your father?"

"My mother never spoke of him."

"Come, child. Let me see your mark." Alviss's hand beckoned her forward.

Keeping a death grip on Thoren's hand, Keara drug her feet toward where Alviss sat. Was he actually able to tell her bloodline by looking at her mark? Perhaps this is what Ari meant when she said Alviss could deduce Keara's family.

Keara pressed her lips together, dragged a breath through her nose and stuck her arm out. Alviss grasped her outstretched arm, raised her sleeve and peered intently at her mark. A gnarled finger stroked across the dragon imprint before pressing hard. Thoren felt the thrum of magic beat against his palm from where it touched Keara's. Her hand tightened against his as her body went rigid, her teeth grinding hard enough to hear.

And then she went limp.

Thoren caught her around the waist, lifting her

into his arms. Steam poured out his ears, his lip peeling into a snarl. His mate hurt. Reasoning fled, instinct taking over. His mate hurt and the cause of it must die.

Alviss's eyes popped wide and from his peripheral vision Thoren saw Balthor begin to rise. A heavy hand slapped against his back and Thoren snapped at it, his teeth clicking together.

"Hey, now. That was rather exciting, eh?" Enar stepped between Thoren and Alviss, using mind-speak to project his voice into Thoren's head. *Goddess's teeth, Thoren, what do you think you're doing? You can't fight Alviss. Do you have a bloody death wish?*

Thoren blinked as he stared into ice blue eyes. Enar was right. What was he doing? A small hand pressed against his chest and Thoren glanced down into Keara's wide green eyes.

I'm all right, you know. It hurt when the magic went into me, but I'm fine now. Are you?

Closing his eyes, he took a deep breath. "I apologize. I'm not sure what came over me." Which was a lie on so many levels, but as lying was going to keep him from being charcoaled, he was all for it.

Enar thumped him on the shoulder and went to stand where they had been before Thoren started the mated male dragon posturing.

You can put me down now.

Keara's feet bumped against the ground and she grabbed his hand again. Maybe she thought he might use it to strangle Alviss if it wasn't put to good use.

Thoren met Alviss's gaze.

"Does she know?"

What was Alviss talking about now? "Does she know what?"

"Don't play dumb, son." Balthor jumped in.

"What should I know?" Keara asked, looking

between the three males.

Thoren realized where this conversation headed and was in no hurry for it to arrive. "What did you find when you touched her mark?" A change of direction was a good thing, right?

Alviss drummed gnarled fingers against the chair arm. Balthor skipped the nervous twitch and used the you're-going-to-get-a-whipping-when-I-lay-hands-on-you face that had sent Thoren running for cover as a child. He felt a tingle of fear and quickly smashed it out. He was grown. Was his father really going to do anything about Thoren not mentioning Keara was his mate?

"Surely you're not as clueless as you appear?"

Thanks, Alviss. "No sir, I'm not. But I would like to know her linage."

"Ah. That's good. You had me and everyone else here worried for a minute. Her linage. Keara, did you know a Draconi can touch your mark and learn your family?"

Of course she didn't. Thoren hadn't known until recently and he'd grown up in Draconia. Naturally, Keara shook her head, her eyes aglow like she'd received a stack of presents on her birthing day.

"Child. Speak up, old ears have problems hearing. Did you wish to know your family?"

"Please sir. If it would not offend."

"Your father has been dead to us many years past. He left and never returned. Your aunt belongs in service to the Goddess. You've already met her. Your grandmother is dead, many years past, before your father. Your grandfather is very old. Do you wish to meet this old male? Is he worth your time?"

Thoren hissed in a breath as he looked between Keara and Alviss. He had a sneaking suspicion he knew who her grandfather was and it shook him to the core.

"He is. I would very much like to know any

relative. Which priestess is my aunt?" Thoren could tell by her face she hadn't caught on.

"This is quite the shock for your grandfather. He did not think he had a grandchild. You might think him grumpy."

Grumpy wouldn't be the word Thoren would use. More like downright dangerous with a large amount of power.

"I don't care. I would still like to meet him. Who is my aunt?"

"Annaliese is your aunt and I am your grandfather."

Just as Thoren thought. Unbelievable. He'd tried to kill Keara's grandfather. Alviss was going to love it when Thoren announced Keara was his mate. Welcome to the family.

Chapter 17

Keara stared at the oldest person she ever saw. Her grandfather. Thick white locks hung over his shoulders, falling in streaks across his sunken chest. Wrinkles collapsed on wrinkles, framing thin red lips. But his eyes sparkled emerald fire, while his aura glowed strong, and Keara knew that despite his withered appearance he held powerful magic.

Magic he'd already demonstrated when he touched her arm and she almost fainted. How embarrassing.

Thank the Goddess Thoren had caught her so she didn't look as bad of a fool. Not that she had time to worry about feeling foolish. She'd been too busy trying to overcome the pain coursing through her veins.

And then Thoren had acted like he needed to avenge her death. Yes, the pain was bad, but it wasn't the kind to kill her. His protectiveness chased away the hurt, leaving a warm center in the middle of her chest. No one ever stood up for her like that. No one.

And it meant so much.

Just when she'd thought things couldn't get any better, Alviss announced Annaliese was her aunt and he was her grandfather. That explained the bond she felt with the healer, but did nothing to explain Annaliese's age. She didn't look much older than Keara.

Yet another thing she needed to ask about.

After she talked to her...grandfather. Oh

Goddess, what if he didn't like her? What if he thought her an aberration like her grandmother had?

Keara tensed her calf muscles, trying to make her legs stop shaking.

"Well, child, speak up."

"I am shocked, sir."

"Stop sirring me. You may call me Gramps. I like the sound of that. What about you?"

The Council gave Alviss looks as if they thought his mind had taken an extended vacation and left an incapable substitute in its place.

Alviss beamed at her. What's not to like about a cute, wrinkled old male?

She smiled back at him. "Gramps, it is."

Using his cane to push himself to his feet, Alviss turned to the male Draconi sitting next to him. "Continue the questioning. I find I wish to talk to my granddaughter. That has a nice ring to it, does it not? Granddaughter."

The male nodded at Alviss, clearly dumbfounded. Maybe her newly found grandfather was not as nice as he seemed? She glanced at Thoren and got no help. His face hung pale and limp as he gaped at Alviss.

Or maybe that was a clue. Obviously Alviss's attitude toward her was completely out of character. Not that she cared. She'd take dear old Gramps anyway she could get him.

Provided he didn't mind her. What if he thought her strange? Or evil? Thoren's presence in her life made old thoughts of evil vanish. But what if Alviss didn't like Halflings?

As he thump-shuffled over to her, planting his cane and shuffling his feet, she realized the thought for what it was—insecurity. *Get it together, Keara. He either likes you, or he doesn't, and that's that.*

She watched Alviss grow closer, and taller,

much taller than he looked hunched over in his chair. Even leaning on his cane he topped her, his bushy white eyebrows covering sharp green eyes.

"Well, child, are you ready for a talk?" He held out an arm.

Keara grasped it, planning on helping him to the door. "That would be nice."

"Hang on."

Her body shattered into a million pieces and swirled through space, rejoining some distance away. Her head spun, her limbs shaking as they took shape next to a bench under a shade tree. Transporting was such a rush. And to think, if Thoren hadn't rescued her she would never have learned the ability.

"Sit, sit," Alviss pointed to the bench, shuffling over. "Old bones can't hold themselves up for long."

Keara held his arm until he flopped into a seat, watching as he planted his cane between his stretched out legs. She sat next to him.

"What's that building?" The circular structure squatted on the edge of the horizon, its stone walls surrounded by a copse of trees.

"Ah. That's where we were. This is much more conducive for talking, don't you think?"

"It is prettier."

"Yes, yes." He patted her hand, his bent fingers warm. "Now, tell me about yourself. Let an old grandfather know what excitement he missed in your life."

How long did it take to talk about what a pariah she had been? Too long. She ended the brief and boring rendition of her life with the best thing that happened to her.

"And then Thoren found me and brought me back with him."

"Thoren mentioned you arrived here several days ago. You met my daughter, Annaliese?"

"She said I could help her at the Temple and learn healing."

"What does Thoren think of that?"

Keara looked at her hand resting in Alviss's. "Why should he care?"

"Oh-ho. He hasn't told you?"

"Told me what?"

"We had a Seer at the Temple for many years who used to predict whether or not a Draconi had a mate. The females who had no mate became priestesses, which is why Annaliese serves the Goddess in the infirmary."

What did this have to do with Thoren? More specifically, what was Thoren supposed to tell her? Politeness kept the smile frozen on her face.

"Anyway, before she died, the Seer predicted Thoren's mate would be special and would perform great magic."

A streak of jealousy slammed into her, bringing an insane urge to commit murder. *Smile, do not snarl.*

"You are who the Seer predicted."

Blink. Breathe. "What?"

"You are mates."

"Nonsense. He married me according to my town's laws, but claimed that wasn't what he meant to do. So I guess that means we're divorced. Besides, Aryana said—"

"Don't pay her any attention."

The tone of his voice didn't waver, but the anger roiling off him slammed into her like a gust of wind. How could he not like Aryana? What was the story behind the anger?

"What's wrong with Aryana?"

"Let's choose another subject. You said you did not know what happened to my son, your father. Is that correct?"

"I never knew who he was. Neither did my

grandmother. What I really want to know—"

Alviss rolled over her words like she hadn't spoken. "So you don't know what happened to him?"

Didn't she just say that? "No, sir."

Alviss sighed. "He left one day as he often did. Said he'd be back and that he had a surprise. I can only assume the surprise was you, but he never returned. A Draconi does not willingly leave the fold for long.

"We waited," his voice broke, "but he never returned. We sent our spies, but without knowing where he went...they didn't find a trace. After the required time he was declared dead. Draconi don't have many children and for me to be blessed with two...But I lost one. And then you came today." A long pause. "The pain of my lost son is still inside me, but you have helped ease the hurt."

Keara patted his hand with her free one and blinked rapidly. Draconia tended to bring on tears no matter where she went.

"I'm glad to meet you too."

Alviss stared at the horizon, face turned from her, obviously not wanting her to see his weakness. Not that she found grief a weakness, but men—and she assumed Draconi males fell into this category too—considered a show of grief to be a show of weakness. And Goddess forbid they appear weak.

"Do you know the symbolism of your mark?" Alviss turned toward Keara, one finger pressing on her mark. Did he have a kaleidoscope of thoughts running through his mind? Because he sure had a hard time staying on topic. Discussion of Draconi marks had been the last thing on her mind.

"It means I'm a Draconi."

"Yes, yes. But in the hands of a powerful sorcerer, that would be yours truly, it can be used for other things. For instance, seeing into your magic, discovering whose family you belong to, controlling the person whose mark you touch. Not that I'd condone that, but you should know about the ability."

Ah. She'd thought Thoren had used some sort of a spell to control her when he'd married—oops, rescued her. Nice to know she'd been right.

Alviss's finger rubbed across her skin, his magic probing hers. She bit her lip to hold back the scream as fire poured from his fingertip into her veins, streaming through every part of her body. And just as quickly as it came, the pain disappeared.

Keara jerked her arm out of his grasp. "You really need to stop probing me like that. In case you don't realize it, it hurts."

Alviss's eyes twinkled. "Now, now, I wouldn't hurt you on purpose. I'm just trying to find out what magic you have."

"You could just ask." Keara crossed her arms.

"Do you know all your powers?"

Clearly, he didn't think she knew. "I absorb illnesses."

"And energy too, do you not?"

"I suppose."

"Of course you do. That's how you survived Thoren's Change, am I right?"

"He told you that?"

"Answer the question."

"Yes. That's how I helped him through his Change. I absorbed his energy. I didn't realize you were supposed to throw it away."

"It's a rare ability, absorbing illnesses, or energy. It's a skill my mate, your grandmother, had. She worked in the Temple as a healer, but that is how she healed. That is not how she helped me through the Change, but she could absorb a great deal of energy. You remind me of her. A little in the face." Gnarled fingers touched her cheek, his eyes darting away.

"Did she have...other magic?"

"What other magic are you referring to?" His sharp gaze returned to hers.

Keara shrugged. "Could she heal in...other ways?"

Alviss's eyes narrowed. "Not that I was aware of. Annaliese might know more. Why?"

"Just curious. No reason." He might be her Gramps, but she didn't yet trust him enough to reveal her secret.

"Well, it looks like our talk is over. Look who is coming to pay us, more like you, a visit."

Keara followed Alviss's finger as it pointed at the Council's Chamber. Two figures, tiny on the horizon, left the building. As she watched, the raven-haired one came their way.

Thoren.

After what Alviss said about Thoren being her mate, she needed to have a word with the male.

Alviss patted her hand. "It's time for me to go. Someone wants to speak with you. Would you be willing to meet with me again? I would like to know you better."

Keara smiled. "I'd love that. I'm glad you're my grandfather." She threw her arms around him in a hug.

His thin arms tightened around her waist, surprising her with their strength.

"Good-bye, granddaughter."

"Good-bye, Gramps."

Alviss smiled and disappeared out of her arms. A grandfather. She had a grandfather that seemed to like her. How wonderful was that?

Her new problem was coming fast. Keara turned toward Thoren and watched as he strode across the grass, his long legs making quick work of bridging the distance between them. Her heart fluttered at the sight of his black hair shifting against shoulders that filled out his tunic. Magic wrapped around him like a blanket, coating him in its power.

According to Alviss, Thoren was her mate.

So why had he denied being married to her?

"How'd it go with Alviss?"

"Great! I can't believe I have a grandfather." *And that he likes me.*

Thoren started to sit on the bench.

"Wait!" He halted halfway down. "I have to return to check on Jamie." In her excitement over meeting her grandfather, she completely forgot about her apprentice and his injuries.

What kind of apothecary was she to forget about one of her patients? Her only excuse was the day had been filled with excitement that now started to turn into a vague sense of anger.

Thoren offered her his arm. Keara paused before taking it.

"What's wrong? Did he hurt you?" He growled the last words.

Keara darted a glance at his face and pulled back. Hard planes created shadows, giving an appearance of vengeance. Goddess, Thoren looked like he would kill Alviss if he thought the old male had hurt her. A smile started to blossom as she thought of his protectiveness toward her, but she squelched it.

"No, no! Alviss didn't hurt me," she refused to mention the second magical probing, "He just mentioned something."

Thoren's face returned to normal. "You look upset all of a sudden. Don't worry about Jamie. I'm sure Annaliese or one of the acolytes took care of him."

"It's not Jamie. Well, it is a bit. I got so caught up in talking to Alviss that I forgot about him. But what I'm wondering about is," Keara took a deep breath. "Alviss mentioned we were mates."

Thoren stiffened, his face turning red. He knew. He knew they were mates and he refused to tell her. He knew before Aryana had even tested them for compatibility. She felt steam in the back of her throat, snaking out her ears. Keara yanked her arm out of his.

"You knew! You told me we weren't married. Why did you lie?"

"I did not lie! We weren't married. I never agreed to marry you and it's not my problem that your town has such crazy laws that by rescuing you from that sniveling lord you thought I married you."

"Yes, yes. And Draconi have a mating ritual. That's beside the point."

"That is the point. I did not marry you in your town. I did not know when I rescued you that you were my mate. I discovered that later."

"And kept it to yourself! I've been wondering how to get you to be interested in me and here you knew we were mates."

"I was waiting to tell you."

"For what? The Goddess to pop in for a visit?"

"I needed to be sure. Once I'm mated, I can no longer be a reconnaissance specialist. I love my job. I had to be sure you were my mate before I told you how I felt."

Ouch. That hurt. "So your job is more important than me?"

"I didn't say that. I had to reconcile myself to the thought of no longer doing my job."

"What changed your mind?"

"You." Thoren ran a hand through his hair and fixed her with a penetrating stare. "You. I couldn't stop thinking of you. And going all dragon-crazy every time you were threatened."

"Alviss was not a threat."

"I know, but I can't help it. A male, any male, even your grandfather, acts like he is going to hurt you and I can't help it. I want to kill him. Just thinking of you being hurt, in any way, is enough to make me kill."

"That's...sweet."

"Sweet?"

"I like it when you get all protective. But I don't like it that you didn't tell me about being your mate. What if I said no?"

"You can't. You can say no all you want, but the truth is there is no other male for you besides me. Only one mate for each Draconi. And you are mine."

"You still should have told me."

"I know. I'm sorry."

Keara looked at the walls of the Temple as they jutted above a stand of trees. Had he really thought his job more important than her? She pressed her lips together as she remembered her observations of people in River's Run. Men there tended to think of their jobs as their life. Draconi might be part dragon, but they apparently thought the same way. No wonder Thoren felt torn if he knew that by mating he would be giving up his job.

That didn't excuse the fact that he forgot to tell her she belonged to him.

Thoren opened the back gate to the Courtyard, allowing her to walk in first. She needed to think, to pull her thoughts together. All the excitement of the day left her feeling worn out, tired, emotionally drained. She wanted Thoren, but she didn't want him to think he could treat her like this. That he could leave her out of decisions that concerned her.

"Thoren, I need some time to think."

"There is no thinking. You belong to me and me to you. What's to think about?"

"You withheld truth from me and yet you expect me to let it go. I can't do that."

"I explaincd "

"I know and I still need to think. I know you

didn't mean to hurt me, but you did. And what about your job? If I am an apprentice at the Temple, what will you do?"

Thoren's face shut down, closed her out. "It doesn't matter."

"Yes, it does. If you don't do something, you'll grow to resent me and I don't want that. I need to think and you do too before we go through with the mating."

"Keara, please. I'm sorry I hurt you. I want you more than anything."

"I know and I feel the same way about you. But I still need time to think. We can talk tomorrow. It's almost dark now." Keara leaned toward him and gave him a peck on the cheek. "Goodnight, Thoren."

Taking a cue from Alviss, she transported away from him before his arms encircled her waist. Before she acted on her heart and invited him into her room for the night. She appeared in front of Jamie's room, two doors down from Conr's.

When she finished with Jamie, she needed to see how Conr was doing. Not that Annaliese had problems treating the lad. Seeing to the ill was a calling Keara had no control over. Her blood begged her to attend and she followed.

Thoren probably felt the same way about his missions.

Keara turned the dragon's head knob and pushed open the door to Jamie's room. Annaliese stood over the boy, holding a cup to Jamie's lips. Both sets of eyes locked on her as she entered.

"He needed some water. I hope you do not mind."

"Of course not. I got transported away before I could tend to him. Thank you for your help."

Jamie seemed a little groggy from the aftereffects of the datura. His words slurred as he spoke, "Hey, how're ya? Where'd ya go?" He flopped his good arm to Annaliese. "She jus' up and disappeared."

Keara walked to him and stroked his shoulder as he turned his face into her hand. She ran her fingers through his dirty hair.

Annaliese paused, holding the cup as she watched Keara's hands. Keara met her gaze. Her aunt. Why had she not noticed before? Their noses were different, but everything else looked identical.

"Did you know?"

"That you are my niece? I suspected when I saw how you healed Conr."

"I didn't heal him."

"You helped. He is much better today. I took away the containment field over his bed."

Keara's breath caught. "He is?"

"I just said so."

She smiled. "I didn't think I helped. Does it upset you to know I'm your niece?"

Annaliese set the cup down. "Why should it? I'm pleased to know my brother left a part of himself behind. And it's nice to know I wasn't imagining things when I saw Mother in you."

A family. She had a family. That seemed to like her. Who would have thought? "I'm glad we're related too." Keara blinked. Draconia and its tear-forming air got to her. "So Jamie," she sniffed, "how do you feel?"

Jamie ignored her, continuing to look between Annaliese and Keara. "Ya bof look alike."

"I'm glad you're observant. Now tell me how you feel."

"I'sss fine."

"Are you in pain?"

His head flopped back and forth on the pillow. "Nuh-uh."

"Perhaps you would like me to teach you a spell to mend his bones."

"There is a spell to do that?" Instead of running her hands over the bones and healing them, a spell would do the same thing? Interesting. Anything to take her mind off Thoren.

"Yous iss puttin' spells on me?" Jamie waved his free hand.

"It will make you feel better," Annaliese grabbed his waving hand.

"S'all right. Feel a little hazy."

Keara patted his shoulder. "It will be all right."

"When you heal a broken bone, you first set it, like you have. Once you are sure the bones are set correctly, then you cast a spell to heal the break. Watch and listen."

Annaliese spoke words Keara had never heard and a glow appeared around her hands. She placed her hands on Jamie's broken arm, leaving the glow surrounding the splint. She then did the same thing to his leg.

"And that's it?" Keara held her hand above the blue glow surrounding Jamie's arm, feeling the pulse of magic.

"You may touch the magic. Yes, that's all there is to it. The spell will dissipate once the bones are healed."

Keara lowered her palm, feeling the magic beat against her own skin as it reached inside her, trying to heal her bones. Yanking her hand back, she looked at Annaliese.

"And I can learn that spell?"

"Of course."

"What language was that?"

"The language of the Goddess."

"And I am allowed to learn it?"

"Of course."

What a different place. Wrapping her mind around women—females—being allowed to speak to the Goddess was enough to leave her speechless.

Maybe speechless was a good thing. She could use this time to think what she would say to Thoren the next time she saw him.

How could he not have at least told her she was his mate? While she understood his dilemma, it still left her feeling like he didn't care about her.

"Keara? Would you like to learn the spell now?"

"I'd like that." Anything to take her mind off Thoren.

****

Thoren sat at the table with Ari, shoveling food into his mouth like it was his last meal. Enar went somewhere with Lily, undoubtedly enjoying a moment of bedsport, while his best friend sat on a bench with the High Priestess instead of Keara.

If it had been Keara sitting to his right instead of his aunt, he would have suggested activities more along the line of Enar's current one.

The chance of that happening now headed into the range of not so lucky. Thoren stuck a piece of meat into his mouth and chewed. What a fool he was. How had he ever considered his job more important than his mate?

Too late now to do anything about it. He explained his foolish actions to Keara and the choice was hers.

He hoped she chose him soon, but what were the chances of that? For all he knew, she'd stay angry at him forever and where would that leave him? With a job and no mate.

Had he mentioned what a stupid fool he was?

"You seem to have a lot on your mind."

Great. Now Ari wanted to talk. He jabbed a vegetable stalk onto his fork and popped it into his mouth.

"Mmph."

"Your father is insistent upon you finding a mate. I can understand where that would get a little old."

"That's not it." He chased the vegetable substance down with a good swallow of wine and peered into his cup. He could do with a little more of the stuff.

"I'm waiting."

He shrugged. Lying was not an option. Neither was discussing his apparent journey to the land of selfish and stupid.

A splitting headache saved him from both options, the call of the Council banging around inside his skull like an anvil. Twice in one day? Not that he complained. It beat answering his aunt.

"The Council?" Ari placed a hand on his back.

"I've got to go." Now that the pain stopped, he needed to show up in front of the Council before they decided to call him again.

He doubted his head could take another round of the Council's call.

"You'd think they'd come up with a better way to call their spies. What if you were in the middle of a fight or something when they called? You'd be dead."

"They only call when you're in Draconia so the assumption is you would not be fighting. I'll see you later."

Before she started with another round of what's-the-matter, he transported to the Council's Chamber.

The thirteen males sat in the glowing candlelight that cast long shadows upon their faces, giving them a haunted appearance. No one spoke at his arrival.

"What's wrong?" Something had to be. It had been less than an hour since he'd left and things were fine then.

"Be patient," Alviss said. "We'll let you know shortly."

Thoren didn't have long to wait before the heavy

wooden doors thudded against the stone wall as if a gale force hit them, ushering in one infuriated Enar. Dust sprinkled on Thoren's head as the doors slammed shut. Enar stalked past his best friend, stopping directly in front of Viktor.

"Twice in one day? I have a life outside of this Council."

"Not by my wishes, you don't," Enar's father hissed at him.

"Silence!" Alviss's voice boomed throughout the room as he gestured for a snarling Enar to stand beside Thoren.

"You have been called because intruders have been spotted in Draconi territory. We thought you would like to handle it." Alviss's eyes sparkled as he looked at them.

"Why us?" Thoren asked. Usually reconnaissance specialists did not fight off intruders. On the rare occasion an intruder crossed into Draconia, the Council used their special set of Watchers and Draconi trained to handle that type of thing.

Judging by Enar's face, he was itching for a fight. Thoren glanced at Viktor who glared at Enar like he crawled out from under some rock. Enar might be itching for a fight, but it wasn't a fight against intruders.

"Because of whom we suspect the intruders are." Alviss waved his hand, causing a ball with flickering images to hover mid-air. He beckoned Thoren and Enar to peer into the depths.

White mist swirled in the seeing ball, coalescing into clouds that separated in half, forming a vision. Thoren squinted as he stared at the flickering images. By the Goddess. How had he crossed the ward lines?

Simon and a figure wearing a cloak hiding his face sat around a campfire surrounded by a contingent of soldiers. A cold fury washed through Thoren. These men were the ones that took Keara. That drugged Keara. That planned to rape her. His hands cranked into fists, nails stabbing into his palms. His lip pulled into a snarl, as steam poured from his ears.

The bastards must die.

"Where are they?" Thoren growled.

"So they are the ones that captured Keara?" Alviss asked.

Thoren swallowed steam and managed to get his claws to retract into fingers. He didn't bother removing the snarl. "Yes."

"Is the mission capture or destroy?" Enar fingered the hilt of Blood Seeker.

"Destroy," Thoren said staring at Alviss. The old male better not refuse him his vengeance.

Alviss's wrinkles convulsed into a smile. "Destroy. These are the ones that harmed my granddaughter." He peered closer, his eyes blinking. "Is the one in the cloak a Draconi?"

"According to Keara he is."

"Then you must capture him and bring him to us for questioning. Then you may kill him after we speak to him."

"It will be my pleasure."

"They are right inside of Draconi territory. The wards must be weakening for them to have crossed the border, or that rogue Draconi has more power than he should. After you have secured the territory, see if you can determine the strength of the wards so we can send someone out to restore them. May the Goddess bless your mission and may the ones that considered defiling my granddaughter die in pain."

Sounded like a plan to him, especially the dying in pain part. Thoren grabbed Enar's arm and transported them to the woods where the soon to be dead men camped.

Five fires burned brightly in a small clearing in the woods. Six men sat around each fire. If Simon and the rogue Draconi had prepared well, they would have several men patrolling the perimeter of the camp. No more than forty men to their two. Not a problem.

Although the hooded Draconi gave Thoren pause. What magic did he have? Why was he here and what did he want from Keara? What was it about Keara that caused the Draconi and Simon to chase after her, even into Draconia? Furthermore, how had they crossed the wards? Thoren knew the questions pointed to the rogue Draconi, but the answers remained shrouded in mystery.

Solving mysteries was not his forte.

Killing those who harmed his mate, was.

"Blood Seeker is thirsty. Are you going to sit on your arse all night or do we get to have some fun?" Enar held his sword reverently, his finger lightly stroking the blade.

"Simon and the Draconi are mine." Thoren flexed his fingers, not needing a sword. Energy balls worked well, thank you very much.

Enar inclined his head. "May the Goddess go with you."

"And also with you."

Enar crept away from Thoren some distance before letting out a war cry, startling the soldiers sitting around the campfires. They scrambled for their weapons, some of them losing their heads in the process. Thoren turned from Enar's fight, looking for Simon and the Draconi.

He didn't see the Draconi, but he did locate Simon hiding behind a tree. It seemed the lord wasn't so tough now that his men were being killed.

Thoren stalked toward the man, picking his way through the undergrowth, skirting the periphery of the camp. Cries came from the soldiers as Blood

Seeker drank from the slain men's wounds, empowering Enar with their life's strength. A magic sword in the hands of a Watcher was a dangerous thing.

Simon didn't see Thoren, his eyes fixated on the slaughter of his soldiers. Thoren spoke the words of a stunning spell, forming the magic in his palm. Once Simon had been questioned, he'd be killed.

Good riddance.

Thoren threw the blast.

Before it reached Simon, it scattered into the trees, chipping out bark to rain down in a cloud of wood. What just happened? Thoren stared at Simon, as if the man knew the answer.

"See, Simon. I told you he'd come for us." The hooded Draconi stepped out from the tree next to Simon's.

How had he missed the male? Even if he hadn't seen him, the male's magical signature should have tipped him off. And yet Thoren hadn't felt a thing.

"Who are you and why are you here?" Thoren took a step toward the hooded Draconi.

"Who am I? Why, the one who will watch you die, of course. It's nothing personal. You have something I need and the only way to get it is to kill you. My revenge is close at hand. Happy dying!" The Draconi waggled his fingers at Thoren and ran into the woods.

Reacting faster than Thoren thought possible, Simon yanked his sword from its sheath and charged him. So much for chasing after the Draconi. Thoren shot a blast of energy at the lord, staring at his hands when nothing happened. How could nothing happen? Magic did not disappear.

He sidestepped Simon's sword thrust and tried to form another energy ball. Before he could turn around the worst pain of his life tore through his gut. His breath came in short bursts as he looked down. Oh Goddess, no.

Thoren fell to his knees, his hands clasped against his stomach where the tip of Simon's sword poked through. A boot pressed against his hip, shoving as the sword was yanked from his body. Thoren toppled face first into a carpet of leaves, his hands bloody as they pressed against the hole in his abdomen. He tasted the coppery ting of blood in his mouth, felt his heart quicken as his life's blood saturated the earth.

"Isn't titanium grand?" Simon slammed the sword into the ground in front of Thoren's eyes.

"No!" Enar rushed toward him, sword raised.

A blast of light came from the trees, slamming into Enar, sending Blood Seeker flying from his hand and dropping him like a rock onto the blood-soaked ground.

"No!" The word had no strength in Thoren's mouth, little more than a whisper. Enar was dead and he was dying. His eyes closed.

Keara. His mate. Would she mourn him? Or would she be glad he no longer bothered her? Oh, Goddess, if he lived he would ensure Keara knew how much she meant to him. If only he could do it all over again, he would admit she belonged to him. Who was he fooling? He'd admit it to himself. None of this job-is-more-important-than-mate lies. No, he would do things right.

He would declare his love.

"Now we wait."

Too weak to move, even open his eyes, Thoren heard the Draconi approach.

"They killed my men! Now who will protect me?"

A long sigh. "I said I would, but did you listen? No, of course not."

"I want the woman."

"And you'll have her. After me. After my revenge."

"But that's too long!"

"She'll come. She'll be drawn to him."

"How long?"

"Not long."

No. Not Keara. They couldn't be speaking of Keara. He needed to warn her of their plan. He needed to tell her how much he loved her.

Keara. His mate. His love.

A cold peace beckoned him, touched him, his body turning numb. He felt the blood slow its race between his fingers, a small trickle like dew dripping onto the leaves. Death called to him, tempting him with peace. But he only saw a face framed with curly red hair, green eyes sparkling as she looked up at him from where his body covered hers.

Keara! He cried, sending her all of himself before the darkness of death overcame him.

Chapter 18

Keara dropped the cup, hearing it crack against the wood floor as if from a distance. Thoren's voice echoed in her head, crying her name.

"What's wrong?"

Looking at Annaliese, she shook her head. "I don't know."

"What did you hear?"

"How do you know I heard anything?"

"Don't hide it. I could tell by the expression on your face." Annaliese clasped her hands and pierced Keara with her green gaze.

That look would make a hardened criminal confess. Keara didn't stand a chance.

"I heard Thoren cry out my name and then I saw woods with a campfire. And bodies." Keara shivered as the images of headless dead bodies flickered in her mind.

Annaliese moved so fast Keara didn't track her until the priestess grabbed her arm. "Where? Was Thoren injured?"

"I think he was. I didn't see him, but my vision came from the ground, like I was lying down. I think he's hurt. I need to find him."

"You can't. Go to the Council. Go to my father, your grandfather. Explain to him what's wrong. He'll send out a search crew to find Thoren. You can't go alone!"

Keara patted Annaliese's hand until the other female dropped her grip on Keara's arm. "All right. Will you take care of Jamie until I come back?"

"Of course. Be quick. Visions like the one you had are portents. Go!"

Keara scrambled out the door, running down the hall. Why was she running? She should transport. It was quicker.

But wait. If she went to Alviss then by the time he sent a search crew out to Thoren it would be too late. Thoren would be dead. She had felt the blood pour from between Thoren's fingers, heard his heartbeat pound in her ears as it tried frantically to pump blood through a dying body. Only Keara could save him. Only she had a magical ability that would heal him. Alviss would never let her go search for Thoren.

She had to find him on her own.

Taking a deep breath, she concentrated on what she saw when Thoren contacted her. Woods. That didn't help. Trees grew abundantly in Draconi lands. Blood. Oh, Goddess, there was so much blood. On the ground. On Thoren. Where was he? Fire. How many woods had fire? She closed her eyes, her breathing rapid, her muscles tense. Could she find him?

She had to. Failure was not an option.

Closing her eyes, she concentrated on Thoren's face, his eyes, his smile, the way his muscular body moved as he walked. Where was he?

Her body shattered, torn apart bit by bit, and as a cloud of dust, she flew out of the Temple and across the ground. Trees and fields passed in a blur, dark blobs in the night as she soared across them. And then she dove, crashing through limbs and leaves, reforming as she landed on the ground.

Trees surrounded her, their branches creaking in the wind, leaves rustling together. A shiver darted down her spine, the hairs on her neck rising. Straining her ears, she listened for any sounds besides the tree limbs croaking a warning. Nothing.

Not even insects chirped.

And then she heard the crackling of a fire.

Sticking to the shadows, Keara followed the noise, creeping up to a clearing. Five fires flickered in the open. The scent of dead bodies assailed her nostrils, and bile rose in her throat. Several heads lay scattered, eyes and mouths stretched wide. She swallowed. Those dead were beyond her help.

Keara crept closer, wondering who had the strength to remove a man's head. Certainly not any of the soldiers in River's Run with their small swords. Her foot tripped over something on the ground and she stumbled, palms slapping against the nearest tree as she caught herself from falling. Turning she stared at the dark ground, trying to find what she had tripped over.

A body. Keara felt a chill slide down her spine and she almost walked away until she noticed the abundance of blond hair. Goddess, no! Kneeling, she brushed the hair out of his face, slamming a hand over her mouth. Enar lay on his back, eyes closed, his shirt singed in a circular pattern, same as an energy ball made. But who would throw an energy ball at him?

Her fingers felt for the pulsing vein on his neck and pulled away.

Dead. Her eyes darted around the clearing, but saw no movement outside of the shadows cast by the fires. Where was Thoren? If she wanted to find Thoren, she needed Enar.

Since the night Thoren unlocked her magic, healing did not leave her as tired as it used to. But the episode with Conr shook her confidence. How could she help Enar if she hadn't been able to draw the illness out of a small boy?

Nothing left but to try.

Keara placed her hands over the scorch mark on Enar's chest, closing her eyes. Her palms began to tingle as she imagined his body healing. From deep within her came the power to counteract his death, to absorb what had happened to him and change it into life. Her magic coursed through her veins, winding its way to her palms, where it flowed into Enar's lifeless body. Using her imagination, she guided the power to his heart, forcing the chambers to fill and empty, until with a shudder it beat on its own. Channeling the magic into his burn, she repaired the charred skin, watching as the flesh color bled into the blackened area. So much for the tunic. She was a healer, not a tailor. She kept her hands on his chest until he drew in a gasping breath, his eyes flying open.

One hand snuck out, grasping her wrist with the desperation of a starving male being shown food.

"You're hurting me," she hissed and he released his grip.

"What are you, female?" Enar whispered, his voice raw.

Keara saw pinpoints of light on the periphery of her vision as she shook her head at Enar. Returning the dead to life left her more drained than healing an illness. Although this time wasn't as bad as the time in River's Run.

Keara shivered as that healing memory visited her conscious. The only thing then that had saved her from certain death was that no one but her knew the girl died. Keara thrust the memory away. Now was not the time for remembering.

"I am me."

Enar raised his head, staring at his chest as he brushed his hand across the singed tunic. His eyes narrowed on Keara. "You are special. I owe you my life, it seems. Last I saw, Thoren was this way and he was in trouble."

Keara's breath hitched. What was wrong with Thoren? How far away was he? Would she be able to heal him? Her heart pounded and she wiped her palms on her legs.

Enar rolled to his feet, shaking off her hand as he steadied himself. He bent to pick up his sword before starting through the trees. Keara followed behind him and tried not to gag. The stench of death hung in the air like a palpable cloud.

Don't breathe, don't breathe, don't breathe.

She yanked the neck of her tunic over her nose. Whew. That helped cut the stench down a bit. At least Enar stuck to the tree line, not venturing into the clearing. Did he not notice the odor? Maybe as a warrior he was used to the smell of blood. Enar grabbed her arm, pulling her down with him behind a bush.

"It looks clear, but I last saw Simon and the Draconi here. Thoren was over there," he pointed to yet another tree, "and he'd been stabbed."

"Stabbed?" Her voice came out in a high-pitched squeak.

"That's the way it looked, although how he let Simon stab him is a mystery. Your job is to heal Thoren and get him out of here."

"Can you transport him? Because I just learned how to transport myself. I've never tried taking anyone with me."

"Best learn. Heal him up well enough and he'll transport himself. Now go, but be careful."

"Where are you going?"

"To make sure we're alone."

"How will I find you?"

"Don't worry, I'll find you."

Enar touched her shoulder as he disappeared into the trees, the shadows claiming him. Great, how was she going to get Thoren back to the Temple? What if she tried to transport him and injured him in the process?

Stop worrying and cross that stream when you

get there.

Hunched over, she skipped from shadow to shadow until she came to the tree Enar had pointed to. Her gaze searched the ground, her heart beating double-time. A shadow glittered where light struck it, sparks like midnight diamonds coursed through strands of hair. Hair that was attached to a head, that was attached to a body covered in a black tunic.

Thoren.

The feel of blood seeping over her hands, her body growing cold as her blood seeped into the ground slammed into her and her breath froze inside her chest. Was he dead?

Keara rushed to his side, crushing leaves underfoot, not bothering to conceal her steps. Her mate lay injured, dying. She dropped to her knees, checking his pulse, not believing what her eyes told her. Dead.

No! He couldn't be dead. He couldn't leave her without him. What would she do without him? His body grew fuzzy and she blinked rapidly. She had to heal him. She had to. But could she?

Before Enar, she had only raised the dead once and it occurred immediately after the girl died. Raising Enar took more power than when she raised the girl. Would she be able to raise the dead twice in a night?

She had no choice. Without her, Thoren would remain dead.

Rolling Thoren onto his side, she smoothed the hair off his face. Dark lashes rested against his skin, looking peaceful despite the pain lines radiating from his eyes and mouth. Blood stained his tunic and leather pants, stiffening the material.

She placed one hand onto the hardened blood covering his back and the other hand over the wound on his stomach. Closing her eyes, she imagined her magic rising in her, flowing through her until her palms tingled with its force. Her body grew heated, the magic begging to be released, to heal. She shoved that power out of her hands, pushing it into Thoren's wounds, forcing it to heal his injuries.

In her mind's eye, she saw the tears in his abdomen and back and drew the jagged edges together, her magic sewing the wounds closed.

So far, so good. A little dizziness never hurt anyone. And what was she supposed to do? Lie down and rest? Thoren remained dead and until he breathed, she needed to continue pouring her magic into him.

He had lost a lot of blood. What spread across the bed of leaves couldn't be returned to his veins, so she needed to start from scratch. His blood supply needed replenishing. Shooting another wave of magic into him, she pictured drops of blood expanding, growing, filling his veins. She forced the blood through his circulatory system, warming his limbs. And then she sent a burst of power into his heart, restarting it.

Thoren jerked as the power wave shot through him. She watched for his chest to rise and fall, but it remained unmoving. Why wasn't he breathing? What did she do wrong?

Oh. A body needs air. Judging by the black spots dancing along her peripheral vision, she might need a breath too. She took a deep breath, rolled Thoren onto his back and breathed into his mouth. His chest rose and fell. The blackness crept through her vision, reducing it to pinpricks of light. She would not faint. Fainting was not an option.

Another deep breath. Another exhale into Thoren's mouth. This time after his chest fell, he sucked in a breath. And then another.

Keara smiled. Her magic worked. Thoren lived. The pinpoints of light at the edges of her sight cascaded across her vision until Thoren disappeared from view. Peace mingled with exhaustion washed through her as she toppled beside him, succumbing to the darkness, oblivious to the leaves cushioning her fall.

****

Thoren gasped, his limbs jerking, pulling him from darkness. His lids flew open but all he saw was shadows darting in the leaves. What just happened? With a sickening thud, it came flooding back to him: losing his magic, being stabbed with a titanium sword, dying. But he couldn't have died if he still breathed. His hand slapped over his stomach, feeling the dried blood and gashed tunic.

By the Goddess. It wasn't a dream. Then that would mean Enar was dead. He rolled to his side, turning toward where Enar went down.

No tall, blond body. Plenty of soldier's bodies littered the area. His nose wrinkled. Death stank.

All right. So if Enar wasn't where he fell, then where was the Watcher?

Leaves rustled as feet pressed against them. Thoren started to turn, then thought the better of it. Not that he was a coward, but he felt weak, drained of energy.

Like he'd died and been brought back to life.

"You were right. She came."

Time didn't diminish the whiny nasal tone of Simon's voice. But the whine wasn't what struck him. Who was the she Simon referred to?

"I told you. I have my female and it looks like you took the bitch's nephew down." Draconi. Magic layered his voice, an unmistakable Draconi trait.

The bitch's nephew? Was he referring to Ari? And which female? Where was the rogue Draconi? Thoren listened, trying to extrapolate the locations of Simon and the Draconi based on the noises they made.

"Did you discard the sword?" The Draconi again,

this time closer to Thoren's feet.

"Of course. It's thirty paces from here. That's far enough away, right?" Simon's voice sounded from Thoren's back, close to the ground.

"It is. Now take your sword and finish this one off."

"But I thought we were taking her with us?" Thoren winced at the whine in Simon's voice.

The Draconi sighed. "Not her, you dumb goat. Him."

"But I already killed him."

"Obviously you didn't because he's still alive."

"Are you sure? He looks dead."

"Stop arguing and kill him."

He was not going down without a fight. Thoren rolled, focusing his magic into his hand, but before he lobbed the energy ball at Simon, blood exploded in a rain over his face and torso. Two thuds sounded as he wiped the blood from his eyes.

Enar stood over him, Blood Seeker dripping red. Simon's head lay in the opposite direction from his body. Thoren's eyes met Enar's, both males blinking. Blood must have splashed in his friend's eyes, since he'd never seen Enar tear up. He had no room to talk, Enar's figure fuzzed out and it had nothing to do with Simon's blood on his face. Thoren drew his sleeve across his eyes.

Clap, clap, clap. "Thank you. He was getting annoying."

Thoren lowered his arm, head turning toward the voice. The Draconi stood clapping his hands, his face hidden in the shadows of his cloak's cowl. Thoren ran his gaze down the Draconi's body, trying to find some clue as to who he was, but the drapes of the cloak hid any identifying features. Even his feet hid in shadows.

A flicker of light caught his eye, drawing his gaze to a lump lying on the ground close to the

Draconi's shoes. Red hair sparkled as shafts from the firelight danced upon it. Curly red hair.

Keara.

Thoren's lip pulled into a snarl and before his brain gave the command, his body moved, leaping to his feet. He tried to shoot an energy ball but nothing happened. The Draconi jerked, glancing between his hands and Thoren. His face might be hidden in shadows, but surprise radiated off him.

Which would be the last thing the bastard felt. Energy balls might down the enemy, but nothing beat the satisfying thud of his fist. The male wanted Thoren's mate and for that, he must die.

Thoren sprang forward, tackling the Draconi around the waist, slamming them both into the ground. His fist pulled back, but before it hit flesh, the male bucked his hips, throwing Thoren onto his back, the heavy body of the male landing on him with a breath-jarring thud.

The Draconi sat on his legs, trying to cast a spell and getting nowhere. Enar jumped into the melee, kicking the Draconi in the shoulder, flipping him off Thoren. The Draconi rolled in a smooth movement, crouching. Thoren sprang to his feet as Enar pointed a sword at the Draconi.

"Titanium is a bitch, eh?"

The Draconi's head wavered as he turned to Enar and then Thoren.

"Bid your aunt greetings from me." Jumping to his feet, he spun and ran, his cloak disappearing into the shadows. Enar sprinted after him, Blood Seeker in one hand, the titanium sword in the other.

Thoren scrambled across the ground until he reached Keara. How did Keara get here? Did Simon and the Draconi harm her? His hands flew over her body, checking for wounds. Nothing. Then why was she unconscious?

"Keara!" He shook her a little, hoping for a

response, getting nothing but a moan.

Her brow felt cool to his touch as he stroked her hair from her face. Her chest rose and fell, her pulse fluttering against his fingers. Once again, he needed to take her to the Temple to be healed. No other male he knew took their mate to the Temple for healing this often. Maybe she was better off without him.

As if dragons could live without their mates. He might act like a fool, but he loved her. There. He admitted it. He loved Keara and he'd be a poor excuse for a male if she died out here in the woods.

He gathered her against his chest, preparing to transport them to the Temple. His body should be splitting into pieces, floating through the air and yet, nothing happened.

Footsteps approached, running, twigs snapping. Thoren laid Keara back on the ground and spun on his heel, still crouching. Enar broke through the shadows of the trees carrying both swords, breathing like a dragon chased him.

"Lost him," Enar gasped, dropping the swords as he bent over, hands on his knees.

He didn't care about the rogue Draconi when his mate was injured. "She won't wake. I need to get her back to the Temple but that sword is prohibiting it. I don't know what's wrong with her!"

"It might have," he gasped for breath, "something to do with her...raising both of us...from the dead."

"We died?" Wasn't he a barrel of intelligence? Of course they died. Hadn't he seen Enar dropped with an energy ball and felt his own life slip through his fingers?

Enar, still breathing loud enough to hear a mile away, picked up Blood Seeker and wiped the blade on Simon's tunic before sheathing it. "Being skewered generally does that to a person."

Thoren glanced to Keara. How had she raised them? He ran a hand through his hair. A bloody hand. He cursed.

"I need running practice." Enar knelt beside Thoren, slapping a big palm against his back.

"Or bigger lungs."

"Thank you." Thoren clasped Enar on the shoulder. Enar shrugged.

"What do we do with the titanium sword?"

"The Draconi mentioned a safe distance of thirty paces. If you hide it, can you remember where it is?"

"Do I look like a dumb goat?"

Thoren stared at Enar.

"Thanks. It's nice to see you again too. I'll go hide the sword. Don't leave without me."

Thoren wrapped his arms around Keara, listening to her ragged breathing and stroked a hand through her hair. She raised them both from the dead. No wonder she lay in a coma. Using strong magic had a tendency to drain the user of energy. And he was hard pressed to think of a more draining example than raising a person from the dead.

He hadn't even known that was possible. Had she known about this ability? Obviously she had, or she wouldn't be here now. What a rare gift she possessed. Myths featured tales of Draconi raising the dead. At least he always believed them myths until now. Maybe Enar was wrong. Maybe they hadn't died.

And maybe dragons didn't know what to do with their wings.

Along with having a powerful healing talent and the ability to absorb magic, she was a death raiser. Once the knowledge of that little ability got loose, peace would become non-existent. Everyone would be knocking on their door for her help when a loved one died.

He refused to let that happen. She'd be drained

of all life if she raised everyone who died.

He'd have to hide her ability. Only a few could know and those few must keep the secret closely guarded.

Her hair felt stiff under the stroke of his palm.

His mate came for him. Faced his enemies for him. Risked her life for him. His job meant nothing compared to Keara's love.

"It's done." Enar placed a hand on Thoren's shoulder. "Is it far enough for you to get us out of here?"

Thoren focused on forming an energy ball in his palm. Yes, the sword was far enough away.

"Hold on."

Thoren closed his eyes, imagining the Temple, imagining them all landing in the Courtyard. Their bodies shattered, driving through the air in a cloud of dust, reforming in the Courtyard. Thoren ran inside, carrying Keara, running until he reached the infirmary wing.

Where was Annaliese? Thoren called the healer with his mind. The air swirled in front of them and with a muted pop Annaliese appeared.

"What...By the Goddess! Bring her in here!" She shoved open a door and Thoren rushed inside, laying Keara on the bed.

"What happened? She left to tell Father about a vision she saw of you injured. Are you well?"

"Well enough. She won't wake. Can you help her?"

Annaliese placed a hand on Keara's brow and closed her eyes. Thoren watched Keara's chest rise and fall, his heart thudding, his mouth dry. Annaliese's eyes flew open, wide and frightened.

"She raised you!"

By the Goddess's teeth, how did the priestess know that? Did she possess the ability to forge her way into another's mind without permission?

"Don't say that out loud. Do you know what others will do if they discover her gift?" Thoren crossed his arms.

"I'm sorry. It's just...not even my mother had the ability to raise the dead. I've never seen it done before."

"How did you know what she did?"

"I need Aryana. Only she has the ability to heal Keara. I'll return." The air shimmered as she disappeared.

"You get the feeling she doesn't want to speak on how she knew Keara was a death raiser?" Enar slumped against the door, arms folded.

Speaking as he moved, Thoren grabbed a chair and placed it by Keara's side. "Just because we can mind-speak doesn't mean we can invade another's mind. Unless we project them to another, our thoughts belong to us."

"You sure about that?"

Thoren held Keara's chilled hand. *Come on, love, wake. Don't die. Don't leave me alone. I need you.*

"Thoren?"

That's right. Enar was carrying on a conversation. Or trying to. What was the question?

"I don't know." *What you're saying, what I'm doing, if Keara will live.*

"She'll live. Ari will work her magic—"

"Ari? You're on a pet name basis with my aunt?" A Watcher did not bed the Draconi High Priestess. Even if said Watcher was his best friend. The females they met on Thoren's journey across the land to please Balthor had been one thing. No harm done, both parties enjoyed themselves, who cared?

But his aunt?

Any male besides a Draconi who touched the High Priestess did so on punishment of death.

Son of a bloody goat.

Enar's red cheeks gave it away, his darting gaze

sealed the deal.

"You didn't."

Enar shrugged. "I have Lily now."

"She's my aunt!" *And the High Priestess.*

"You didn't have a problem with it when it was a female in some village."

"But Ari is not a female in some village. She's my aunt!"

"It's over. We ended it."

"You ended it? You mean it was more than once?"

"Do you really want to hear this now?" Enar gestured to Keara. "What's done is done. In the past. Over."

Thoren shoved a hand through his hair, locking his jaw to keep from leaping at Enar. His hand cranked into a fist and he fought to straighten it out.

He would not hit his best friend. He would not hit Enar. He would not.

Pop! Pop!

Aryana and Annaliese appeared in front of them, both females hurrying to Keara's side. Ari stopped, though, and looked from Thoren to Enar and back again, her eyes narrowing. One finger pointed at Thoren.

"We'll discuss your discussion later."

Since when did the priestesses start invading minds? Or had they been doing it all along and Thoren just now realized it?

"Move away from the bed." Aryana motioned him back and Thoren scooted the chair against the wall.

He shut his eyes and focused on controlling the anger before it controlled him. His mate was dying, his best friend and his aunt had an affair and his knees threatened to embarrass him by giving out. What else could go wrong?

Oh yes. The rogue Draconi escaped.

Thoren took a deep breath. As Enar said, what was past was over and done. No use getting riled up. He needed to let all his emotions go and focus on Keara. She was the only thing that mattered.

When he opened his eyes, Enar stood in front of him. Thoren slugged him on the shoulder and walked to the bed.

Aryana rested her hand against Keara's brow, eyes closed, her face relaxed.

When she spoke, her gaze fixed on Thoren. "She is drained of energy. Annaliese told me what Keara did. I'm sorry, but it will have to be reported to Alviss."

"I know. I just don't want everyone knowing. Can you heal her?"

"I can try. No guarantees."

Annaliese placed both hands over Keara's heart and Aryana placed hers on top of Annaliese's. Chills broke out over Thoren's skin as Aryana chanted in a language he'd never heard. The singsong words rose and fell, filling the room with a spell as old as the Draconi race, a spell of powerful magic. Aryana's hands started to glow, the light spilling into Annaliese's.

A current shot through the room, ricocheting off the stone walls, bathing them in a blue glow. Thoren felt the magic push against his skin, wanting his power, his strength.

The gentle touch pulled back, returning to blast into him, sucking on his magic, drawing out a small portion of it to hover over the priestess's joined hands.

Thoren gasped, remaining upright by pure will. Enar yelled as the blue current pierced him, as it pulled out a piece of his energy. Rather strange, that the spell would affect Enar, since it seemed to be a spell for finding magical energy and Watchers held no magic. No matter. As long as it helped Keara,

Thoren didn't care where the energy came from.

More energy filled the room, blue light pouring through the windows, the cracks in the door, the walls. Small magical portions from who-knew-how-many formed a ball of blue energy that hovered above Aryana's hands, growing larger with each stream of light that entered it. The priestesses exchanged a look, a silent communication, and removed their hands from Keara's chest. The ball slammed into Keara, bowing her off the bed as it covered her with its glow. Keara gasped in air, her body slamming into the mattress as the blue glow intensified.

"What did you do?" Thoren rushed to Keara's side, but hesitated to touch her.

"Don't touch her! The spell might target you instead." Annaliese grabbed his arm.

"I gave her more energy," Aryana said. "She'd drained hers raising both of you. Do I even want to know how the finest reconnaissance specialists ever managed to get themselves killed?"

Keara's chest rose and fell, rose and fell, in a steady rhythm. At least her breathing seemed stable. That had to mean something.

"They had a titanium sword," Enar said.

"Titanium?" Annaliese gasped.

"How did they discover the effect titanium has on a Draconi?" Aryana's eyes popped wide.

He wondered the same thing. "I don't know, but the Draconi—"

"A Draconi?"

"He was working with one of the lords from Keara's town. He said he wanted revenge. He seemed to recognize me, though, because he referred to me as the 'bitch's nephew' and told me to give my aunt his regards. I'm assuming he meant you."

Aryana stopped breathing as she exchanged a look with Annaliese. "What did he look like?" Her

247

voice shook.

"I don't know. He wore a cloak that concealed his face."

"He ran fast," Enar chimed in. "I lost him and I don't normally lose my prey."

"Maybe that had something to do with you gasping like an old dragon."

"You try running after being killed with an energy ball and then rising from the dead. See how fast you go."

"Enough!" Aryana sliced a hand through the air. "You need to report these findings to the Council."

"Report away. I'm needed here with Keara."

Annaliese placed a hand on his arm, her face a mask of healer's kindness. "Keara is going nowhere nor is she waking until the energy is released into her body. See how it's still visible? She'll wake when the blue disappears, which won't be for some time. Go make your report and return."

Thoren snarled and Enar yanked him back. "Relax, Thoren. She's right."

He needed to stay by her side. Keara needed him. What if she died when he wasn't here? What if she died while he was?

Shaking off Enar's hand, Thoren turned to his aunt. "We need to talk."

"No, we do not. My body is mine to give as I will and you will not report it either."

"What's to stop me?"

For the first time in his life, he saw a malevolent glitter in his aunt's eye that gave him pause.

"I know something you don't want told and you know something I'd like to keep secret. We are at an impasse, are we not?"

Aryana, his aunt, the High Priestess, was using blackmail? On him?

And using it quite successfully, might he add.

Why was he so upset with Enar and Aryana?

Because she was his aunt? Because his beliefs had been violated? Or was he upset over Keara and channeling his anger elsewhere?

Thoren ran a hand through his hair and glanced at Keara, who lay with a peaceful look on her face. Was his sense of right and wrong worth her life?

"Deal. You have my word I will not mention your...indiscretion if you do not mention Keara's ability."

"I'm glad you see things my way. Now go and report. Return by morning and Keara will be as you left her."

Thoren clapped a hand against Enar's back and transported them to the Council's Chamber. Instead of sitting in their chairs, the thirteen males clustered around the seeing ball.

"How is my granddaughter? I cannot see her in the ball," Alviss shoved his way out of the pack of males and shuffled toward Thoren.

"How..." oh that's right. The seeing ball. "Aryana performed a spell to replenish her energy. So you saw everything?"

"Not everything. Enough to know what Keara can do. Enough to see my best reconnaissance specialists get their arses kicked into the grave. We've been discussing Keara since then and missed the rest. Where's the rogue?"

"He got away." Enar glared at the males.

"You lost him. No whelp of mine—" Viktor snarled, his face red.

Alviss pointed his cane at Viktor. "Quiet! I'm tired of your squabbles." He turned back to Enar as Viktor continued to snarl. "How did the Draconi escape?"

Enar shrugged. "He ran, I chased. He disappeared. I looked around and nothing. Keara was injured so I returned. The titanium sword is hidden for your retrieval."

"And do you know who the Draconi is?"

"No sir."

"He apparently knew Aryana. Said I was the 'bitch's nephew' and to give my aunt his regards," Thoren said. "May I go now? I need to see Keara."

His palms itched to leave as his heart thudded hard enough to move his tunic.

Balthor's face wrinkled into a smile. *It's about time you admitted Keara is your mate, son.*

Before he made a sarcastic comment to his father, Alviss's next words cranked his fists into tight knots.

"We'll bring Aryana to us. You will stay to hear this."

Removing the snarl from his lip took some effort. His mate needed him.

Two blinks and a popping noise later and Aryana stood beside him. Her face pale, her eyes snapped wide, she stared at Alviss. Taking a deep breath, she exhaled through her nose.

"Alviss. How nice of you to bring me here without warning."

"Aryana. Thoren tells me the rogue Draconi who attacked him seemed to know you. Do you know who he is?"

Aryana cut a quick glance to Thoren before returning her glare to Alviss. "My nephew did not describe the male, only that he wore a hood. Not even I can definitely determine who someone is without a description."

"Give us your best guess."

"I have banished a couple of Draconi during my service to the Goddess. The most recent banishment occurred four months ago. My guess would be Fasolt."

Alviss's eyes narrowed. "You banished someone without my knowledge?"

"It is not required for me to inform you of those

250

who are banished. In case you forgot, I am the High Priestess. Part of the duties involves banishing those that need it. And Fasolt needed it." She snarled.

"Why did you banish him?"

Aryana's fists clenched. "He assaulted one of my priestesses, claiming it was her fault he did not see the Goddess during his session with her. She almost died. His face was...damaged in the struggle to subdue him. He swore revenge upon me. It sounds like him, but again, I was not there to see."

"Did either of you know Fasolt?" Alviss turned to Thoren and Enar.

As one, the two shook their heads.

"No, sir," Thoren answered for the two of them.

"This presents further issues for us to discuss. You can go now," Alviss waved his hand and Aryana disappeared. "You may go too, Thoren. No, Enar, you stay. We need to know how to recover that titanium sword."

Enar nodded at Thoren. Thoren slapped a hand on Enar's arm.

I'm sorry for overreacting.

It's all right. Get back to your female. Wish I could see my woman now.

You will soon.

Yes, but not soon enough.

Picturing the healing room, Thoren transported to Keara's side. The blue haze still covered her, cloaking her in light. His mate. His love. His life.

He pulled the chair next to the bed and sat. When she woke, he wanted to be the first thing she saw.

Chapter 19

Warmth insulated her, cocooning her like a blanket on a cold day. A heavy warmth. Very heavy. Almost suffocating. Keara pushed at the heaviness, trying to find the corner on the blanket to yank it off her body. Maybe if her eyes would open she could see what to do. But her lids felt heavy, almost as heavy as the weight covering her, and the effort to get them open spent energy she didn't have. Better to try to remove the blanket sightless.

She shifted, but the heaviness remained. Blue light snuck under the seals of her lids, bathing her in its glow. It wanted inside her, to grow, to live. Instead of running from it, she embraced it, a trace of a thought telling her the blue light was there to help.

The light shot through her, filling her with its energy, its power. She felt bits of strength from many sources within the light, all working together to empower her. Nothing to lose by accepting the gift. Opening herself to the power, she let it course through her veins, through her heart.

And as fast as it came, it left.

What in the name of the gods was that? She felt energized, powerful, a mountain among hills. Until she opened her eyes and saw a mural of dragons flying over clouds. She lay flat on her back in a healing room.

Again.

She tried to push the covers off, only to be stopped by a warm hand. Turning her head, her gaze ran up Thoren's arm, meeting his eyes. She smiled.

Before she could take a breath, strong arms yanked her against a muscular chest. She breathed in Thoren's scent and her body lit up like a fire on a cold day. He lived. She lived. Relief flooded her. What had she been so mad at him about?

Thank the Goddess you're alive. You had me worried. Don't ever do that again.

Back at you.

"You're holding my granddaughter too tight."

Thoren's grip relaxed, but he didn't let her go.

She twisted in his arms until she saw Alviss sitting on the opposite side of the bed.

"Hey, Gramps."

"Hey, yourself. How do you feel?"

"I feel...weird. As if pieces of others live in me. Odd, eh?"

"Not really." Annaliese stepped into view, her hands folded in the sleeves of her gown. "We used a spell that took a little energy from each Draconi in the Temple to replenish what was missing in you. That feeling will wear off over the next several days as their energies disperse."

Thoren reluctantly released her and Keara scooted back against the headboard. She wanted to be alone with Thoren, but as no one made a move to leave, she knew it was a pointless wish.

Alviss patted her hand. "Do you feel like telling us about the rogue Draconi?"

Keara shrugged. "He and Lord Simon captured me in River's Run. He said he needed me to get revenge on his enemies. I'm not sure why. That's about it. I didn't see him in the woods when I found Thoren. I...passed out," she was not going to mention why, "and here I am. What happened?"

Eyes widening, she listened as Thoren recanted what happened after she lost consciousness. So the rogue Draconi had a possible name, a possible motive and was on the loose. While important, more pressing matters worried her.

Did Thoren know she raised him and Enar from the dead? What would happen to her when he realized her secret ability? Would he still consider her his mate, or would it be too much for him to handle?

"Now about you." Another pat from Alviss followed by a serious expression.

Uh-oh. This didn't look good.

"How long have you known you could raise the dead?"

Keara's breath caught. Froze right up, leaving her wide-eyed and sweaty palmed. Alviss knew. They all knew. By the Goddess, what would they do to her? It didn't take a genius to realize that while the Draconi might be a race seeped in magic, even they didn't have raisers of the dead. Fear wrapped its tendrils about her heart.

What kind of an aberration was she?

More hand patting, Thoren joining in. She grasped his palm and he squeezed back, that one small motion freeing the locked air, allowing her lungs to move.

"I did it once before, but no one knew the girl had died. They just thought I healed her, which was strange enough, but they would have killed me if they'd known what I was capable of."

"Your gift is rare—"

Thoren snorted at Alviss's words. "That's the understatement of the month."

Alviss gave Thoren a glare that made Keara happy she wasn't on its receiving end. And to think, Gramps seemed like such a nice old male. "As I was saying. Your gift is extremely rare and as such, we need you to keep silent about it."

"Huh?" Of all the things she expected him to say, this one never crossed her mind. Silent? What did he expect? Her to stand on the Temple roof and shout that she could raise the dead? What kind of an idiot did he think she was?

Where was the censor? The fright? "You're not scared of me?"

"Scared of you?"

"Why would we be scared of you?" Thoren squeezed her hand.

"Because I'm different. No one has the ability to raise the dead."

"I suspect Mother did and just didn't tell anyone."

All eyes turned to Annaliese, who blushed. So she wasn't the only one with odd abilities. She took after her grandmother.

"I also suspected. But if your mate doesn't want to tell you something, you shouldn't force it." Alviss narrowed his gaze on Thoren. "Keep that in mind, hatchling, and things will go well for you."

"You really don't mind?" She'd been so worried about their reaction, afraid they'd disown her, return her to River's Run. For them to not mind was...shocking. And yet, gratifying.

"Mind?" Alviss waved a hand. "No. But I caution you in this gift. Do not promote it. I'd prefer you not even use it except in an emergency. And even then be careful with it."

Not a problem. Raising the dead left her with a foot in the grave and that she didn't care to experience again. "Agreed. Unless my mate is injured."

Thoren squeezed her hand. *Mate? So you will join with me?*

Of course. I love you, even when you thoroughly aggravate me.

Me? Aggravate you?

"Ah. So you accept him as your mate?" Alviss let loose with a wrinkled grin.

255

"I do." Keara looked Thoren in the eyes, smiling at the love she found in his gaze. Her mate. Forever.

Annaliese clapped her hands together, her normally calm face exploding with excitement. "A mating ceremony! I love the mating ceremony. It's so touching. I'll go let Aryana know." With that she disappeared.

"I should do the same. Go that is." Alviss pecked Keara on the cheek. "I'll see you at your mating." He disappeared in the time it took her to blink.

"You will mate with me?" Thoren's face was a mask of pure joy as he looked at her.

"I said I would."

"So I'm forgiven?"

"I didn't say that, dragon. I love you and I'm more than happy to mate with you, but I don't want you thinking you can hide important things from me."

Thoren lowered his gaze. "I was wrong. I just didn't know what I would do since I couldn't continue doing my job."

"I don't understand why not."

"Only unmated males are reconnaissance specialists."

"Then why don't you work for the Council? Maybe they have an opening."

Maybe that was the wrong thing to say seeing how Thoren stared at her like she grew a third eye. Without warning, he grabbed her in a tight hug, pulling her against his chest.

"I'm so glad you're mine. Are you all right? Do you mind if I leave for a bit? I need to take care of some things before the mating ceremony."

"Wait a minute. The mating ceremony is today?" Her squeaky voice was an embarrassment, but that's what happened when a female found out her mating day was today and by the feel of things, her hair still had leaves in it.

"Of course it is. It'll be held at sundown as is normal."

"What do I need to do?" How could he possibly expect her to be ready in time? She still felt weak. But weakness wouldn't stop her. She wanted him like a parched throat desired water.

"All you have to do is show up. Repeat the words back to the priestess."

"What words?"

"She'll tell them to you. I'll let the rest be a surprise, but it will end in a joining."

"I know that. Wait. No one else sees this joining, do they?"

"What kind of voyeurs do you think we are? Of course not. The joining happens in private."

Keara exhaled a breath she didn't realize she held. "So—"

"Ah-ha! The soon-to-be mated pair." Aryana and Annaliese popped into the room, excitement in their eyes. Aryana walked to Keara's side and waved her hand at Thoren. "Shoo. We need to prepare Keara for the ritual. Go do something else with yourself."

Thoren kissed her, a quick buss on the lips that left her aching for more. Tonight. Tonight she'd have all of him she wanted.

"See you later, love." The air shimmered where he sat, condensing with a small pop as he disappeared.

Aryana placed a hand on Keara's arm. "Are those leaves in her hair?"

Annaliese peered closer. "We have a lot of work to get her ready for tonight."

"Come along, Keara. The day's half over and we haven't even started working on you yet."

Hustling her out of bed, the two priestesses shuffled her into the bathing room.

It looked like she'd be ready for her mating day after all.

Chapter 20

Keara stood to one side of the altar in the chapel and stared at the stained glass windows lining the room. Heat rose in her cheeks. Were those really pictures of dragons in intimate poses? In front of the Goddess's altar? Not that she was a prude, but she still had a lot to learn about Draconi culture. A grin crossed her lips as she thought about the looks of mortification on the faces of her grandmother and the priests in River's Run if they saw pictures like these hanging in the Goddess's chapel.

Good thing they weren't here.

Although, to be fair, she wouldn't mind her grandmother being present for her mating ceremony.

Thoren smiled and the reality of the situation slammed into her. Today she took him for a mate. Until she died, he would be hers. Someone who accepted her completely, without reservation. Someone who thought her magic was wonderful. Someone she loved more than life itself.

Never in her wildest dreams had she thought to find a mate. And yet here she stood in front of Draconi witnesses and intimately posed dragons to prove to all she belonged to Thoren and he to her.

Thoren's gaze raked her body as heat gleamed in his eyes. Even she had to admit Annaliese and Aryana had done a wonderful job dressing her.

After washing her three times in perfumed waters, they rubbed her skin with oils until she felt like a piece of meat prepared for consumption.

Which, judging from the look in Thoren's eyes, wasn't too far from the truth.

She smoothed her palms over the green fabric of her dress. The nicest dress she'd ever had the privilege of wearing. Made of silk, the dress's long sleeves hung in points past her wrists and left her shoulders bare to the cool breeze circulating in the chapel. A girdle woven from gold hung about her waist and a circlet of yellow and blue flowers sat on her head.

It might be vain, but she knew she looked good. Thoren winked at her and her heart knocked against her ribs.

His black hair hung freely about his shoulders, thick and straight, begging for her fingers to run through it. His tunic was green silk, matching her dress and he wore black leather pants that hugged his finely sculpted arse and thighs. He rolled his shoulders back and Keara felt wetness between her legs. One side of Thoren's mouth curved into a grin. Did he smell her arousal?

If her face got any hotter, someone would need to throw water on it.

A squeak of hinges, followed by a rustle of fabric, sounded from behind the altar, and Keara turned, seeing Aryana glide through the door. Dressed in her finery, the High Priestess looked liked a beautiful handmaiden of the Goddess. Her black hair hung in a straight line to her waist, her face a mask of perfection.

Good bone structure. Keara giggled at the thought and then clamped her lips together. What a thing to think of on her mating day. How nervous was she? Amazing how she wanted to mate with Thoren more than anything and yet she apparently had a case of nerves.

Aryana held out her hands as she faced them. Thoren placed his left hand in Aryana's right one.

When Keara didn't move, Aryana wiggled her fingers indicating Keara should do the same. Keara grabbed the priestess's outstretched hand with her right one. If she needed to hold hands, someone should have explained that earlier.

As long as she got Thoren in the end, she didn't care.

"We are gathered today to witness the joining of Thoren, son of Balthor and Moira to Keara, descendant of Alviss." Aryana placed Keara's hand in Thoren's. "Do you Thoren, take this female for your mate?"

Thoren squeezed her hand. "I do."

"And do you Keara, take Thoren for your mate?"

Did she ever. "I do."

"May the Goddess shine her pleasure on your joining and bless you with many offspring." Aryana pulled a red ribbon from a hidden fold in her dress and wrapped it loosely around their wrists. "With this ribbon to symbolize your joined blood, I present your union to the witnesses here."

Thoren's family, Alviss and Annaliese stood up first, clapping, the rest of the witnesses following. Thoren belonged to her now. Keara let a happy grin plaster her face as Thoren's and her family surrounded them. Even Jamie managed to come, hobbling around on his recently mended leg, proclaiming to anyone listening that Thoren and Keara were adopting him. Hugs and names were given, compliments on her dress and hair spoken, fingers touching the silk of her gown. A veritable whirlwind of family and friends rushed around her, pulling her into the vortex, accepting her as one of them.

Wasn't life grand?

****

While waiting for the tipsy priestess to refill their wine glasses, Thoren watched his mate laugh with his mother, the two females chatting like they'd known each other forever. Waiting to have her alone caused an ache between his legs that no amount of shifting squelched.

"I'm leaving."

Shifting might not squelch his erection, but Enar's words withered the thing right up.

"Leaving?"

Enar stood beside him, arms crossed. "You know, that thing you do when you depart one place for another?" Thoren closed his eyes and shook his head. When he opened them, Enar had a half-grin in place. "I'm taking my woman home."

"No more missions for you?"

"None. I'm your Watcher. Since I'm assigned to you, if you stay, I stay. No more missions."

"What will you do?"

Enar shrugged.

"I'm going to sit on the Council—"

"Holy altars, Thoren. What were you thinking? Oh wait, you obviously weren't."

Thoren shook his head. "Just because you don't like the Council doesn't mean I don't like it. It gives me a chance to work at a job that I enjoy. It's close enough to going on missions that I'll enjoy myself. Maybe you can join me."

"When dragons prefer staying on the ground instead of flying."

"You might like it once Viktor leaves."

Blue fire flashed in Enar's eyes. Not that Thoren blamed him. The word "bastard" didn't go far enough in describing Enar's father. "As I said, I'm leaving tomorrow."

Always the master of avoidance. "I wish you and your woman well. Know that you're always welcome in my home."

Enar thumped him on the back and Thoren returned the hug. Thoren watched as Enar walked to where Lily stood by Keara and Moira. He might not have a seer's precognitive abilities, but he knew Enar's path would lead the Watcher back to him. It was the how of that knowledge that would prove interesting to watch.

Not that it mattered now. One glance at Keara and he wanted to seal the mating ritual, wanted to join with her, to bond with her, wanted to claim her as his. How long did it take a tipsy priestess to pour two glasses of wine?

"Thoren!"

Thoren stiffened at the sound of his father's voice. For so long tension existed between them, he barely remembered a time when he had been close to Balthor. His father must be pleased that he had found his mate, yet the ceremony ended awhile ago and this was the first time Balthor sought him out.

"Father."

"Your wine," the priestess giggled as she thrust two glasses into Thoren's hands. Perfect timing.

"I know we've had our differences."

Thoren forced his raised eyebrow to lower.

"And I wanted to apologize for it. I shouldn't have rushed you into finding a mate."

Of all the things his father could say to him on his mating day, this took the prize. What was he supposed to say? No harm done?

"I...thank you for admitting it." Was that the best he could come up with?

Balthor laid a hand on Thoren's arm. "I'm proud of you, son. Never forget that, even if I huff and puff at you."

"Thanks, Father. I'm heading over to Keara now." He raised the glasses.

"Ah. I'll walk with you."

For the first time in a long time, walking next to his father left him relaxed instead of frustrated.

"Thoren! Your mother was just telling me about

when you were a boy." Keara reached for her glass.

Great. Leave it to his mother to tell all his embarrassing moments. Not that he was mad. She loved him, he loved her and the stories were told in good fun. Good fun at him, but hey, it made Keara smile and that counted for a lot.

The only thing marring this day is that Lily is leaving. Keara's voice whispered in his mind as she glanced to the entryway.

Thoren looked at Enar leading Lily out of the reception room. *You'll see her again.*

I know. But it's still sad. I promised to see her soon.

Bet I know how to cheer you up. He waggled his brows.

Keara's green eyes twinkled at him and his body reacted, his arousal pressing against his leathers. How much longer did he have to stand around waiting to leave?

When can we leave? She sipped her wine, eyes glowing with love.

I don't know, but I'm ready to get you alone.

Red splashed across her cheeks, causing his erection to grow harder than he thought possible.

Me too.

Who cared what the guests thought. They could eat and drink all they wanted. And if it bothered them that he and Keara left, that was their problem.

"Mother, Father, we're leaving."

"It's about time." Moira kissed him on both cheeks. "The mating ritual is not complete without the joining. Don't worry about the guests, they have plenty of food and drink to keep them occupied."

"It was nice meeting you." Keara touched Moira's hand.

Before his mother replied, which had the potential of delaying them even more, Thoren grabbed Keara and transported them to his room in the Temple.

"It's about time. I didn't think we'd ever be able to leave." Keara kissed him, leaning into his body.

He wrapped his arms around her waist, pressing her against him, the feel of her body sparking tremors that shot down his spine. Running his hands up her back, he touched his tongue against the seam of her lips, a silent entreaty to open. Her lips parted for him, her tongue dancing against his.

Small hands untucked his tunic, shoving it upward. Thoren released her mouth, yanking his tunic over his head. His hands fumbled against her back, seeking the clasps for her dress, finding nothing.

"How did they get the dress on you?"

"Magic."

"All right." He waved his hand and the dress vanished from her body, reappearing draped over a chair.

Keara gasped, looked down her body and slowly raised her head. "Well, that's one way of undressing a female. Seems that you're a little overdressed for this party."

He snapped his fingers and put his leathers on top of her gown.

"Much better, love. I like you like that." A fingernail ran down his chest, burning tendrils shooting outward from its path.

He ran his gaze over her skin, which gleamed in the soft light of the globe lamps. Her hair hung in red spirals down her back, a circle of blue and yellow flowers rested against her head. She smelled like lilacs, intoxicating and pure.

His.

The one female created for him.

Thoren smiled.

"You look like a dragon that just took his first flight."

"You make me happy. I can't believe I found you."

"I know what you mean. I'm so glad that you rescued me. I love you."

"I love you too. Would you bond with me?"

"Didn't I just do that?"

"We mated. By bonding we lock our life-forces together."

A grin lit her face. "Of course I will. What do I need to do?"

"We exchange blood."

Her eyes popped wide. "Really? I felt that urge. Earlier. When we first met. I wanted to bite your neck."

"Now you'll get to." Placing both hands on her face, he kissed her, plundering her lips, branding her his.

She leaned into him, running her fingers through his hair, across his back. He walked her backward, never leaving her lips, until her knees hit the bed and she tumbled onto the mattress.

"Oomph. Wait a minute. Let me scoot back."

She settled onto the bed and he crawled up her body, a predator after his prey. Her nipples budded for his touch and he obliged them, circling a finger around one nub until it hardened. Flicking the bud with his tongue, he took it into his mouth, as she clasped his head against her breast with a moan of pleasure.

Why stop with just a moan?

Keeping his tongue in place, he circled her other nipple with his finger, feeling it tighten in response. Alternating his mouth and finger, he played with both her nipples until her breaths came in moans. Licking his way down her stomach, he circled her navel with his tongue, one finger separating her inner folds as his mouth continued its caress across her skin.

"Ooohhh, that feels good, Thoren."

Grinning, he flicked his tongue across her clit, circling around and around while his finger matched the motions inside her warm core. He felt her pulsating against his finger as her breaths came in short pants.

"Come for me," he growled and she did, shattering around his finger, her cries filling the room.

Rising above her, he pressed into her warm opening that sheathed him like a glove, filling her with one long thrust. Her legs wrapped around his waist taking him deeper, her nails raked against his back before one hand cupped his arse, urging him faster.

He set their rhythm, thrusting into her, meeting her stroke for stroke. Moaning with pleasure, Thoren thrust against her, until he didn't know where he ended and she began. Being inside his mate, his love, took him to heights he never realized possible. With each thrust, each little sigh escaping her lips, he felt their love deepen. Little moans left her lips, her breathing a series of pants.

He licked her neck, tasting the salt of her skin. Her tight sheath gripped him rhythmically, drawing him closer to his release. She cried out and his balls tightened, drawing up. He echoed her cry as he pumped into her, his orgasm exploding, giving her his soul along with his seed.

This time he didn't hold back, he locked inside her, beginning the bonding ritual. Magic flowed across their skin as their life-forces began to mingle. Keara pulled his neck to her lips and with a stinging strike bit through his skin.

He felt his blood flow into her mouth and returned the bite, his teeth sinking into the skin of her neck. Blood and magic mingled inside him, linking him to her. Forever and always. Bonded mates.

Freeing her neck, he ran his tongue over the bite marks, closing them. Keara did the same as he released his inner grip on her core.

Thoren collapsed on top of her, her arms tightening around him. He loved her so much and tonight she was his.

"That was wonderful." Her hand stroked his hair.

Afraid of crushing her, he rolled them to their sides, still nestled inside her.

"So what now?" Keara's finger circled his nipple.

"We repeat that?"

"No. I mean, yes, we will repeat that, but that's not what I meant. I mean where do we live? How long until we adopt Jamie? What do we do now that we're mated?"

In the excitement of the mating ceremony, he forgot to tell her his news.

"I spoke to the Council and they took me on as a new member."

"That's great! I imagine you're really happy about that."

"I am. There can only be thirteen on the Council and one of the males wanted to retire so it all worked out."

"Good. Now when I come to the infirmary you won't have to sit home all alone, pining away, waiting for me to come home."

"Silly female. I wouldn't pine."

"Uh-huh, sure you wouldn't."

Thoren kissed the tip of her nose. "Jamie's adoption is scheduled in three days. Goddess help us."

"Hey, now. He's not that bad. Until you came along he was nice and quiet. Although he did have a penchant for falling out of trees."

"Don't worry. I happen to like the infirmary.

You'll be there. He'll be there." Thoren grinned.

"Silly. So where will we live?"

"We'll live here until we build a place of our own. How does that sound?"

"As long as I'm with you, I'm happy."

"That's a good thing because it looks like you're stuck with me."

"I wouldn't have it any other way."

Neither would he. Having a mate was the best thing that ever happened to him. And he wouldn't trade her for all the reconnaissance missions in the world. He kissed her again before proving just how much he loved her.

A word about the author...

By day, Karilyn works in the research department of an oncology clinic. By night, she tells the stories of her imaginary friends.

Karilyn and her most wonderful, ever-patient husband share their home in the great state of Texas with two partially psycho dogs and a handful of colorful fish.

You can reach Karilyn at
karilyn@karilynbentley.com.